Marianne

By Charles F. Roost

Marianne

By Charles F. Roost

Copyright © 2011 by Charles F. Roost, D.C.
Lansing, Michigan, USA

Cover design by Merriam Marketing

All rights reserved. No portion of this book may be reproduced without written permission by the publisher or author.

Published in the United States of America by DC Publishing
ISBN 978-1461065265

722 N. Creyts Rd.
Lansing, MI 48917
www.Delta-Chiro.com

Marianne

LIST OF CHARACTERS

PEOPLE
Marianne Frack – twelve-year-old
Pete Frack - Marianne's father
Molly Frack - Marianne's mother
Steve Frack - Marianne's older brother
Pastor Dave Merryl - Youth Pastor
Samantha (Sam) Merryl - Dave's wife
Art Malgiddo - pornography ring leader
Henry - pornography slave trader
Jennifer Tarry - Marianne's friend
Mr. Al & Mrs. Caffer - prayer warriors in the church
Lieutenant Lydia Mochek - Detective on Marianne's case
Pastor Mark Miller - Senior Pastor
Toby Wallace - Music Minister
Elders: Ted Eastwell
John Stirming
Fred Hatch
Tammy Tesch - Friend
Danielle Buchannon - Steve's girl friend
Other Police Officers -
    Ted - Autopsy
    Tom Barrington - Diver
    Paul Timmons – Investigator

DEMONS	**ASSIGNMENT**	**ANGELS**
Badger	Pete Frack	Brilliantly2

Previous assignment - Cain & Able
Spiritual appearance – spider

Bagda	City of Alagonic	Aggrevious

Rome's fall into immorality
Spiritual appearance - huge ogre

Crimnog	First Evangelical Ch	Maniroff

Furrgstan	Steve Frack	Catellian

Spiritual appearance – amoeba

Gramsting	Pastor Dave Merryl	Aglow

Attempted assasintation of Hitler
Spiritual appearance – lizard

Grayly	Youth Group	

Spiritual appearance - imp w/ long tail

Molech	Regional Principality	

Assigned to Lenin and Stalin
Spiritual appearance – huge skeleton in armor

Murkinator	Marianne Frack	Ajourney

Murder of Archduke Ferdinand in 1914 starting WWI

Spiritual appearance – salamander

Puutor   Lieutenant Mochek

Schmellenuff Pastor Miller   Freely3

Skallum   Molly Frack

              Al Caffer   Clayton
              Mrs. Caffer   Merely
              Samantha Merryl   Salient
              Danielle   Symphony

Introduction

The tragedies of life are so hard. So painful. Sometimes they feel entirely senseless.

But what happens in this life is never wasted – never meaningless. For behind the scenes, a mere breath away from our physical senses, is a larger, more 'real' world than we've ever seen. Separated from us by a mere dimension is a world of conflict and deep meaning that explains 'why'.

Why does disaster strike? Why do good people suffer? Why does tragedy find its way into the lives of even God's people? Why does a child like Marianne become the target of an abduction? Why does this godly, innocent 'tween' have to endure the plans of evil men? Why does her family have to wait, knowing nothing of what she is experiencing?

The world beyond our five senses is more real, more solid, and more impactful than anything we experience here on earth. Yet we can impact, and in some ways control, what happens there.

Marianne would tell you, "Hold fast! Press on! It is worth it – whatever you are going through."

Prologue

The ebony eyes of the salamander-like demon glared at the angel over the multi-colored head of the twelve-year-old human girl. His moist, gleaming skin rippled under the sheen of his opponent's inward glow, and drips of vaporous poison clung to the folds in his hide. Transferred to this case only four weeks earlier, the slimy demon knew of only portions of the plan coming up from the Pit. He, as a sergeant in the demonic hierarchy, had replaced a mere private when the plan took its final form, making Marianne, this seemingly innocuous girl much more important than her few years or mundane station in life would indicate.

Murkinator was his name, and the crowning glory of his long resume of evil was the orchestration of the murder of Archduke Ferdinand in 1914, igniting a short fuse to the first of the human's World Wars. His salamander body reflected, not only the light from his opponent's spiritual glow, but also his own personality – an oily, insinuating, flexible approach to his missions.

The hierarchy through which he had dropped over the last six thousand years had assumed a military ranking system that ran from lowly privates – disrespected peons who were assigned to individual humans with absolutely no leadership role in the Satanic master-plan - and corporals – who would be attached to humans who played slightly more important roles, such as school administrators or small-time politicians – down to powerful generals, like Molech, (Murkinator trembled simply thinking of the power in that demon's talons) who was assigned to oversee the entire eastern seacoast of the United States.

Murkinator himself was a sergeant, and apparently the Enemy (may Satan blast His name) had finally realized that Marianne was more than just another human puppet, for only yesterday the level three angel staring at him over the human girl, a level three by the name of Ajourney, had shown up to supplement the little level one who had been her guardian since her birth. That poor schmuck had nearly faded from fright when Murkinator had suddenly appeared, dismissing the demon private from the case with a snarl and a backhanded swipe at his head. Murk smiled at the memory, though he had to admit, the little angel had stood his ground at the time –

as was his right with a daughter of the Enemy who sought to follow the bright path as Marianne did.

Well, level 3 or not, the heavenly host would soon see how their precious Marianne stood up under pressure.

For his part, Ajourney was puzzled. Not that he questioned his orders or disliked his assignment, but he had no idea why the Infernal Power would send a powerful sergeant to work on someone like Marianne. It was extremely unusual for a birth-angel to be replaced in the middle of their human's life, but when this girl was suddenly raised up in the Infernal plan, the heavenlies responded by sending Ajourney to support the defenses offered by the outmatched level one.

Now the glowing angel stared calmly at the demon. Slimy and ugly and obviously malevolent, Murkinator was a perfect example of an evil heart manifesting hideous form over the course of millennia of malicious action. Ajourney knew that he would have to stay alert every second in protecting his new charge.

The young girl was a pleasure to guard. Watching her as she went to school, as she interacted with other students and her parents, and as she just enjoyed life as an twelve year-old should. And through it all, tying it all together, he admired her deep, and still-growing devotion to the One True God. Ajourney basked in the power of her spiritual devotion to God. Truly a pleasant assignment. Still, he couldn't help but wonder, what was so unique about her that he and Murkinator had been assigned to her?

Chapter 1
I'll wait for you out here.

Steve crashed through the front door, slammed it shut, threw his school bag in the corner of the kitchen, and started down the hallway to his room. "Friday!" he sighed. "What a relief to be done with school for a few days." Blond and lanky, he and his sister both took after their mom in their looks. At least they both did until Marianne had dyed her hair into multiple hues of blue, green and hints of orange last weekend. He admitted to himself that it looked pretty good on her once you got used to it.

His dad's hair was a couple of shades darker and his build stockier. He had played a year of football as a halfback in college. Face marred by old acne and by the stress of a job he did not enjoy. He was not outgoing but was still liked by people in the circles he kept.

Steve's own hair was also straight and blonde, though shorter than hers, of course. His frame was thin and angular, his arms and legs way ahead of his body in length and in uncoordination due to his latest growth spurt.

Constantly knocking into things when he reached for a glass or walked through a room, it was now a family joke. Although almost five years separated them, he and his sister looked a lot alike in facial structure, too. Good looking kids who were likeable and happy growing up.

Lately this had changed for Steve, however. He argued more with his dad over the littlest things. He spent more time in his room or behind his earphones than out with the family. He was having a tough time sailing the teen years and looked more and more to unhealthy ways to cope with the turbulence that comes with discovering who he was and how life worked.

Now he was finding that early May was the toughest time to focus on school, too. At the end of his junior year, he knew he still had another whole year to focus on getting his grades back up to where they used to be, so he wasn't worried about that. The days grew longer and warmer, and the school year felt drawn out and as boring as a televised golf tournament.

His mom, Molly, called from the laundry room, "Hi, Steve! How was school?"

He rolled his eyes in exasperation. "Okay," came the mumbled reply, but he kept moving down the hall. He had hoped to avoid his mom for as much of the day as he possibly could.

"Shoes off in the house!" his mom reminded him, and his lips moved in almost perfect sync with her words as she went on, "Anything exciting happen at school today? Any home work?"

"Nope!" he answered, and then shut himself in his room. He pulled his shirt off, and changed into shorts and a sweat shirt, before throwing himself down across his bed. His room was clean, with all his things put away, and the bed neatly made. But it was only from habit, definitely not a reflection of what went on in his mind. Nobody had a clue what was going on in his mind.

Knowing his mom would leave him to his homework for at least the next hour, he pulled a tightly rolled joint out from his stash in the back of his junk drawer and lit it, carefully exhaling out the window.

As happy as their family appeared to friends and neighbors, Steve was one undercover, mixed up kid. The trouble was, he couldn't figure out what it was that had him so messed up. Why couldn't his mind work as smoothly and nicely as everyone else's seemed to. Why did he have to struggle so hard with deep and disturbing thoughts; thoughts that all too often led him to dwell on how hopeless he felt; thoughts that would not quit until he finally gave in again and cranked up his music and lit up another joint to make the depression go away.

The days of their family being happy and immersed in fun family activities seemed long ago and only dimly remembered. Vacations packed into the back seat of the family van, swimming in the warm, shallow waters of various coastal cities during spring break, and Christmases at their grandparents all faded further into his brain as the smoke filled his lungs.

As usual, the sweet, soothing smoke did help for a while. But time after time, he would find himself side tracking into the same old depressing thoughts. The gnawing anger, bitterness, and confusion at his situation dragged him deeper and deeper into depression. He pinched off the end of the roach and scattered it out the window.

The knock at his door jolted him back to the present, and he yelled, "Yeah?"

"Can I come in?" his mom asked.

"Sure," he grudgingly conceded after looking around to make sure he hadn't left any incriminating papers, bags or ashes lying around.

The door opened, and his mom said, "Marianne just got home, too, and she asked if she could spend a couple hours at the mall with Jennifer and Tammy this afternoon." Steve kept his stare on the ceiling, and his mom went on, "But someone has to stay here to let the washer repair guy in."

Steve scrunched his lips into a crooked frown, knowing that he was the "someone" who would have to stay. Then his mom went on, "Could you run her over in about an hour?"

At first Steve was shocked, but then grinned. Almost seventeen years old, he had gotten his license over a year ago, and still rarely got to take the car out without his folks in the car. Even if it was a mini-van, he loved to drive – any car, for any reason. "Sure! That'll be a blast!" He grabbed his phone to call Danielle, his girlfriend, to see if she could meet him at the mall in an hour and a half.

* * *

Bagda nodded to the demon lieutenant and growled, "That's what we were waiting for. Marianne will be at the mall in twenty minutes. Go with plan A-121. Set it in motion when she steps out of the car, and," he poked his nail-hard talon two inches into Grayly's patch-haired chest, "make sure it works! I'll see you roast if this falls apart on us."

Grayly pulled away, yanking his boss's fingernail out of his chest with a wet sucking sound and a pained grimace on his face. He bowed, groveling before the major, before backing out of the huge demon's sight.

Both then paused as they felt the fresh infusion of energy that accompanied a new sin participated in by one of the humans under their watchful care. They heard the groans of pleasure that all of the demons involved with this human felt. Looking back at the monitors, they quickly found the human responsible.

"I was hoping that Pastor Dave would keep on with that smut," commented Bagda. Then he bellowed through the spiritual ethers to another underling, "Good work Gramsting!" Looking back at Grayly, he added, "He's in deep enough that it'll take an act of You-Know-Who to break him free."

Turning from the screens, Grayly screamed his orders out, gathering his henchmen, and sending them hustling out on their duties.

He then smiled, glowing in the pleasure of knowing a good plan was about to be set into action. He strained to look down at the pus oozing from the hole Bagda had made in his chest, and snaking his long, narrow tongue out, licked at the yellowish ocher. Shape-shifting to his human form, he smiled and stepped between dimensions to follow the implementation of the plan.

* * *

Pastor Dave sighed with frustration. His prayers felt as though they were bouncing off the ceiling of his tiny little office with a tiny little window. Those prayers seemed to simply ricochet back to bash into the top of his skull. He got up off his knees and sat back in his chair again.

His mind went back to the trash can where he had just hurled the magazine. It was just a magazine! Just a few pictures! Yet it had so much control over him. It amazed him over and over, just as it overpowered him over and over.

He knew that looking at pornography was wrong, knew that it would torture his wife if she knew. He knew that God would be displeased, too, if…

Interrupting that chain of thought, he realized how absurd what he was just thinking was. *If God what?* Did he really think he was hiding anything from God? Groaning at his own hypocrisy, he bent forward and held his face in his hands. "God!" he prayed. "Save me from this circle of frustration and defeat! I am so - so - so..." He couldn't even express what he was thinking.

Slumping back once more, he sat there, reviewing in his mind the areas of his life where he was running into walls; goals that were unreached and seeming more and more unreachable with each passing day.

Prayer life - dead.

Bible reading - dry.

Marriage - okay but lacking something - life, or passion, or something.

The youth group he led ground on, but there was no victory there either. Kids kept showing up probably because their parents made them, but there was no spark. There was certainly nothing that would show the world that this was a group who served a living and powerful God.

Only a few years ago it had seemed so different. He and Sam, his wife of thirteen years, had felt the call of the Lord so clearly. They both knew beyond any doubt that this was where God wanted them. They had arrived full of fire, hope, and crystal clear vision. Yes, the vision of succeeding, of taking this city for Christ, of working right alongside their Friend and God had been impelling and empowering. Yet now - now they plodded. Try as he might, he could not put his finger on what or where things had started to change. And Lord knew he had tried to reason it out. Looking back, he knew that it was his fault - that something inside of him had changed, but he couldn't figure out what it was.

The soft beep of his phone went unnoticed for four chimes, and then he broke from his reverie, sat up, and reached to the corner of the desk for it. "Hello?"

"You sound glum. Are you all right?" His wife sounded concerned.

"Yeah, I was just kind of lost in my thoughts here." Forcing his tone a notch brighter, he asked, "How was your day? The kids okay?" Their three little ones brought the only joy he felt in his life these days.

"The usual. I'm just a bit tired."

He could understand how keeping up with the fast paced needs of two kids in grade school and one still at home could wear a woman out. "How about I bring home pizza tonight?"

She sounded relieved as she responded, "Could you? I was going to have to run out for something otherwise."

"Sure hon. Everything else okay?"

"Yep! I'll see you about six?"

"Six it is. I love you!"

"Me too. Bye!"

He hung up and stared at the picture on the face of the phone. His smiling wife looked back. He flipped it closed and looked at the wall clock. He only had a couple of hours to finish all the details for the senior high activity for tomorrow night. That included calling a couple of the kids that he wanted to encourage to be there, like Sarah, Steve, and James. He also needed to make sure the Hollands were set with the refreshments and double check with the church custodians to make sure the tables and sports equipment would be available.

Before diving back into his work, he reached into the trash can and pulled the magazine back out, carefully placing it in the back of his drawer under some papers. As he returned to his work, his concerns were buried once again in the back of his mind. There wasn't time today to get to the bottom of all his problems. Too much to do.

* * *

Steve rolled his eyes in mock frustration as the three irritating, immature junior-highers tumbled out of the house and into the back seat of the van. But it was worth putting up with their giggling, goofiness and overall immaturity to have the van all to himself for a couple of hours.

He was surprised that his mom had finally given in to Marianne's nagging to go to the mall with just her friends. But he had to admit, Marianne was obnoxiously persistent. He knew that their mom was concerned about three seventh-grade girls on their own in the mall; after all, there were the gangs, (although mom had never actually seen one) and you did hear about things happening at the old Cherry Lane Mall across town.

North Creek Mall, on the other hand, was the smaller and much nicer of the two malls that served the greater Alagonic area. It boasted a Macy's and a Lord and Taylor and about three dozen smaller but still classy stores. It was enough to keep teen-aged girls busy window shopping for days. Compared to what Cherry Lane Mall offered across town, it was clean, relatively safe and expensive. While Alagonic was home to over two-hundred-thousand people, it was still a bit on the slow side when compared to cities of comparable size elsewhere.

There actually were some gangs, quite small-time in Steve's mind, and some crimes, but Alagonic stayed fairly quiet over all.

Their folks hadn't let him go to the mall alone with his friends until he was fourteen! Well, nothing exciting ever happened on this end of town. The mall was situated in the middle of the well-groomed, uppity side of a mid-sized town. More police presence, mall security, and upper-middle class people than over at Cherry Lane. They'd be fine. He was glad his folks were loosening up a bit.

Twenty minutes later he had parked the car, made arrangements to meet the girls at Penny's main door in two hours – they agreed on seven o'clock sharp. Jennifer pulled out her phone, ostensibly to check the time. The other girls rolled their eyes at Jennifer's showing off – the first of them to get her own phone. Marianne was jealous but tried not to show it. Steve rolled his eyes, too, but just slammed the van door and walked off to find Danielle.

* * *

Furrgstan, a demon with the lowly and common rank of private and who was assigned to young Steve Frack for this operation, went to full alert as they approached the mall. When his charge left the van, he nudged Steve's brain, distracting him just enough for him to leave the keys in the ignition when he locked, and then shut, the door. He then nudged him again just enough to ensure that he wouldn't think about them until he came back out to the van later.

Normally such a maneuver would have drained the demon for hours, but he was strengthened by having been in Bagda's evil presence and by Steve's use of marijuana just before leaving the house. He flexed his muscles and stretched, reveling in the feeling of control and power.

He drifted along by Steve's shoulder, unseen by any human as long as he remained hidden in the spiritual realm. As the kids entered the mall, Furrgstan stayed on task and intensely focused, because he knew that this mission was a big one. This one had come up, in minute detail, all the way from the captain down at principality level, and he suspected even deeper than that - perhaps from Lucifer himself. His own job was peripheral, merely to make sure that Steve didn't accidentally blunder into the way of the plan. But he knew that if he blew it, he'd fry for it.

Looking around, he felt that everything was going well. Prayer support for these kids was minimal. The Enemy was present but weakened by apathy, by inattention, and by the subtle sins of the Christians involved - some of the same factors that strengthened the demon horde.

As Steve, along with his evil and invisible escort, Furrgstan, approached Danielle, the demon bristled and hissed at the luminous, faintly shimmering angel standing by her side. Symphony was his name, but his presence was weak compared to Furrgstan right now. He anticipated no trouble from the puny looking angel.

He turned and looked down the mall to see the girls heading for the side aisle that led to the rest rooms - the real stepping off point of this plan. Plan A-121 was in motion, and if it came off, this city was theirs for the taking.

* * *

Marianne complained, "You guys! We've only got two hours. And you want to go to the bathroom already?!"

"It'll only take a sec. C'mon!" Jennifer loved to primp and absolutely had to make sure her hair was 'just so' before doing the mall thing on their own for the first time.

Too excited to wait with them inside the restroom, she said, "Oh, brother! I'll wait for you out here," and she stopped short of the door to the ladies room. The door swung shut and she backed up into the quiet hall, resting her back against the painted brick wall. The wall was painted a glossy tan that felt cold and tacky to the bare skin on the backs of her arms. Dropping her bag to the floor, she closed her eyes and counted to ten to slow her beating heart.

Her first time at the mall without her mom or dad along. Very exciting. She couldn't wait to get back out to the main mall and start walking down the big hall, window shopping, taking her time, going in stores when she wanted, hanging around the fountain if she wanted. How totally cool!

The shuffle of a shoe down the hall by the opening to the mall startled her, and she turned to catch a glimpse of someone just moving out of her view. She looked back the other way and noticed the closed door of the men's bathroom, and further down the dead-end hall, big brown double doors with "Fire Escape" painted in red letters across them. The mall bathroom halls always creeped her out, even when her mom was with her. They felt shady and isolated and, well, creepy. They echoed with whispers and noises without sources. She moved to the bathroom door and opened it a crack. "Hurry up, you guys!"

"We'll be there in just a minute," the other two answered together.

Marianne let the door slowly shut and started to turn around to pick up her purse. Out of nowhere, a strong arm came around her face and another around her chest, pinning her arms painfully to her sides and squeezing the breath from her lungs. The arm around her face moved to press a wet cloth over her mouth and nose; then the other arm loosened enough to let her gather a breath to scream. But as she gasped the sharply pungent smell of some noxious chemical in the cloth made her gag, the fumes seemingly shooting directly from her lungs out along her nerves and into her brain. Her muscles immediately lost all their strength. She sagged in her attacker's arms, all control gone. She was conscious but had no control of any of her muscles. She felt a curious detachment, knowing that she was in deep trouble, knowing that she needed to call for help, knowing that she should be fighting, yet not able to move, or cry out, or fight at all.

She felt herself lifted up and carried toward the fire exit doors. In his hurry to get away from the scene, the man shoved against the handle of the door and smacked Marianne's head against one of the metal posts. In her already dazed state, it hardly hurt at all, though she realized that it should have. The shock sent bright sparks into her eyes, but regardless of the fear and her recognition of what was happening to her, she felt only warmth - a peaceful feeling of safety wrapping her in a kindly embrace. She pictured her dad holding her late at night, following a nightmare. Darkness welled up, replacing the stars, and she knew nothing.

* * *

So far, so good. The Murkinator, a demon sergeant in the form of a salamander, rubbed his hands together, and looked at the big, stupid demon who had his talons deep in the heart of the man carrying Marianne. The Murkinator was not his true name, but like so many of the demons of his rank, he had a penchant for picking up on the fads of his humans, and his choice of names was an example. He liked the looks of this operation. His assignment to this Christian girl was risky, but held out chances for great reward if the plan succeeded.

Yes, everything was going just fine. The only thing that troubled him was the completely inexplicable behavior of Marianne's guardians. The big one was the only angel involved in this operation that could have messed up their plans, but he merely walked by her side holding her in his huge arms, and murmuring something in her ear. The Murkinator couldn't hear what he was saying, but the demon felt the raw power issuing from the guy. And stranger still, the Murkinator could swear he saw tears running down the smaller angel's cheeks, as he gently cradled her heart in his arms.

The Murkinator was set to fight the angel if he started to interfere. The powers lower down had channeled strength to the sergeant from others for this occasion - strength far beyond his normal capacity. He flexed his muscles, feeling the power - reveling in the sensation. Not all of the children of the Enemy had a level-three guardian assigned to them. But the Enemy apparently thought Marianne needed a strong one now. Even so, Ajourney and her birth angel were walking with her but doing nothing to stop the operation. So far Ajourney had merely stood by, watching and talking to Marianne. It's a good thing too, because Ajourney looked tougher, brighter, stronger and more intense than any Murkinator had ever faced alone. Looking at the brightly glowing guardian, deep down Murk doubted that, even with his new hell-sent power, he could take him in an all-out fight.

He nearly chortled with glee, literally drooling with joy, when the human kidnapper accidentally bashed the girl's head on the door. But it was the birth angel's head that rebounded as though it had been his head that hit the door, and a deep blue bruise instantly formed on the side of his forehead in the same place that Marianne had struck the post. The Murkinator frowned as a little smile of peace crossed her face before she succumbed to the drugs and the blow to the head and passed out.

Then he understood. The angel had entered Vicarious Mode. Everything that they did to Marianne would be taken by the angel, felt by the angel, absorbed by the angel. This happened every once in a while for a human who was somehow special enough in the Enemy's eyes to warrant it. None of the demonic hierarchy had yet figured out the pattern for when it happened or with whom it worked.

While this took some of the sweet thrill of witnessing Marianne's pain away for the

Murkinator, it was still going to be a grand day, as he watched the shining angel tarnish and bruise and slowly come apart, one piece at a time.

The Murkinator still kept careful watch as the man carrying Marianne, a tough looking and roughly dressed thirty-seven-year-old wearing holey jeans and chains hanging from his pocket and belt loops, guided by his incredibly ugly demon, moved through the door and dumped Marianne inside a shiny, black, new-looking van waiting outside the door.

Then, to Murkinator's great shock, he heard the screaming voices of the other two girls, as they opened the emergency exit and saw the van door close on their friend and her kidnapper. Eyes wide and round with fear and fingers pointing, there was nothing they could do to stop the kidnapping at this point. But the Murkinator knew heads were going to roll for the demons who were supposed to have kept them occupied in the rest room until they were clear.

Belatedly, Dean, the young driver, gunned the engine and roared away from the mall, tossing the thug and Marianne unceremoniously in a heap at the back. The thug cursed Dean as he tried to leverage his bulk off from Marianne's still unconscious form. The driver's demon allowed him to speed to the corner and then twisted his talons deeper and forced the human to slow to an unhurried pace to avoid undue attention.

The plan went on to phase two.

Chapter 2
We should be doing something.

Just being with Danielle was great. Walking hand in hand as they slowly made their way down the mall, he thought of little other than the feel of her hand in his, the sight of her smile, the sound of her voice, her laughter. There truly was nowhere else he would rather be.

Steve groaned when he heard the screams of the girls. He turned to watch them running toward him. "Geeze! You can't take these girls anywhere!" He looked at Danielle, but she was looking at the approaching girls with widening eyes.

"Where's Marianne?" she asked Steve.

"She's with those goofy..." He was interrupted by Jennifer's cry.

"She's gone! Some guy in a van took her!"

Steve looked askance at the girls, expecting to see through the joke, and waiting for them to laugh at him for falling for another of their endless pranks. That moment never came though, and he felt the weight of disbelief and horror settle into his stomach; a sick, choking feeling that sank into the fog of his brain, swirled down to his guts and then tightened as he realized that Marianne's friends weren't kidding at all.

"Where? When? Who?" came Steve's panicked questions, but Jennifer was so out of breath that she could only point in the general direction they had come from.

Steve didn't wait for more but took off at a sprint. Ten steps down the mall he realized that the people who had snatched Marianne would not be at the back of the mall waiting for him, and he changed direction, sprinting for his own van.

"It was a black van!" Tammy called at his hurrying back.

People stared at him running by, dodging around happy groups of shoppers. As he slammed through the mall's tall glass doors, he thought they would break, but he kept on going at a sprint across the sidewalk and into the road. Squealing tires shocked Steve to a stop, and a shiny black van lurched to the side to avoid running him down. Steve caught the wide eyes and open mouth of the surprised driver as it drove past. The driver goosed the engine and raced up the drive and out of sight.

Realization hit him instantly. That must be the van his sister was in. Driving himself into motion again, he turned first to follow the fleeing van, and then back in the other direction to go to his van. Caught between the two impulses, his mind still mushy from the weed he had smoked back at home, he finally dashed the rest of the way to his van. Reaching the driver's door he fumbled for his keys and nearly fainted with despair when he realized that he had locked them in the ignition.

He pulled back his arm and smashed his fist into the window, but the glass held. He glanced in the direction of the vanished black van and began frantically beating on the window, harder and harder. A crack appeared in the glass, but with his next blow he heard a snap, and a shooting pain speared up from his wrist. He cried out, and slowly sank to his knees, cradling his broken wrist. It was only at this point that he recalled that he could have at least gotten the license plate number of the black van, and he bashed his head against the side of the van in exasperation.

Only then did he think to call 911. He had to twist awkwardly to pull his phone from his pocket with his unbroken left hand.

* * *

The police had finally gone. He could hear their car door close and the engine start. But now Pete, Marianne's dad, wasn't so sure he was glad about that. The house was silent save the continued, soft moaning of his wife seated on the couch. Molly had taken the news of Marianne's abduction by sinking into a chair, mouth agape and clasping her hands into her lap. One whispered, "No!" painfully strained through vocal chords tense with shock was all she said.

The shock still kept reality from rising up to the part of Pete's brain where he could think about it. As the father of the house, he should be able to do something – to come up with a plan – but his thoughts were locked in a worthless, desperate circle. Marianne gone?! Why? Why her? Why us? These things happened in other cities, to other families. Not his family, not to his little girl!

So, the police had come and gone. They had filled out forms, chosen a picture to circulate, given Pete instructions to stay by the phone, and finally gone.

They had given him a business card with the name of a detective and a phone number on it, but nothing had been accomplished, there were no leads, no news. And although the sergeant sounded sure and hopeful, Pete feared the worst.

It was real and not a dream. His daughter was likely never coming back.

He checked the negative thoughts, and made himself imagine her coming home safe.

He crossed the living room, and went around the glass-topped coffee table to the couch. Slowly he lowered himself to sit next to Molly. Her only response was to move her leg out of his way. Her gaze was turned away from him, away from here and now, toward some secret place where, who knew what she saw. It was a gaze that he was going to grow accustomed to over the days ahead.

"Molly," he said, his voice stressed as though he lifted tons with it. "Molly, what are we going to do?"

She shifted her gaze to look at him for a moment, but then looked away again without speaking. Her pretty, straight, blond hair neatly pulled behind her ears was at odds with the strain that was just beginning to show on her face.

"Hon, we should be doing something..." His voice wound down as he realized that he hadn't the slightest clue what that something might be.

As he watched her, fresh tears started flowing, and her hands sought and found one another and began wringing together, knuckles whitening with angry strength, as though she were trying to wrest the safety of her sweet daughter back away from the unknown strangers who had taken her.

* * *

Major Bagda whistled a strange chord in a minor scale and Lieutenant Grayly, the demon assigned to cover the youth group and overseeing the portions of this plan that effected that part of the church, now dressed in a three piece suit and wing tip shoes to celebrate a smoothly running plan, shortly appeared in front of him. The well dressed demon, in the body of a middle aged man, looked just like a human but for the red glint in his eyes, which he hid by keeping his face averted and his eyes partially hooded. He was a lieutenant with two sergeants and thirty grunts under his field command and often took more pride in his rank than was pleasing to his immediate superior.

Grayly bowed deeply and smoothly, with the air of a country gentleman. Bagda grunted and gave him a back-hand that knocked his head to one side and skewed his tie to the other.

"What was that for?" whined Grayly. He wiped greenish yellow drool and red, slimy blood from the side of his mouth that his superior had just split open.

"Cut the crud, you piece of sniveling slime!" came the retort. "Your section is in the heat of the action for this next phase, and I want some sort of assurance that you're up to it. Can you give me that assurance?" He glared at the lieutenant, who took a breath to answer.

The captain waved a hand negligently at the well dressed but cowering demon, and the fine clothes and human looks were immediately replaced with his natural appearance: that of a naked, scaly, reddish-brown imp with a scabby, hair-covered chest and a four foot tail that he incessantly either tripped over or trod upon. Others took great pleasure in stepping on it, too.

Grayly glared up at his superior, who sneered, "Well? You got a problem with my management style?"

Grayly pulled his temper back into control, bowed again, but with more sincerity this time, and said, "Everything is prepared your lowness. Each student is covered day and night by his demon, and you've seen for yourself how well Gramsting is handling the young pastor. All is ready."

"It had better be. If you screw this up you'll be shot back up to patrol so fast you won't remember the way back down. But if we pull this off, we'll both be moved down the ladder a couple of notches."

The two soaked up the possibilities for a moment, until Bagda shook himself and said, "Wait here a moment, I want to call Badger and 'the Murkinator,'" he twisted the words and grimaced as he spoke the demon's chosen name. He hated these human fads, dressing like and taking names like the humans. He saw through such facades to the deeper root issues that never changed. That's why he was the major. "I want to call them in for a conference."

He blew a couple more off key chords, and almost instantly the other two demons joined them in the vaulted cavern. Both bowed deeply, and stayed hunched over until Bagda grunted and allowed them to rise.

"That's the kind of respect I expect from you," and again he swatted Grayly. The other two, not daring to laugh outright, darted glances at one another and squelched the urge to grin.

"Report!" barked Bagda, and both began spilling their guts simultaneously into an unintelligible mix of words.

"Shut up!" screamed the captain. "You first, Murkinator," pointing to the larger of the two, whose true form was something like a large lizard or salamander.

"The girl is under control, and in spite of what the humans do to her, her guard does nothing to defend her. How long do we get to keep playing with her?" His voice betrayed his fear that they would have to turn her loose soon. He was having so much fun!

"Aren't you leaving something out? Something important?" Bagda asked the salamander-shaped demon, who noticed the threat in his major's voice. The sergeant's demeanor suddenly become quiveringly fearful. Bagda added helpfully, "Something that starts with the letter 'v'?" There was a blank look on Murk's face.

Bagda leaned closer to the salamander's face and lowered his voice to a cruel slur, "Something that starts with 'vike'?" When there was still no sign of comprehension dawning in the mind of the Murkinator, Bagda reached back, wound up and smacked the lizard, breaking his arm. He then followed the flailing demon, took a deep breath and shrieked, "Does the phrase 'vicarious mode' mean anything to you?!" He was now screaming right into the demon's face, his own face swollen, veins distended, red eyes bulging with rage.

"Ye - ye -yes, sir!" chattered the salamander with his face pressed tight against the floor.

"When I say report, I want a full report, you sack of garbage!" And with that he kicked the demon, snapping the damaged arm off, lifting him high into the air, and slamming him against the rock ceiling before the beast could diffuse and disappear back into the worldly realm. A moment later, he reappeared, hurriedly gathered his broken appendage and disappeared, all before the captain could light into him once again.

Bagda slowly turned his gaze on the other demon; this one still in his natural soft, amorphous jelly shape. Badger quivered as only an amoeba can. He knew that if Bagda smacked him, he would be days pulling himself back together. "Tell me about your human - the father. What kind of shape is he in?" The leader demanded.

"He's pretty well doing himself in. He's more and more isolated, feeling responsible for his daughter's disappearance, for his wife's grief, and for his son's rebellion. He's worthless to the Enemy, because his prayers are rare and ineffectual." The demon fairly preened with his own self-worth.

"And what are you doing to insure he stays that way?" asked Grayly.

The underling demon hesitated, knowing that here was a trap that he could trigger with a single wrong word. "I'm watching very carefully, and when he does try to pray I nudge his thoughts along diverging pathways so he can't concentrate on You-Know-Who." He paused, looking at the two powerful demons he served, trying to anticipate their reactions.

Bagda nodded. "That's good. You seem to have a good grasp of what needs to be done. Just be careful to maintain that balance between letting him out of your control and pushing him so hard that he realizes you're there and calls for more help than you can handle."

The captain grabbed a handful of each of the others' hides and pulled them over to a vent hole. Pushing their noses up close, he held them in the smoke and fumes that jetted out, at the same time snorting a long lungful of the pungent, fetid smelling air himself. "Aaahhh!" all three sighed, when he let go.

"That's the greatest!" gushed Grayly.

Then, at a dismissing wave of Bagda's hand, the lieutenant and his private faded out of view and back to work in the shadow land known to the humans as the 'real world'.

* * *

Steve groaned and rolled over again. The ache in his heart like a weight pushing down on his chest, his soul, his mind, until he thought he couldn't draw another breath - until he was sure his heart would burst. *It's all my fault!* he screamed out in his mind. The words seemed to echo, bouncing from his guilt to his inadequacy, and amplified by the drugs in his system.

It had been six hours since he had broken his wrist on the van's window. Six hours since his little sister had been taken and he just stood there like an idiot while the guys that did it drove right past him. What a fool!

The couple of hours in the emergency room were bad enough, not knowing if they had managed to find the van, but this was worse. The pain in his wrist faded to insignificance beside the pain in his heart. And he feared that this would never end; this knowing that she was really gone, that she might never come back, that the kidnappers might be doing anything to her, and that it was his fault.

Dear God, he thought, *there has to be a way to fix this, because I can't take this pain much longer.*

The voices of the cops had silenced, and he no longer heard his dad trying to get a response from his mom. He groaned aloud, rolled over and reached into the back of his nightstand drawer, fumbling for another joint and his lighter.

* * *

Brilliantly streaked toward the rendezvous with his mentor and superior, Agrevious. He pondered the five levels of angels in the heavenly hierarchy. The levels indicate levels of responsibility as well as capability in carrying out the will of the Father, and capacity for giving service and worship to the Creator. Stopping a foot or so in front of the huge, level-four angel, Brilliantly asked, "Sir, is this going to work? It sure seems as if a lot of the pieces of this plan are out of place and heading in the wrong direction."

Agrevious slowly nodded his head. Looking at the enthusiastic, and aptly named, level-two angel, he chose his words carefully. "Brilliantly, remember the Great Victory when our Lord chose to give His greatest gift to these humans?"

The smaller one nodded, and Agrevious went on, "Of course you do. We were all stunned at the boldness and perfection of the plan that God had set in motion millennia ago, the plan to win His children back from Satan's clutches. But what we didn't understand until it was over was that He had it all planned out from the start, from before He even made us."

"Yes, sir, I remember," Brilliantly answered respectfully. "but..."

"Try to keep that in mind as the demon operation unfolds and the Father's plans are fulfilled, because we are not told everything, only what we need to know to do our job properly. All does not seem to be under control, but you know as well as I do that we have our people in place. The prayer support we need is not there yet, but at the right time... well, we shall see.

"In the mean time, continue to do your assigned job with Peter Frack, and keep supporting Ajourney in any way you can, because he is, by far, bearing the brunt of this mission, at least until our Lord steps in to take that role."

"Will that be soon?"

"Soon enough," he admonished firmly. And until then, the girl is in good hands. He'll make sure she suffers no more than our Lord allows. He has made promises to her, you will recall."

"Yes," the smaller angel acknowledged. "And He is faithful and good, isn't He?"

The larger angel nodded and smiled, "He is good indeed." Then in a more stern tone, "And He has a plan, too. Always. These events will turn out for His glory and our charges' good, if they will only allow it."

* * *

Lieutenant Lydia Mochek lifted another file from the stack on her desk. It was thin, but when she saw the contents, its weight grew heavy in her heart and in her hand. In her 20 years on the force, she had seen many such cases, but repetition didn't make it any easier to accept another kidnapped child.

"Marianne Frack," Lydia whispered the name typed on the form quietly. Scanning down the page, she read, "Twelve years old. Abducted from the North Creek Mall at about six o'clock this afternoon. No clues, two witnesses - make that three. A description of a black van. Nothing else of use yet." Lieutenant Mochek looked up at the cobwebbed corner of her small office, and sighed. She refused to let this case get past her professionalism; refused to take it onto herself. That would only impair her ability to help this family get their daughter back. As the only female, black female no less, on the Missing Persons desk, she could not afford to fail to perform at her best on this case. Yet her eyes filled with tears, tears of anger, frustration, and fear that another child was lost for good.

* * *

Later that night, Pete and Molly Frack lay in bed, but neither of them slept. Pete lay there in agony. There had been no call, no demand for ransom, no sign of the van. And just as bad, there had been nothing he could do to break through the walls Molly was building, nor to cross over the deepening emotional moat that Steve seemed to be digging around himself.

Pete felt his life was in tatters, pieces of it blowing away in the shearing winds that howled through his heart and mind. How could God allow this to happen? What had he done to deserve this kind of disaster?

Tears that burned like acid poured from his eyes as he silently howled back at God, *How could You?! How could You let them take my daughter? How could You let this happen?!* Silence filled the room while the storm raged in his mind. There was no answer. How could there be, with such a cacophony in his heart?

Lurching from the bed, he stopped to draw the covers back over Molly's quiet form, and then strode angrily from the room, down the hall, and into the family room. The darkness of the room was broken only by gray street light filtering through the sheer curtains covering the bay window and shadows crept from every nook and cranny, every corner of the room.

Without warning, fear welled up within him, even cutting through his inner storm of anger and doubt. He stopped suddenly, sweating and physically shaking with trepidation. As he tried to think through what he was suddenly so afraid of, the fear crescendoed, cresting into a near panic, filling his mind with blanketing dread and terror. Turning his back on the nameless, formless fear that filled the darkness and threatened from the shadows, he stumbled from the dark room and hurried back to their bedroom.

As he moved back down the hall, the fear rapidly receded, filling him with such a sense of relief that he failed to even wonder about the incident. He fumbled in the dark for the phone book, knocking his phone off the nightstand with his elbow.

Molly stirred, and asked in a clear voice that let him know that she hadn't been sleeping either, "Pete, what are you doing?"

He sighed, and answered, "I'm calling the Merryls. Pastor Dave and Samantha will want to know what's happened." His tone was unsure, but Molly said nothing more, so he picked up the phone from the floor and turned once more to the phone book.

Since Molly was awake, he flipped on the light and quickly found the listing of Merryls'. There were eight of them, and two D. Merryls, but looking further he noticed the Rev. suffix behind the second one, and lay his finger under the corresponding number. He hesitated again, thinking of the lateness of the hour. The clock glowed its silent 12:32 at him, but he knew that Pastor Dave would want to know what was happening. He dialed the number, and after only three rings, a voice answered that was amazingly free of sleepiness.

"Pastor Merryl's home," came the woman's voice.

"Uh... yes is Pastor Dave there?" Pete asked, unsure of how to proceed. "This is Pete Frack."

"Oh yes, Mr. Frack, I'll get him for you," she responded without hesitation, or reference to the hour, for which he was grateful.

A moment passed, and he heard a change in the phone noise as another extension was connected. An enthusiastic tenor voice said, "Mr. Frack! What can I do for you tonight?"

"I'm awfully sorry to bother you so late, but..."

"Not at all, Mr. Frack. I get late calls all the time. What's on your mind?"

"It's Marianne, Pastor Dave. She's been kidnapped. She's gone. They took her this afternoon, and..."

"Wait. Are you sure?" Dave sounded confused and hesitated before going on. "Of course you're sure, it's just that I thought you were calling about Steve. But go ahead, when did this happen?"

"Steve? What about Steve?" It was Pete's turn to be perplexed for a moment, but he quickly gathered his thoughts and explained, "No, it's not Steve. It's about Marianne. We're in big trouble."

Pete could feel Pastor Dave's attention shift and focus on the new subject. "What's the problem, Mr. Frack?"

"She was taken from the mall at about six o'clock this afternoon. The police are working on it, but it doesn't sound good. There has been no ransom demand, no contact of any kind with the kidnappers." Pete's voice was so matter-of-fact sounding, that it seemed unreal, both to Dave and to Pete himself. How could his voice be so quiet in the middle of such a disaster?

Silence stretched across the phone lines as Dave sorted through the thoughts whipping through his mind and wondered what in the world to say to Mr. Frack. The pause lengthened, but finally Dave said, "Mr. Frack, let me make some calls, and I'll come over first thing in the morning. Would that be all right?"

Pete replied, "Sure. Sure. We'd appreciate your visit."

"And Mr. Frack? We'll be praying for you, okay?"

And with that they both hung up. *Well,* thought Pete, *that was pretty unhelpful.* He had a vague sense of having handed a burden off to someone who had no idea how to handle it. And yet, he felt at the same time that he had done something that needed to be done. He felt as though part of a load had been lifted from his heart, as though he had broken through somehow to a level of action rather than just sitting and stewing in his helplessness. It seemed as though the room, and the weight on his shoulders, had lightened just a bit.

He sat for a moment longer, and then clicked off the light, crawled into bed along side Molly, and gently held her in his arms. They still didn't sleep, but together, silently, they helped one another through that longest of nights.

* * *

Badger gnawed on his multi-knuckled finger, relishing the agony that came as the leathery skin split. The fresh pain eased the fear that welled up in him as he thought about Grayly or Bagda finding out about this slip-up.

It was only a minor lapse, a tiny hiccup in a small part in the otherwise smooth flow of operation A-121. But he knew Bagda would have an unholy fit if he heard of it. Badger glared at the battered form of Brilliantly, Pete's guardian angel. Badger had been distracted by the sudden appearance of the incredibly powerful Agrevious, who was the angel watching over the whole city.

Being the object of this glowing, potent being's attention was decidedly not Badger's idea of a good time. The heavenly being had shown up for only a split second, and then had departed again without ever laying a hand on him, but the spiritual after-image on Badger's eyes had distracted him and had taken long enough to fade that Ajourney had had time to prod Pete into calling Pastor Dave.

Badger lit into the angel like a terrier into a rat, pummeling him with his fists, feet, and knees. But the demon knew it was too late. What was done was done, and it only remained to be seen just what damage had actually been dealt to the plan. The panting demon watched the angel with one eye and kept most of his attention on the human who was just hanging up the phone.

It seemed as though Pastor Dave had remained as ineffectual as usual. Gramsting must have handled his end of the conversation well enough to cover for Badger's own mistake. And Pete seemed nearly as full of despair as he had prior to the call. Perhaps this would be all right after all.

Badger made a decision to try to patch up the operation on his own rather than reporting this small, itsy-bitsy mistake to his boss. That was preferable by far to admitting to his lower downs that he needed help with his pitiful little part in the mission. Why get smeared by Bagda for it if it could be made right with no one the wiser. Yes, he would just beef up his efforts and hope that he could smooth this mess over again before anyone noticed.

Badger walked over and gave Brilliantly another solid kick to the ribs, smiling at the effect, and then turned his attention back to Pete, subtly working his demonic claws back into the fibers of Pete's heart.

Chapter 3
Her time was well spent.

Pastor Dave Merryl slowly hung up the phone. He was an athletic thirty-two-year-old who stayed fit by running and playing basketball with the boys in the youth group. He was blond, six feet, one inch tall, and still built like the wrestler he had been in high school. But no matter how fit he was physically, he knew that he had blown it. At the moment, he had been so overwhelmed with the news of Marianne's kidnapping that he had completely lost his focus on how he should try to help the Frack family. Of all the times for a big disaster like this to happen! He knew he was emotionally and spiritually unprepared to handle this crisis. He rested his elbows on the counter and rubbed his face with his hands, sighing deeply.

Sam, sitting at the other end of the counter, asked, "What is it? What's happened?" Concern filled her voice as well as her eyes. Her short stature belied her huge heart for Christ. He had never met anyone as consistently focused on their relationship with God.

He raised his head to meet her gaze, "Marianne Frack has been kidnapped," he replied shortly. "She was abducted from the mall this afternoon, and hasn't been seen since."

Sam's hands flew to cover her mouth, muffling her gasp. Her eyes widened, and she shook her head as if to deny the message. "Dave, we've got to pray. And we've got to let others know to pray, too." Her words seemed to strike to the root of his spiritual dilemma, and his head jerked as if she'd slapped him.

Were his thoughts that obvious to her? "Yes, you're right. We do need to pray. Let me call the elders and get them in gear, and then we will."

In his heart, he knew that should have been his first action - even while he was still on the phone, he knew he should have led Peter Frack in prayer for Marianne. But as dead as his own prayers had been, he knew he couldn't have pulled it off with any conviction. Now his wife was showing just how far he'd fallen. She still had her relationship with God: alive, vibrant, powerful. But his was just a dried up husk of what it had been. So he constantly fell back to what he could do, what he could accomplish on his own strength - like good programs at church, and now mobilizing people - rather than what he should do - like calling out to his God for help in a situation he couldn't possibly solve, but God certainly could.

Humiliation filled his heart as he realized that he couldn't let on, not even to Sam, how far he felt from God. Sam's face looked hurt as she quietly acquiesced to his unspoken refusal to join her. She said, "All right, hon. I'll be in the other room," and left to begin her prayers for the Frack family.

He heard the floor squeak as she knelt at her "prayer spot" in front of the easy chair in the living room. He could picture her there, head bent over folded hands. He had seen her there so many times, envious that he couldn't seem to make the same connection with God that she so easily fell into. He reached for the phone again, simultaneously pulling the church directory over.

* * *

Separated from the Merryls by the thinnest of barriers, a curtain made of a mere twist of a dimension, was another scene entirely. Three demons squared off against two angels; the three hell-bent on savaging the lives of the two humans before them, while the two angels focused intently on salvaging. Aglow, Pastor

Dave's guardian angel, was not nearly strong enough to defeat the combined might of Gramsting, Dave's personal demon, combined with the prowess and power of Grayly, the demon assigned to the youth group.

Gramsting had come early into this battle, assigned to Dave when Dave had made his first intentional step into the pornography lifestyle. Since that time Aglow had suffered through one lost battle after another. Trying to get through to Dave was like shouting against a hurricane. Nothing seemed to get through to him, to break the blindness that Gramsting's lies had caused.

Samantha's angel, Salient, was in a little better position to resist on her human's behalf. Sam still maintained a soft and repentant heart, as well as an active prayer life. But even though he was able to protect his charge from direct assault, he could do little to stave off damage to this family. This had all the makings of a very rough time for the Merryls.

* * *

Sam's heart was broken as she thought through and spoke to God about all that was on her heart. *"Dear Father,"* she poured out from her wounded soul, *"What are we to do? There is so much! So much on my heart, I don't even know where to begin, what to pray."*

Dave had made several phone calls, to Pastor Miller and to three or four of the church elders. That had not taken long, and he had gone to bed shortly after he hung up from the last call. Sam didn't understand why he wouldn't join her here in prayer. She chased those thoughts around and around in her mind for awhile until the house quieted, and then slowly her mind followed suit.

There in their little house on the worn carpet, with her thoughts stilled for a while, she was reminded of the verse in Romans chapter eight that told of the Holy Spirit praying for her because she didn't know the words to say. This was the first time she really understood what Paul meant by those words. She was greatly comforted even in the middle of her overwhelming feelings of loss and loneliness.

She continued to pray through her list of troubles, starting again with the deepening chasm between her and Dave, a chasm that had steadily deepened over the last ten months or so. She expressed her concerns for the Frack family and, of course, for Marianne and her safety. She again praised Him, kneeling quietly and realizing that she was, in a very real sense, in the throne room of Almighty God – the God who had created everything and who held everything together moment by moment with His awesome power. The God of love who treasured humans so much that He had sacrificed His own Son to give them a way back to fellowship with Him. Her love for God deepened as she was reminded again of His love for her.

Over the course of a few minutes, a growing conviction made its way into the front of her mind. She pictured the faces of an elderly couple in the church. A sweet old man and his wife by the name of Caffer to whom she had only rarely spoken. She could picture their faces, wrinkled and surrounded by their gray hair, and felt an urge to call them, a burden placed on her heart by the Lord. "Not now, Lord. It's so late!" she thought. But the conviction held, with even more strength.

Looking up at the clock on the VCR, she saw that it was 3:38 a.m. and that she had been curled up in front of the chair for nearly two hours. She walked quietly to the kitchen and sat at the counter. Thumbing slowly through the church directory, she recalled the spelling of their names, and thumbed over to the Caffer's phone listing.

Finally convinced that she should go ahead and call, she punched in the numbers and listened for the ring on the other end. It rang four times and she nearly hung up, but her heart kept telling her to hold on even when her mind said, "Hang up." Five rings. Six. Finally she heard the phone lifted off its cradle at the Caffers' end of the line. "Hello," an obviously elderly, female, fragile sounding voice answered. Sam thought to herself, *Almost 4:00 a.m. and she sounds wide awake!*

Aloud, she spoke into the receiver, "Mrs. Caffer, I'm so sorry to call you at this hour. This is Sam Merryl, from First Evangelical. Can I speak with you for a moment?"

Mrs. Caffer interjected, "No, no, my dear. You don't need to apologize. Mr. Caffer and I were up anyway. What can I do for you, dear?"

Sam's curiosity was prickling, but she held herself to the point of her call, rather than asking what in the world they were doing awake at four a.m. "Mrs. Caffer, something terrible has happened to one of the children in the youth group at the church."

"I see." came the soft reply over the phone. "Can you tell me more, dear?"

"Yes, ma'am. Marianne Frack was at the mall today, and was abducted from there by a man in a black van. No one has seen or heard from her since then."

Mrs. Caffer was silent for a moment. "Mrs. Caffer? Did you hear?" asked Sam.

"Yes dear. I was just mulling over how God works in such mysterious ways. You see, the reason Mr. Caffer and I are awake is that I had a dream - an incredibly vivid dream that woke me up. And when I woke up, I had this overwhelming desire to pray for the youth group and for you and Pastor Dave. So I woke up Mr. Caffer and we went to prayer. As we prayed, the Lord impressed upon me the image of a young girl. So we've been praying over those things for the last hour or so."

"Mrs. Caffer! That's amazing!"

"Well, dear, what you shared with me certainly explains why the Lord placed those things on my heart. But it's not the first time He's awakened me or my Allen in order to pray."

"Oh, Mrs. Caffer! I'm so glad! And I'm humbled by your sensitivity to God's voice. Thank you so much for your prayers."

"Well, honey, we'll pray with more details and more authority now. I'm glad you called."

"God placed you on my heart as I was praying. I couldn't just ignore it."

"No, you certainly couldn't do that."

"I promise to keep you informed, Mrs. Caffer, if I hear anything else. But probably not in the middle of the night next time." Both women laughed, and Sam said goodnight and hung up the phone.

Comforted by the fact that there was another prayer warrior on the job, Sam finally relaxed. Breathing a small sigh, she listened to the sounds of the night and heard nothing but a ticking clock, the whisper of the wind in the trees outside, and an occasional passing car. Even at this hour the city didn't completely sleep.

She wondered if Marianne were sleeping.

* * *

Meeting with them in the attic of the Caffer home, Agrevious nodded a "Well done" to Salient, Clayton and Merely, the three angels assigned to Sam Merryl, to Allen Caffer and to Alice Caffer. The angels saluted smartly and returned to their duties. Having pushed back the forces of darkness long enough to bring these three prayer warriors together, they now stood guard, holding the ground that had just been taken back from the darkness.

* * *

Across town Murkinator worked with Despair, a tiny demon who tried to worm his way into Marianne's heart but who was turned away time after time. It was as though there was a wall around her heart which offered no chink or hole through which he could creep. Finally Murkinator banished him with a snap of his fingers, deciding to rough up Ajourney some more in an attempt to further weaken his defenses.

It was very disappointing to watch Marianne go on with such self control in the face of the physical, emotional and other abuse which her captors were inflicting on her, and it was Ajourney's fault that she was so peaceful.

* * *

Marianne was certainly not asleep. Her captors had finished with her moments ago but had left her tied to some cold pipes in an acutely uncomfortable position in a corner of a room that was empty other than the bed in the other corner. There wasn't even a rug covering the rough, scarred hardwood floor. They had also left her in pain, but over the last couple of hours a renewed sense of peace and comfort had come over her.

The drugs they had given her had worn off long ago, but her confidence that she was in the arms of her Savior was strong and sure. No matter what the men did to her, no matter what the tireless camera recorded of her abuse and humiliation, her heart was at rest. She couldn't believe how simple it seemed at times to trust Jesus with all that was happening to her.

Her streaked hair was still neatly brushed, and though her face still felt tight from crying, her tears had been washed away. The film crew had put makeup on her face that now felt stiff and awful to her.

It had been a tough time when they locked her on the floor in this room. A time when hope seemed to ship-wreck on the shoals of her loneliness and helplessness. But then she had turned her head to the wall, leaning her forehead against the rough, cold plaster and prayed. It took a moment, but as she sought Him, she drew near again to His presence, and again His comfort filled her heart.

Now she waited. She was not sure what she was waiting for, but her stillness was more than simple idleness. She was not just sitting and passing time, she was waiting. And not only that, but she waited with confidence, knowing Who planned her future, knowing in Whose hands she rested, and knowing that she did not wait alone. For a twelve-year-old girl, alone in a dangerous situation, her time was well spent. Still and quiet and mostly unmoving, Marianne waited.

* * *

Ajourney, bruised, bleeding, and weary but still taking all of Marianne's pain on himself, shifted himself to fit under her body, insulating her more thoroughly from the cold floor and hard pipes. He felt again the renewing strength that flowed through him with Marianne's prayers, the Caffers' prayers, and the prayers of Samantha Merryl. A pitiful few warriors for such an important operation, but, he reminded himself, the Almighty doesn't need large numbers only contrite hearts to work his purposes. And these few were true - true to God and to His word. They would suffice, at least for now.

He smiled and settled in for a long night. He knew that unless something drastically changed, and soon, Marianne's time on earth was growing short, and that the Master Himself would be coming to comfort her in the middle of this journey. In the meantime, Ajourney knew that she was strengthened and comforted by his own arms, and by the arms of the Comforter Himself. This was a very difficult time for her, but he was so proud of her. Her conviction that she was safe in God's plan despite her circumstances was largely responsible for his ability to protect her so. His heart fairly glowed with love for her, and tears slipped down his face; not tears of pain, nor of sadness, but tears of pure love for this young saint.

He couldn't help giving a threatening glare to the demon who called himself the Murkinator. The lizard ducked as though Ajourney had thrown a punch at him. Though Ajourney's orders were for defensive action only, the little lizard got insufferably cocky if he went too long without a reminder of who was on the Lord's side.

Ajourney wondered at the bruises on the Murkinator's face and shoulder. Earlier the lizard had disappeared for a few moments, and then returned looking far worse for wear and acting a bit edgy. The other demon, the little demon of despair, had been sent packing after several futile efforts at breaching Marianne's defenses. With the solid shield of Marianne's faith, Ajourney had had no trouble countering Despair's thrusts toward Marianne's heart. Now it was just the two of them, weary angel and skittish demon, and they settled into their positions, squared off, warily watching one another over Marianne's head as the night passed.

* * *

Saturday dawned bleak and dreary in more than just Pete's heart. The weather had turned over night as a low-pressure front passed through, bringing clouds with it, then rain, and finally sleet. Pete took grim satisfaction in the weather – it reflected his mood so well.

Pastor Dave had called at nine o'clock to let him know that he and a few of the church elders would be over at eleven. Now, at ten-thirty, he and Molly were up and dressed. Steve had only gotten up just long enough to take another Tylenol III for the unending ache in his heart as much as for his broken wrist. He had then returned to his room, leaving Pete and Molly alone in the family room; she sitting silently on the couch, he staring out the window to the back yard. In the light of day he barely remembered the fear that had come over him in this very room the night before. He shrugged it off as a case of the jitters, a side effect of the trauma of the last day.

He brought a cup of coffee to Molly, placing it carefully in her compliant hand. She murmured an automatic "thank you" and continued staring at the wall across the table from her.

He paused, considering Molly. How things had changed. While Molly had always been introspective, she had always rolled with the punches that life threw her way. When crises arose, Molly always seemed to be able to stand and think clearly – a steady, strong oak in a storm. When Steve had cut his arm skateboarding, she had calmly wrapped a towel around it and hustled him off to the emergency room. He could list one occasion after another that showed her as a person in control of herself. But this event had apparently pushed her too far. He had never seen her like this – unreachable. He had no idea what to do for her.

A few minutes later, the doorbell rang, and he set his own cup down and hurried to the front hall to open the door. Four men stood on the porch, all looking uncomfortable and wet from the pouring rain.

"Come in, please!" he said as he backed away and held the door open. They paused as though none wanted to be the first across the threshold, and then all shuffled in, shrugging out of their dripping jackets, and handing them to Pete. Each gave his name with his coat. "Hi, I'm Ted Eastwell," said the first, a tall thin man who didn't seem to want to look Pete in the eyes.

"John Stirming, Pete. Sorry to hear about your daughter." This came from another tall man who shook his hand as though they were closing a loan.

"Pete, I'm Fred Hatch," pronounced the third, who was dressed in a dark suit, making Pete wonder if he was on his way to a funeral. Fred locked eyes with Pete and stared with a gaze that was quite uncomfortable - eerie in fact. Pete tore his eyes away, looking to Pastor Dave for a familiar face.

And the fourth was Pastor Dave Merryl, looking weary, as though he had just gone ten rounds with a heavy weight champ. His eyes were dark and swollen, and his hair looked limp and dull. It was quite a contrast with his usual well groomed appearance. He looked much older than a youth pastor ought to.

Pete hesitated, his arms full of wet jackets. Then he pointed toward the family room and said, "I'll put your coats in the other room and join you in the family room in just a minute.

There's coffee on, make yourselves at home." The four visitors made their silent way back through the house, nodding at Molly as they passed the kitchen.

Pete rolled his eyes, thinking that this was going to be awkward as well as a waste of time, but hurriedly laid the collection of wet coats across the arm of a chair in the kitchen and returned to his guests.

"Can I get coffee for anyone?" he inquired, and when three of the four nodded, added, "Sugar? Cream?"

He noted their preferences and walked out of the room with, "I'll be right back." He was as glad to have something to do as the three elders and Pastor Dave were to have something in their hands to hide their nervousness.

It took several minutes of fussing to get each his chosen combination of coffee, cream, or sugar, but finally all settled into chairs or the couch. Pastor Dave cleared his throat. "Ah, Mr. Frack? Pastor Miller couldn't come this morning, but he wanted me to let you know that he'll be praying for you, and will try to call you later today. Why don't you bring us up to speed on what's taken place." Nodding at the others, he went on, "I gave them the outline of what took place yesterday. Has there been any new development?"

Pete nodded his understanding of Dave's words, and then slowly shook his head in response to the last question. "No. Nothing new has happened. There is still no word from the police or from the kidnappers."

As he spoke, he thought, *This is crazy! I can't believe I'm speaking these words. This should be a script from a movie, not something I'm saying about my own daughter!*

The others variously nodded their understanding or shook their heads in commiseration. After an uncomfortable silence, the others looked at John, who looked as though he'd had to fold himself to get into the chair. He took the cue and, like an experienced business man, led the conversation toward the purpose of their visit. "Pete, we're here as representatives of the Board of Elders. We want you to know that we're here to help you and your family in any way we can and that we'll be praying for you and your family." He paused to allow any others to speak, but when no one did, he went on, "Let's pray now, shall we? Pastor Dave, why don't you lead us?"

They all bowed their heads, and Dave cleared his throat, thinking, *Oh, boy, the pressure's on now. Praying in front of board members is not my favorite thing to do.* But after what he thought would be recognized as a thoughtful pause, he began, "Oh heavenly Father, we ask for these, your children, an act of grace. We ask that You would bring about the rescue and return of Marianne, and that You would give grace and peace and patience to each member of the Frack household. We thank You for all You do for us and pray these things in Thy Son's holy name, Amen."

His clenched hands belied his otherwise outwardly relaxed posture. He felt miserable as he carefully picked his words to sound proper for the church leaders. None of them had come from his heart, though he really did ache for Marianne and for her stricken family. His mind was so caught up in his own guilt, and in the knowledge that his relationship with Christ was damaged, that he couldn't pray with any sincerity. He knew without a doubt that not one of his words had reached any higher than the ceiling over his head.

The others muttered their 'Amens' as well, and looking around for confirmation, rose in unison to leave. They all made their silent way back toward the entry door.

"Pete, we'll be praying for you," Fred said in a nearly automatic mode, as he finished pulling on his jacket and reached for the doorknob. "We trust you are using this sad occasion to think through what God might be trying to teach you. I believe He speaks most clearly to us in our times of pain."

Pete looked at him with his mouth hanging open, trying to make even a little bit of sense out of what Fred had just said.

"Yes," agreed John, "We will trust God to bring Marianne home to you in good health, but we must be willing to learn from this. You do agree, don't you, that God is trying to discipline you, His child?"

Ted simply kept nodding his head, looking from one face to another like a puppy, anxious to please.

Pete looked at Pastor Dave, who had turned a deep shade of red, clearly embarrassed by the insensitivity of the two elders. "Uh, I think we'd better go now, gentlemen."

Pete gladly left the room to retrieve their coats, and returned as Dave spoke again, "Pete, I'll give you a call later to keep in touch." A cold gust blew in as he opened the door. Then he ushered the three elders out into the blowing sleet, looking back over his shoulder with eyes rolling to show his disunity with the three.

Pete leaned his head against the closed wooden door and tried to collect his thoughts and warm his heart. Bad enough when the elders had demonstrated such a superficial use of prayer, the situation had turned ludicrous when the two had taken their parting shots. Could they really be implying that Pete and his family somehow deserved this horror due to something they had done, some sin they had committed?

Sighing, he slowly turned and went back to the kitchen. Molly still sat, coffee untouched and now cold in front of her on the table, wringing her hands again, which looked red and irritated. He pulled out a chair next to her and sat, joining her in silent and futile contemplation of what they could be doing to bring Marianne back safely.

* * *

Badger rubbed his hands together in glee, and then, unable to contain his joy, swept around the Frack family room giving high fives to the other demons. They had successfully derailed this first puny, weak, ineffectual attempt of the humans to tap into the only source of help that would do them any good. The others all responded except for Gramsting, the sergeant assigned to the youth pastor. He only looked worried.

He continued to focus on his host, the good Pastor Dave, knowing that his responsibility here was greater, and that if he lost control of the pastor, the operation was in deep danger, and so was he. Gramsting saw clearly how close the humans involved with operation A-121 were to the truth, and how little it might take to set them firmly on the narrow way to You-Know-Who. The key lay in balance: balance between using the truth and weaving in lies so subtle that humans didn't quite notice them, yet significant enough to keep them on the smooth, broad downhill road to hell. He was good at it, and though the others would never admit it, they could learn a lot from him, just as he had learned much from Bagda over the centuries.

* * *

Lieutenant Mochek put off the call until early Saturday afternoon. But finally she knew she had to get in touch with the parents of case number MF-87563-92. There wasn't much she could tell them, and the conversation was heavy with despair, despair which she could do nothing to dispel.

"Mr. Frack, I'm sorry that there is so little to tell you at this point. We have several leads which we are following up. The van is the most solid one at this point. But the M.O. is very similar to several others that have occurred in the last few months."

"What?!" came his angry reply. "You mean to tell me that there have been a series of these kidnappings and you've told the public nothing about it? Nothing to warn them to be more careful? Who do you think you are, hiding this kind of information?"

"Mr. Frack, some of the information is withheld to protect the progress of our investigation, and other parts are held for a time to protect the privacy of the families involved."

"Well their privacy may have cost us our daughter. And you tell me - is it worth it?"

The line hummed with tension, but there was silence between the two for a moment. Lieutenant Mochek remained silent, fighting the resentment that Mr. Frack's comments aroused.

In a quieter, and infinitely tired sounding voice, Pete went on, "Do you have anything else to tell us?"

She forced calm into her voice, "No, Mr. Frack. I'll let you know if we hear anything. But don't be afraid to call me at any time." Then, much against her professional training, she closed with, "I'll be praying for you and your daughter." The words, meant to be encouraging, sounded hollow and impotent to her own ears, which had heard more bad news than any ears should.

They ended their conversation, both of them feeling empty and helpless.

* * *

Marianne rubbed her wrist where the handcuff had rubbed the skin red. She still hurt from the filming earlier today, and as they headed down the hall, she knew they were going back at it again. Two of the men came for her; the big one who had taken her from the mall led. She didn't know his name, but he was one of the "actors" and she had named him Moe in her own mind. And another, the boss whom every one called Art, followed, keeping up a running monologue. The man never stopped talking, and it made her mad.

As they turned the corner to head across the dirty kitchen to the basement steps, she took in the sad state of this house. The linoleum floor curled up at the corners, and was covered with papers and spilled food. There was a sour smell of garbage in the air, and dirty dishes filled the sink. A black garbage sack overflowed, leaning in one corner.

As they neared the open door to the basement steps, she saw the back door with its peeling white paint and the cracked, black-painted window panes. She noticed its loose doorknob, and then she noticed the hasp was open with the padlock hanging loose on the latch.

Without pausing to consider the odds against her, she shoved Moe into the stair well and got great satisfaction from hearing him crash down the steps, cursing all the way. Without hesitating, she used that shove to push off to dash for the back door, reaching the door in a split second.

Art was taken by surprise, and looked at Moe's feet disappearing down the steps before reacting to Marianne's escape. He made an aborted move to go help Moe, but realized that the greater need was to get Marianne. With a shouted curse he got under motion, following her across the kitchen. Half a step into his chase, he slipped on some unidentified food smeared on the floor. As Marianne yanked open the door, letting the setting sun to flood into the filthy room, he recovered and set out after her again. Marianne leaped down the two cement steps into the grass of an overgrown back yard and started wading through the knee high grass toward the gate, hanging open at the back. The long grass pulled at each step like knee deep water, but she pressed on, freedom just a short sprint away.

* * *

Ajourney grinned as Moe's demon tumbled down the steps in synch with his human. Unlike the human, however, the demon was back into the fight in a flash. Ajourney gave him a solid poke in the face as he flew around the edge of the door, stunning him and slowing his advance.

He looked just in time to see Marianne leap off the porch and set out through the long grass. Just in time, he caught up and guided her around the bucket of water hidden in the grass, pointing her in the direction of the only break in the fence.

He had little hope that he could get her out of the yard in this desperate attempt, but knew that any commotion they created might at least get some help from a nosy neighbor, or passing car. He also knew that they had to at least try. And now here she was, almost to the gate! Might she actually make it?

* * *

Marianne felt Art's hand grab for her shirt tail and miss, and she dodged to the right around a rusty bucket filled with scummy water hidden in the grass. Art planted a foot right in it, stumbled and swore again, but kept coming after her.

Her hopes soared as she reached the gate and saw a woman across the alley hanging up laundry to dry in the evening air. She gathered a breath to call out to her for help, but just then her foot tangled in a pile of rope and wire sitting in the gap of the fence. Art's hand grabbed a big fist full of her hair, yanking her up from her fall, and her breath fluttered out in a weak moan of pain. Art yanked again, and dragged her back into the yard. Marianne saw the woman look over her shoulder at the noise, but was nearly certain that the neighbor had seen nothing that would make her suspicious enough to get help.

* * *

Ajourney felt the blow on his left shoulder, and lurched to his knees, now within reach of the fence. The monstrous demon who was Moe's possessor loomed over him, daring him to move against him. But Ajourney's head was spinning from the pain, and all he could do was watch as Art reclaimed his hold over Marianne. In spite of the pain, and in spite of two huge demons, one of them wielding the club that had felled him, he moved to protect the child, but the monster slammed the club into the side of his head and darkness claimed him for a time.

* * *

Art clamped his hand over her mouth so hard she couldn't breathe, and dragged her by her hair and face all the way back to the house. By the time he had hauled her into the house and slammed the door shut, her vision had darkened with lack of air, and her scalp felt as though it were coming right off the top of her head. She gasped for air as Art took his hand away from her face, gagging with pain. Stars filled her vision for the time it took to regain her breath.

He threw her across the room into Moe's waiting arms and snarled, "You little witch! Don't you ever do that again. I'm going to teach you to stay put. You'll learn to obey so well you'll be asking if it's all right to breathe!" He was screaming at her, and finally stopped to catch his breath. "Take her downstairs, and get her cleaned up again. We've got filming to do yet today!"

Moe dragged her away, limping on a sprained ankle, as Art ran his hands through his hair, trying to regain his composure.

Chapter 4
It's a beautiful thing to see.

Steve had drifted in and out of sleep, riding the alternating waves of pain and too-strong pain medication. He thought about Danielle, who had called and texted several times expressing her concern. But he couldn't bring himself to talk with her. His guilt was too heavy to bear by himself, yet he couldn't face his girlfriend with Marianne's absence weighing on his heart either.

The ringing of the land-line phone pierced the sleep and drug-induced fog shrouding Steve's brain. He groaned and reached over to the nightstand next to his bed. His knuckle brushed against the glass of water sitting there, knocking it to the carpeted floor with a splash, but not breaking the glass itself. "Geeze!" he muttered and then lifted the receiver to his ear and pushed the 'connect' button just in time to hear his dad answer on the kitchen extension. He held the breath he had taken to say hello.

"Hello," came his dad's voice, with a tired edge that even Steve, in his medicated state, noticed. "Pete, this is Jerry... Jerry McGee from the church. I heard about your daughter, and the description of the get-away van."

"Yeah Jerry, thanks for calling," Pete answered, without much conviction, and thinking what an odd first sentence that was.

"Well, I wanted you to know that my boy, Ted just saw a van that matches the description of that van over on Maple Street at the dry cleaners near the bar there."

Pete hesitated for just a second as he thought about what Jerry had just said, and then replied, "Did you call the police?" Pete's voice was much sharper now, interest piqued by the news. Steve, too, perked up his ears.

"Not yet. I didn't think that I should on just the sighting of a black van," came the hesitant reply.

"Well, how long ago was it? And which way were they heading?" Pete's voice was quick and impatient now, and Steve quietly let his breath go as Mr. McGee asked for more details from his son. Steve knew Ted, and was surprised that the kid had noticed anything going on around him. He was such an air head.

"Ted says it was about twenty minutes ago, and that the van was just pulling out onto Hubbardston Road heading out of the city. He said that he came right home to tell me. I don't know if it's any help, but ..."

"Let me get off the line and call the police. Thanks for calling, Jerry." Pete's voice was hurried now, but Jerry apparently didn't catch the urgency.

"Well, Pete, I felt you might want to know, and to know that we're thinking of you guys. It's got to be tough right now for you all."

In his mind, Pete was thinking, *Get off the phone, you idiot!* But aloud he said, "Listen, thanks Jerry, but I think I'd better call the police now. Thanks for calling."

Neither of the men heard the light click of Steve disconnecting.

Steve could hear the murmuring of his dad's voice from the other room as Steve grabbed a couple of things from his dresser, pulled his jacket on, and walked down the hall to the garage door. At the corner of the door to the kitchen he paused until he heard his dad talking. Peeking around the corner he saw his dad look toward the back yard and used that opportunity to cross the doorway and out of sight. He quietly lifted the van keys from the hook, gripping them in his fist to keep them from clinking. He slowly opened the door and stepped down the two steps to the garage. The weather seal squeaked just a bit as he tried to close the door without making any noise.

He sat for just a moment in the van thinking about the fastest way to get to Hubbardston Road and whether he should just leave it to the police. How long was it likely to take for them to respond to his dad's call? Then he noticed the still-cracked window where he had hit it with his fist trying to get into the locked car to chase the kidnappers. He jammed the keys into the ignition and hit the garage door opener at the same time.

The door barely cleared the top of the van as he gunned the engine and backed out of the drive. Slamming it into drive, the tires spun on the wet pavement as he headed down the road for the east side of town.

* * *

Ajourney, Marianne's guard, hurt from his head to his toes, and everywhere in between. But what hurt the most was his heart. The men who were treating his beloved charge in this inhumane way felt nothing at all. Their spiritual and emotional calluses were hard and thick and insensate with ages of sin, the covering of their demonic companions, and the long abuse of their consciences. Though he did not fear any of them, still Ajourney winced every time he saw the evil demons riding shepherd over Art, Moe, and the others. Along with the individual demons oppressing them, Lust, Addiction, Envy, and Greed were always present, seeking opportunity to get their specialized digs in and taking great pleasure in further wrecking already depraved lives. The insidious spirit, Addiction, was around, too. Slithering deeper and deeper into each of the men's hearts.

Ajourney craved the times when Marianne was focused on the Lord in prayer but certainly understood the times when she was distracted by the ministrations of these evil-doers. The prayers of that lovely older couple, the Caffers, and of Samantha Merryl offered treasured boosts of spiritual ammunition and energy as well. The ascending, heartfelt, interceding thoughts and prayers of these saints were a balm on his wounds and a source of strength for the ongoing battle. Oh that there were more of these warriors who would respond to their heavenly call to battle-prayer. There would be more eventually he knew, but Ajourney felt the current lack in the aches and pains that he bore for Marianne, especially right now. Marianne's attempted escape, along with his own assistance in distracting Art and the artful placement of the bucket of water hidden in the grass, had almost been enough. But the demons riding herd on the kidnappers were sharp enough that they had thwarted the attempt before any good could come of it. Now Marianne and he had paid a price, a price mitigated by the supportive prayers of those who cared enough to intervene, but a painful price just the same.

* * *

As careful as Steve had been about making noise while he left the house without his parents' permission, his dad had heard the door close, had heard the engine start, and wondered where Molly was going all of a sudden. But he was on the phone with Lieutenant Mochek by then, and didn't find out for several minutes that Molly was still sitting in the living room, unmoving, still staring at nothing. By the time he looked into Steve's room and then outside to see which direction he had gone, Steve was nowhere in sight.

Pete's head felt as if it were about to burst. The stress was already incredible without having Steve run off without warning. It wasn't like

Steve at all to do this. *Oh, my. Where in the world did we get off track with him?* Thinking back over the years, he could see Steve the first time he had mowed the lawn, the first time he had ridden a bike, the times at the beach: swimming and splashing and taking on the world without a moment of hesitation. Steve had always been confident, certain, positive, always glad to be with the family. And now, well now, Steve was way off somewhere on his own. Even when he was at home, he was off somewhere in another world.

Sure he was dealing with a lot and seemed pretty withdrawn from the family, but he always followed the rules, and one of those was; no leaving the house without leaving a note of where you were going, much less taking the car without permission.

Despair welled up in Pete's heart, so heavy and powerful his knees nearly buckled. He leaned wearily against the wall, heaving a great sigh - nearly a sob - and grinding the heels of his palms into his eyes until he saw stars. As the sparks faded from his eyesight, he looked again at Molly, wondering whether it was worth the effort to tell her about Steve taking off.

Shaking his head at the futility of trying to get through to her, he shuffled back to the phone and dialed Pastor Merryl's number. It was time to bring him up to speed again. Maybe Dave would have something constructive to offer.

* * *

In a break from riding herd on Pete's heart, Badger allowed himself a small, demonic smile of self-congratulations. His team was working well together now, like a finely tuned orchestra, each doing his part to drive this family apart from one another, and even more important, apart from the Enemy. He patted the little Despair demon on his gnarled back, and both of them watched Despondency gnaw away at Molly's will.

Next on his to-do list was to assist Gramsting with leading that Merryl guy further into the pit he was falling into. By having Pete subtly suggest he wanted help with finding the black van, Gramsting could guide Pastor Dave into still more 'self help' by rounding up a youth posse to look for it. And the busier Pastor Dave was with doing useless things, no matter how helpful-sounding, the less time he had for seeking real help for his addiction, or for healing his marriage.

"Ah!" Badger sighed, "I love it when these lives fall apart like this. It's a beautiful thing to see," and continued to nudge Pete's mind, ever so slightly. He exulted with the feelings of an artist creating a masterpiece.

Badger scowled at Brilliantly, who was sitting over in the corner of the kitchen just watching. The angel had been particularly quiet throughout this whole mission. He was no match for Badger anyhow, what with the poor prayer life that Pete had and all. Badger had pretty free reign in this battle for Pete's mind. His soul had almost been lost to the Enemy as a younger man, but Badger had narrowly averted that disaster, and had been successful in keeping Pete ineffective and weak in his spiritual awareness for some twenty years now.

He gloated to himself that he knew very well the secret of balancing control with finesse so that his victim never quite caught on to how much his thoughts and decisions were guided and influenced by the demons attached to his case. It was highly effective to let the humans believe that even if there were demons out there somewhere, such fallen angels were pretty much unable to affect them. The good ghost, bad ghost myths helped matters along too. As if an eternally damned, and hopelessly evil spirit could ever be good. Badger snorted, even a child could figure out the truth of the matter. No demon could possibly be good, other than for the purpose of laying groundwork for an even greater evil.

As Pete hung up the phone, Badger zipped over to the Merryls' house to check with his sergeant. "Badger reporting, sir!" he snapped as he rose to a full attention stance, not very impressive in an amoeboid body, but Gramsting noticed. He wasn't so far removed from being a private that he had forgotten the difficulties associated with that status.

The sergeant acknowledged his presence, and then waved him silent, and refocused his attentions on Dave. Badger watched, trying to learn from his superior's obviously more advanced technique as he skillfully placed thoughts into the youth pastor's mind, leading him down a path of logic based on one wrong belief. That error had emasculated more spiritual plans than he could count. But mankind continued to charge ahead, thinking that they could accomplish great things for God if they simply tried hard enough. "God helps those who help themselves" was the call to arms for hundreds of powerless churches and useless ministries across America.

The end result of Gramsting's ministrations to Dave was a plan of action for the poor sap that not only would not help but that would maintain a sense of self sufficiency, keeping him from seeking help from the only place that could help, the Creator Son. The beauty of the demon's work was in the fact that Dave's actions would affect so many areas of this community for the cause of sin, death, and Satan. Once Pastor Dave arrived at the desired decision, Gramsting could let Dave have some slack. So he then turned his attention back to Badger. "Good work, you smelly, lying slime-ball."

Badger did the demonic analogy of a blush, and murmured, "Thank you, sir. It is going well, isn't it?"

"Yes. These humans are so lost in themselves, they don't even recognize that we are here. But let's not get complacent. Get on back to your post. I'll make sure the lower-downs hear of your good work."

"Thank you again, sir! I won't let you up." Badger backed away, turned and popped back to his position at the Merryls' home.

* * *

Dave was shaking with excitement. Here at last was something he could do that would help. His shaking finger could barely hit the right buttons as he called the first name on the Senior High phone chain. His fingers twisted knots in the curling cord as the phone rang once, twice, three times, four. Finally the answer came, "Tesch's residence."

"Hi, this is Pastor Dave. Is Jordan there?"

"Hi, Pastor Dave, this is Tammy. I'll get Jordan for you."

"Thanks, Tammy." Again a pause, as Tammy's footsteps and muted shout for her brother could be heard over the phone.

"Hello."

"Jordan, this Pastor Dave. I've got an emergency job for the phone chain."

"Hi, Pastor. Is it about Marianne?"

"Yeah, it is. I've come across something that we can all do to help. I want you to get the phone-chain going and tell everyone to meet us at the church in twenty minutes. Can you do that?"

"That's not much time. But, sure I can. I'll be there at..." he paused to check the clock., "...at 6:35 on the dot."

"Thanks, Jordan. Don't waste any time. I'm counting on you." And with that Pastor Dave hung up the phone. "Now I have to get some maps and divide the city up so we can cover each area thoroughly." He spoke to himself, completely absorbed in his thinking and planning.

"Who were you talking to, Dave?" Sam asked. Dave was startled right off the stool on which he sat.

"Don't do that to me!" He gave a guilty little laugh, and then wondered why he felt as if he'd just been caught doing something dirty. "I'm mobilizing God's army, hon. Peter Frack just called and said that he thinks they may have spotted the van that took Marianne. So I'm getting all the kids to go out and help look for it."

Even as he said it, he had to admit that it sounded pretty half baked. But something in the look on Sam's face made him go on to defend his decision even before she said a word of condemnation. "I know it's not much, but it's got to beat sitting around doing nothing or going around with a bunch of elders insulting the Fracks!"

"But hon, are you sure you should take the kids out into what is really police work? It could be dangerous!" Her tone was pleading and fretful, and though she hated it when she sounded that way, the fear she felt for what he was planning overwhelmed her.

"I've thought through all that. I'll be careful. I promise." He gave her a quick peck on the cheek, gathered his papers, and was gone.

Sam was stunned and horrified by what Dave was doing. She knew that he had no business getting the kids involved in looking for that van. Fear seethed in her mind, and she wondered what to do. After several moments of pacing from one room to another, she settled into her prayer spot and quieted her mind, asking God for renewed protection and for a breakthrough for Dave.

* * *

Twelve-year-old Tammy Tesch overheard the conversation between her brother and Pastor Dave, at least Jordan's end of it, and she didn't like what she heard. Was Pastor Dave really having all the senior highers go out to look for Marianne? While one part of her wanted to help, and another part of her thought it sounded exciting, the smartest part of her knew that her parents wouldn't like it one bit.

But when Jordan asked for the car for the evening, her folks barely asked him what he was doing before giving the keys to him. Showing a lot of discernment for a junior-higher, she thought, *This is weird. Since when do my parents give my brother the keys for the car when his only plans are to be out driving around all night? And looking for criminals, no less!*

But off he went, leaving Tammy to sit around the house moping about Marianne's situation, and wondering what had gotten into her folks to act so strangely – letting him go like that. Later that night at bedtime, she said a prayer for Marianne, and wondered if Jordan had found any of the creeps that took her friend.

* * *

Salient nodded gravely, and bowed his head in acknowledgement of the source of his new orders. It was hard for him to watch his charge suffer so. Samantha was so true to who her Lord had made her, and so eager to seek Him, yet she, too, had to be brought through some trying times in order to continue the conforming of her heart to His.

Her prayers, often seeming so ineffective to her, were heard - were savored - as only prayers from a pure, child-like heart would be savored - and were responded to in ways that she might never understand until she, too, was brought out of this shadow land to stand face to face with her Savior. The hardest times were yet to come for her. Yet Salient knew that her soul was safe in the hands of God Almighty. He knew that all that occurred around her and to her was only able to refine her, and mold her into the child of God she was made to be.

It was an exceedingly intricate web of interrelations and authority levels that made up the network of security and protection for these humans whom the Lord loved so much. Salient's supervisor, Aggrevious, had once described it to him as a series of umbrellas of protection over them. Though it had occurred over three hundred earthly years earlier, he recalled the conversation as though it were yesterday.

"The Creator set it all up even before we were made," the level-four angel had begun. "Each of His children is under the umbrella of protection of the Lord. Each is also under other interwoven umbrellas as well."

Seeing Salient's look of confusion, he went on, "For instance, a child is under the protective umbrella of his Christian father and mother, while the mother is under the umbrella of her husband, who is under still other umbrellas – those of his pastor, his employer, and others in authority over him."

"It's very complicated, isn't it?" queried Salient.

"It is, and it isn't," said Aggrevious. "It all works very neatly, each umbrella protecting those underneath from the attacks of the evil one. It is all very smooth and effective, right up to the point where one of them steps out from underneath one of the umbrellas."

"How do they do that?"

"Simply by refusing to honor the authority that God placed in the hands of that 'umbrella holder.' When the protected one disobeys or harbors a sinful attitude, he rejects not only the authority over himself, but also the 'umbrella-like' protection of that authority. The same thing occurs when one of them willfully sins. That, too, is a step out from under protection. And when that happens, he is instantly more vulnerable to the attacks of Lucifer and his henchmen. At the same time, he also permits more vulnerability for those sheltering beneath their umbrella as well."

Salient shivered and added, "And we've all seen what happens then."

"Yes, it is one single step in a direction that is difficult to reverse, and which gets much more difficult with each additional step in the wrong direction."

Salient snapped back to the present with a jolt, thinking of what an avalanche of cascading events had been started when Peter Frack and Dave Merryl had stepped out from under their umbrellas of protection. In their own ways, both of them had sinned: Dave in his pornography, and Pete in his refusal to exchange his system of rules for God's way of grace, love, and forgiveness. In refusing to turn away from their sins, each of them effectively tore holes in their own umbrellas and painted targets on themselves, and on the ones under their own umbrellas, for Satan and his hordes of demons to take pot shots at. The evil one was always alert, always looking for opportunities to get his hooks into another human soul. When the humans stepped away from God's offered protection, it just made it all the more simple for Satan to have his way with them.

  Certainly there was more to it than simply these two men sinning. In a very real way, their sins had opened the door to this domino affect, starting a self-perpetuating toppling of events which now threatened to form a stronghold from which Satan could well gain mastery of an entire city. For this conflict, between the forces of evil and the forces of truth, was on the cutting edge of a larger spiritual operation, one which would make or break the demonic strangle-hold on this city. The spiritual future and the moral compass of the police department, the mayor, the city council, the pastors and leadership of the churches in the greater Alagonic area rested on the way this conflict resolved itself. And all due to man using his free will to reject God's will.

Indeed, the next few days would see some major plans of both Satan and the Lord completed for better or for worse. And through it all, the amazing thing, the mystery, was that the all-powerful Creator of the universe allowed these puny but beloved creatures to have free will - a choice whether they would or would not follow Him. Both Salient and Aggrevious silently contemplated that mystery for a moment, and both slowly shook their heads at the wonder and boldness of the Creator's plans.

Salient shook his head, returning to his present human charge. Samantha was entering what could prove to be the darkest time of her life, and as things stood, Salient could do little other than protect, strengthen, and guide as much as possible. For both she and the one she ached for, her husband, had that priceless gift of free will to use for good or ill.

* * *

The youth group trickled into his office over the course of the next twenty minutes, and by then Dave was ready. "Kids, we've got a mission to accomplish." He paused until all fourteen faces were focused on his, and then went on. "Less than an hour ago, a van matching the description of the one used in Marianne's kidnapping was seen heading south on Hubbardston Road. I think that we can finally do something that might help Marianne by heading out there and setting up watch posts."

The kids showed a mixture of responses from dubious to excited. "Yeah! We can catch the jerks who did this!" enthused Ron, who was a senior, and who lettered in three sports. "We'll find those jerks and make them tell us where they took Marianne."

"Now, hold on," warned Dave, reminded of Sam's words. "We are not the police. We are not to attempt to contact these people in any way even if we do find them. I'm serious here. These are dangerous people, and we are not equipped or trained to deal with them." He looked around, and then locked eyes with Ron. "If and when we spot the van, we get a license plate number and call the police. Period."

Heads nodded in agreement, and then he pulled out a stack of envelopes. "I want you to work in teams of at least two in a car. These envelopes have maps with your areas of patrol marked in red. The areas overlap a bit, so don't be surprised if you run into one another."

Becky raised her hand and spoke without waiting for permission, "I don't know about these guys, but I'll have to be home by eleven tonight."

"Oh, yeah. Good point, Becky," Dave responded. "I realize that we can't patrol the streets twenty-four hours a day. We'll just each do what we can do, and let God handle the rest. I do want each of you to call in every half hour to the number on the front of the envelope. That's my cell phone number."

"But we don't have a cell phone," complained Chad, a short, chunky sophomore who was always kind of a whiner.

Jordan Tesch rapped him on the head with a knuckle, and said, "Didja think he was gonna supply us all with phones, ya nincompoop?" The room full of senior highers all laughed, and Chad blushed a bright red and pushed Jordan's hand away.

Pastor Dave brought the room back into order. "If you don't have a phone with you, you can make sure at least one person in your car has one and call in that way. Any other questions? If not, then let's team up and try to pair up seniors with sophomores and freshmen, if you can. If anyone is left over without a car, you can make threesomes instead of pairs." The kids started to get up, but he said, "Oh! Wait. Make sure you each write your name and number on this sheet before you go."

    The kids jostled their way out of the office, shouting battle cries down the hall and ran out of the church to their cars. Only two or three of them had any reservations about what they were about to do, and those few were swept up in the adventure and the enthusiasm of the others.

* * *

    The next phase of plan A-121 was advancing nicely. "This part should almost run itself now," purred Gramsting, as he ghosted along at Pastor Dave's side. "Not even a thought of prayer from this mob. Hee, hee!" He chortled, "I am so good at this!" He jumped with surprise when Grayly appeared without notice at his elbow. "What are you doing here?" he snapped, forgetting for a moment who was the lower down of the two.

Grayly merely stared at him and effortlessly 'thought' sharp pressure into the lower ranked demon's brain until the sergeant began to sweat with the pain. "I came to make sure you didn't botch this up. It's important that these kids don't start having second thoughts and start calling their precious mommies and daddies until they get out there on their silly little patrols."

The sergeant was beginning to look a little weak kneed, so Grayly let go of the pain centers. After all, it wouldn't do to have Gramsting's attention too distracted at the wrong time. Color crept back into the demon's face as the pain faded to a memory.

The two of them looked around at the shadowy demons hovering by each child, some deeply enmeshed in their hearts, others merely tagging along with an occasional nudge at their minds. The few angels in view were limpid looking, weakened by the impotent, non-vital spiritual life of the church in Alagonic. They appeared as though they were trying to achieve as inconspicuous a demeanor as possible. Grayly snarled at one of them, slashing at him with suddenly long claws, and then laughed when the dully shining angel cringed back behind his charge.

It was apparent that the situation was, indeed, well under control. This demon-inspired and human-engineered operation would not only keep these kids and their pastor too busy to pray, but with any luck, would also result in the great fall of Pastor Dave, the budding porn addict. How the church would reel when that news broke. Grayly began to hum a dirge and rub his hands together with anticipation. Gramsting looked at him, and cleared his throat, bringing him back to the present.

"All right, Sergeant," the lieutenant grudgingly conceded, "it looks good so far. But don't get complacent and sloppy here. An awful lot is riding on this part of the operation."

"You can count on me, L.T." the scaly, bat-faced lizard responded. "I'm on a roll, and we are going to mop up this city before we're done here."

"Just see to it that we stay in control. You know how much easier it is to control these humans when they think they've got all the answers." And with that, he transformed into a vapor and puffed away on the breeze.

"I hate it when he shows off like that," muttered Gramsting. "I'll have his position by the time this job is through. I hope Bagda got my report." He snickered as he recalled how thoroughly he had trashed Grayly in that ten-page report.

Little did he know that Bagda, the demon-lord over the entire city, received such reports constantly from greedy demon overlings, who had less power and talent but as much greed and avarice as the lowest and most powerful demons, and always pitched them without reading them, though not before making a mental note to the future discredit of the backstabbing author.

* * *

Sam sat, alternating between praying and fretting. She was very concerned, seeing consequences for her husband's actions to which he was apparently blind. One of those consequences was the possibility of his ending up hurt - or even one of the kids. As each new and progressively worse possibility played out in her mind, she winced as though she were in pain. Her neck and shoulders were sore with tension, and she rolled her shoulders to stretch the muscles.

Finally, after twenty minutes of futile attempts at prayer, she picked up the phone and called Mrs. Caffer. The elderly woman's warm greeting helped to quiet her trembling heart. "Hello, Mrs. Caffer. How are you doing tonight?"

"Fine dear, just fine. Any news about the young Frack girl?" the older lady inquired.

"Not directly, no. But I do know that the elders went over to pray for the Frack's this morning."

"That's a good thing, isn't it? Though I don't believe my Al was made aware of the visit or he surely would have gone."

"Hmm. Well, I also wanted to let you know what Dave is planning and ask for your prayers this evening."

"You sound concerned. What is Pastor Dave doing, dear?"

"Well, he called all the high school kids over to the church, and they're going to go out to watch the main roads for signs of the kidnappers' vehicle."

Mrs. Caffer gasped, "That doesn't sound safe at all! Why would he do something as dangerous as that with those kids?"

Sam heard a voice beyond Mrs. Caffer's and assumed Mr. Caffer had asked what was happening. Samantha went on, "You're right. I asked him to reconsider, but he had his mind made up and wouldn't take even a few minutes to talk it over with me. I think he has become blinded to some pretty obvious things lately."

There was a pause while muffled voices spoke at the other end of the line. Then Mrs. Caffer came back on, "Could we get together to pray this evening? Al and I are feeling that there are some powerful battles being waged tonight. God just won't let us rest, and we would love to get together with you to intercede."

"Why, sure!" Sam was very pleased. "Could you come over here? I've got to get the kids ready for bed."

"Certainly, dear. We understand. How does a half an hour sound? That will give us just a few minutes to get put together."

"Great. I'll have coffee ready."

The two hung up and began preparing to wage war once again, for Dave, for the Fracks, and for the Kingdom.

Chapter 5
Just the right moment.

As the rest of the youth group swept through the parking lot dividing up on the way to their cars, Steve, unaware of the youth group's actions, drove the family mini van through the city to the mall on the far side of town. Evening was approaching, and though he wanted to get to the right part of town before it got dark, he knew better than to get stopped for speeding. Even though he had disobeyed by coming out here looking for that cursed black van by himself, and even though he was pretty high on pot and the pain medication, he still knew enough to avoid doing totally stupid things like speeding.

Finally emerging from the still snarled traffic in the downtown section, he pulled out onto Hubbardston Road and headed south out of town. This road was a main drag, acting as a vehicular release valve for the traffic pressure that the growing city was experiencing. It was four lanes plus a left turn lane and was packed along both sides with store after store and strip malls every quarter mile or so.

This part of the road was a bit of a nicer island in the middle of a pretty run-down part of town. A mere block or so to either side and the store-fronts and malls changed to run-down homes, slums, and drug houses. You could read of robberies and prostitution busts most any day of the week and even an occasional shooting in this area, and the buildings all had bars on the windows. Between the slums and the Hubbardston stores, bars, and sloppy looking restaurants acted as a buffer between respectful and totally disreputable.

Steve pulled into one of the strip-malls and parked in front of a pizza joint. For a few moments, he simply sat collecting his thoughts and feeling his pot-induced buzz ebbing. Over the course of a half an hour his thoughts grew more cohesive as the effects of the drug gradually faded, and he thought through the little bit of information that Mr. McGee had shared with his dad about the van sighting. Since Ted had seen the van heading south out of town, it made sense to follow that direction, so Steve put the van into gear and crept out into traffic again.

His mind was a whirl of conflicting thoughts: thoughts of guilt over his part in Marianne's plight and guilt over taking off in his folks' car ran through his mind, complicated by feelings of relief that he might actually be doing something to help. The throbbing ache of his wrist combined with his lingering high made it difficult to think clearly, yet he felt proudly pleased with this detective/Sherlock Holmes routine. He shook his head, and muttered, "Maybe another joint will help," and fumbled in his jacket pocket for one.

* * *

Groaning with frustration, Danielle Buchannon looked at the time on her phone and considered calling Steve again. She knew that he couldn't possibly be out with the rest of the youth group looking for that van. She was frustrated that he still wouldn't answer her calls or texts. She was also upset because she was sure that Pastor Dave was wrong in calling the kids out for this. She shook her hands out in front of herself seeking some way to express her feelings of helplessness.

She considered telling her folks but then decided that they would either ignore her or overreact. So finally, she bowed her head and prayed, "Lord, I don't know what to think about this awful weekend. But I do know that Steve is in trouble and that he needs You to help him through this time. Would You please watch over him tonight? Keep him safe, and help him to find You after he's worked his way through this mess."

"Oh, and Lord? Be with Marianne, too. She sure needs You now, too. In Jesus' name, Amen."

* * *

Furrgstan chuckled and raked again at Steve's heart, rummaging around in the human boy's memories for more guilt. What a blast, to watch his host's brain shrivel from lingering, miserable false guilt and other matters for which he had no responsibility, things that could so easily be forgiven and forgotten if he would just accept what the Great Enemy offered.

How ironic, thought the demon, *that humans so often refused the Enemy's forgiveness simply because it was too easy.* The very strongest part of the Enemy's plan, the simple gift of forgiveness, was a stumbling stone for these creatures. The Enemy's gift of redemption for them was so easy that it became a simple matter for a skilled demon to twist their hearts so that they rejected it out of feeling that they didn't deserve it.

The very cornerstone of His gift was the undoing of so many of these pampered, self defeating humans! Hatred seethed in Furrgstan's heart when he thought of the few of his charges who, over the centuries, had seen through the lies which he had so painstakingly woven into their world view, and who had accepted the cursed gift from the Enemy. He had paid dearly for each of those losses, facing a stretch of discipline at the hands of the Corps of Loss for the defection of each soul. The Corps of Loss was the disciplinary arm of the forces of darkness, and Furrgstan had writhed under their ministrations too many times.

Well, not this time. *Steve is mine!* he chortled, as he entwined his talons more intricately amongst the fibers of Steve's will and emotions.

* * *

Marianne sat hunched over, tears streaming down her cheeks, smearing the heavy makeup that the men had applied to her face before the day's filming had begun. *What day is it?* she silently wondered. *How long have I been here?* The hours seemed to just melt together and sluggishly flow by. She felt as if she'd been here forever, yet it also felt if it were just moments ago that she had walked into the mall with her friends. *Why won't someone come and help me? Don't they even care that I'm all alone here?* Her mind wailed with fear and pain and doubt.

This had been a bad time. The worst since she had been brought here by these horrible men. *What was it, a week? No, that's not right,* she countered her own argument. But it felt like it had to have been more than a day of this awful torture. *Where is God now? Why is He letting this happen to me?*

Her mind went in circles; tight, quick circles like a dog chasing its own tail, asking the same questions, over and over again. And over and over she came up with nothing for an answer. Yet, deep inside - much deeper than the suffering her body was experiencing, deeper even than the fear in her mind - was the deep-seated knowledge that God was with her. For a moment, she focused on that truth, and the pain immediately diminished. Gaining assurance from that small reprieve, she tried to send her mind down a new track, putting the events of this day behind her and focusing on what she knew to be true about her God.

"He is love," she murmured. "He loves me and cares about me," she went on quietly, as if affirming it to heaven and to herself. Slowly, the intensity of her situation withdrew from the front of her mind, seeming more and more like a mere shadow of reality. It was replaced by a feeling of peace, and if not actual comfort, then certainly a sense of being in the right place, a sense of belonging to the One who was in control.

She heard the sound of cars on a busy street muffled through the walls. She noticed that the sun was now down near the horizon through the tiny crack visible in the shuttered window. She thought of the pain that Jesus had suffered for her and realized for the first time the real meaning of sharing in His sufferings. A sigh, a relaxing of muscles that hadn't relaxed in hours, a final tear - though one of inexplicable joy now. She leaned back into her corner, draped her chains in a more comfortable place and closed her eyes in sleep.

* * *

Ajourney, too, was weary. He was glad for Marianne, glad that he could bear the brunt of her pain. It had been a difficult afternoon as his strength waned until he felt the fresh influx of spiritual energy as the Caffers and Samantha Merryl, and more recently, Danielle Buchannon, began to pray for the missing girl. Now he sat with his arms around the little girl's heart, guarding her from any new assault that the enemy could mount.

He felt that it could not be long now before the Master called her home to Himself. And he vowed anew that he would withhold nothing in his efforts to guard her and save her from suffering.

He, too, sighed, relaxed a bit, and weighed the darkness of this sinful world against the light and glory of the place that awaited his Marianne. He was very grateful that years earlier she had recognized her real need of forgiveness and had turned to Christ to meet that need. And grateful for the day, more recently, that he had been assigned to this delightful young human, a human who would seek her Maker with a love and devotion that few, even among those who had been saved for years, ever sought Him. She had a singleness of purpose in desiring Him that should have shamed many of the older saints.

* * *

Steve's mind grew wearier with each passing hour. The pain from his wrist and the constant intake of marijuana and pain medication were taking their toll. It was getting closer to eleven o'clock, and he was out of weed to smoke to keep him going. He had long ago lost track of how many times he had been up and down this stretch of road, and he had seen nothing that would help in the least.

* * *

Dave felt good about his plan. The kids were calling in pretty regularly, although Jordan and Chad had only called in once in the two hour period. Dave's car was parked on the corner of Hubbardston and Stony Point Roads, and his mind wandered from thought to thought. Actually, the plan was working so well that he was bored sitting here waiting for the next half hour to pass. He had seen nothing, but he felt confident that sooner or later the search pattern would turn up something.

His eyes caught the form of a girl crossing the street in front of him. She was dressed in a provocative sweater and jeans, and his mind wandered to thoughts that fit more in the pages of the illicit magazines he read than in the mind of a Christian. The girl walked into a bar half way down the block, but his mind continued to form thoughts of her.

As he looked around, he caught sight of a bookstore just a block off the main drag. He found himself considering going in to buy a magazine to help him pass the time. Looking at his watch, he told himself to wait until after the next call-in time when most of the kids would be going home, and then it would be safe to go into the store without being seen.

* * *

Becky, a junior in high school and a friend of Steve's, continued to drive circles through her assigned search area, but her mind was already at home. She said, "That's enough for tonight. Let's call in and head home."

Sherry was slumped in the passenger seat, but she stirred enough to answer, "Yeah. I'm bored, and we're not accomplishing anything. Let's go home."

Becky flipped on her turn signal, did a head check, and moved into the left turn lane. "We'll call in on the way home," and handed the younger girl her phone.

A block ahead of them, a shiny black van pulled out from a drug store and headed down the street away from them. Looking for the traffic to clear, Becky didn't see it, and Sherry was focused on finding Pastor Dave's number. Unnoticed by the girls, the black van pulled into a gas station on Hubbardston, filled its tank, and drove on out of town. Distracted by traffic orchestrated by demons assigned to that chore, none of the kids in the search team ever saw it.

* * *

Dave sighed after the last of the kids called in. None of them had anything to report. All of them except Jordan and Chad were going home for the night. Those two could spend another half hour on patrol, and then they, too, would have to head home. "Ah, well," he sighed, "Most of them can come back out tomorrow again."

He reached forward and turned the ignition to start the car. Carefully looking for a clear spot in the traffic, he crossed Hubbardston, drove the block into the seedier area off the main drag, and pulled into the parking lot of the adult bookstore. He parked in the darkest corner at the back of the lot and walked quickly around the building and through the front door. He hated doing this. His conscience didn't bother him so much; it was just that he was afraid he might get caught doing something he knew others wouldn't understand.

He perused the selection of magazines, and pulled a couple off the shelf that he hadn't yet read. Walking up to the counter, he kept his eyes averted to avoid meeting the gaze of the man behind the counter. In the back of his mind he felt that it would keep the man from recognizing him. Paying quickly, and not bothering to check his change, he left with his purchases under his arm in a brown paper bag.

* * *

Dean shook his head to clear the blur and buzz a bit. As a twenty-four-year-old high school drop out, he had lots of time on his hands, and he used most of it for partying. Even though he had done his part in snatching the girl from the mall, He wasn't allowed to help with the filming in the basement of the house. He was ticked off. He had done what they asked him to do, and done it well. But they still wouldn't let him see what was going on in that basement. He had his suspicions, and wanted in on it. But the answer was always 'no,' and now he was bored.

He didn't think he had never been this high before, at least not this early in the night. The party had been pretty good, lots of tequila, lots of pot, music, girls, and action. Then someone broke out the crack, and Kim, his girlfriend, had made a big scene about his trying it. So what if he had told her before that he'd never try hard stuff? Who did she think she was? His mother? Telling him what he could and couldn't do was not his idea of what a girlfriend should be.

Well, she had blown up over it, so he left. After another couple of shots of Worm, that is. Now his mind was nicely buzzing, and he was driving down back streets to avoid the eyes of cops. He was a very good driver, but as drunk, high and angry as he was, they would certainly notice him and pull him over.

Thinking of Kim and her big mouth made him madder than ever, and the only release he could think of was to step on the gas - hard. The tires squealed under his Olds 442, accelerating him away from the stop sign. He one-handed the steering wheel, slipping around parked cars and screeching around the next corner.

* * *

Jordan was bored and having second thoughts about this whole business. He was also tired of Chad's incessant freshman chatter. The guy just wouldn't shut up for a minute. Jordan wished Pastor Dave had assigned him someone else, but he was stuck with the freshman punk for the whole evening.

The first hour hadn't been too bad, with the thought that they might actually be able to help the police find Marianne. What a cool idea! But time went on, and they drove in endless patterns around their designated area, never seeing anyone else from the 'posse,' as Chad kept calling it, much less any suspicious looking vans. They had already had to buy gas once, and money was not something Jordan could afford to just throw away down his gas tank. And of course freshman-Chad didn't have any money to contribute to the cause. The seat belt rubbed into his shoulder and Jordan unclipped it out of frustration. Chad saw it and said, "You'd better leave that on. It's not safe to drive without it."

"Another five minutes and we're out of here," Jordan managed to insert into one of the rare breaks in Chad's rambling chatter.

"Aw, come on, Jordan," came the younger boy's near whining reply. "We can't quit yet. Marianne's out here somewhere, and we've got to help her." This was the most exciting thing the unpopular guy had ever done, and he wanted to milk it for all the mileage he could.

Jordan snorted, "This is goofy, Chad. We're not going to find that van, even if we stay out here for weeks! They're not stupid enough to be out driving around in public in a van that was used in a kidnapping."

"But we can't just quit. Not yet."

"Five more minutes. That's it." Jordan's tone was final sounding enough that Chad let it drop at that point. "We'll swing down here one more time, and then finish the sweep back up Hubbardston before we…"

He was cut off by Chad shouting, rolling down his window and waving like a goon. "Hey, that's Pastor Dave!" Jordan turned to locate the youth pastor and honked, even though he hadn't spotted Pastor Dave yet. Chad had already turned back to the window to try to catch Pastor Dave's eye.

Jordan craned his neck around, too, leaning forward to try to see past Chad's shoulder, which nearly filled the now open window. They went on by, and Jordan sped up a bit to hurry around the block to try to catch the youth pastor and tell him that they were going home.

***

Dean knew he shouldn't be driving in this condition, much less driving this fast in the dark and in crowded streets, but his anger at Kim was out of control. He spun around another corner and watched his headlights blaze across the front of an oncoming car. He honked and tried to bring the car back into his side of the road. He drunkenly and errantly mashed his foot into the gas pedal thinking it was the brake, and plowed straight into the front of the other car.

***

Another car swerved around the next corner going at least forty – engine racing, tires squealing, and accelerating. His lights were on bright and dazzled Jordan just long enough for him to lose track of where exactly he was in his lane. He heard a horn and took his foot off the accelerator, but didn't have time to move it to the brake before the other car smashed into his. He saw Chad slammed forward into his seat belt, his head smacking into the door frame with a sickening thud. Jordan felt himself flung against the steering wheel and into the windshield, shattering it with his head. He would have gone on through, but his belt buckle caught on the steering wheel, wrenching and gashing his hip and leg, and pulling him partway back inside. His last thought was how much trouble he was going to get into for wrecking his dad's car.

* * *

The demon riding on the head rest in Dean's car grinned and dug his claws deeper into his charge's brain. He reached forward with his impossibly long arm, pushing Dean's foot to the floor on the accelerator. The engine roared as it careened toward the oncoming car. As the two vehicles smashed into one another, hoods crumpling accordion-like, the demon threw his whole force into the back of Dean's head, making sure that the young man caught his chin on the steering wheel, cracking his skull on the windshield.

As the dust settled, the demon slid through the bottom of the car to the road beneath and inspected the damage there. "Tsk. Tsk. That gas tank is almost perforated." Then he bent a piece of the suspension another half inch and made sure that a trickle of gas was spurting onto the hot muffler before nodding in satisfaction. He then drifted back up to Dean's side and proceeded to massage his brain. Timing was crucial here. He wanted to make sure Dean woke up at just the right moment - in time to experience, in exquisite awareness, the death that awaited, but not so soon that he could extricate himself from the wreck. "I love this job," he gloated, whispering into Dean's ear.

* * *

Dean was thrown forward like a rag doll, smashing his head into the windshield. He felt a deep stabbing pain in his rib cage, and saw stars before spinning down into darkness and silence. Unfortunately for him, he would be unconscious for too short a time to miss the painful and lingering death that awaited him only moments away.

* * *

Walking back to his car with his bagged purchases under his arm, Dave heard a horn blare from the road and then his name called out, "Pastor Dave?" When he turned, he saw Chad's face framed in the window of Jordan's car, and Jordan craning his neck past Chad to see if it was really their youth pastor walking out of that adult book store as they swept past. The look on their faces was one of incredulous shock, as though an unanswerable question had frozen their minds into immobility.

Fear ran through Dave's mind and fuel-injected his body as he realized that he had indeed been seen. As his brain scrambled through and rejected the possible explanations that he could come up with to explain his presence at that obviously sinful place, the heat in his face could have burnt toast. *How could he have forgotten that this place was part of Jordan's search pattern?* He stopped dead in his tracks, mouth open, and totally unable to make his brain fashion any thoughts other than berating himself for his stupidity. The boy's car swept on past and out of sight.

As he stood there, rooted in place like a deer caught in headlights, Dave heard the sound of another horn, screeching tires and then the impact of one car smashing into another at high speed. The sound snapped him out of his trance, and, dropping his magazines to the pavement, he dashed out toward the street to see what had happened.

To his horror, he watched as the two wrecked cars settled into a twisted configuration, two hub caps spinning off in opposite directions, fluids spurting onto the street, and steam, or perhaps smoke, wafting into the cold night air. "Oh, please let it be steam," he prayed, watching the potentially deadly fumes beginning to spiral up from both hoods - hoods which were nearly indistinguishable from one another, they were so crushed together.

His disbelieving eyes took in the wrecked bodies of the vehicles, the fragmented pieces of smashed glass and plastic all over the pavement, and then the unmoving body of Jordan hanging out from the front windshield of the car, draped over the wrinkled metal of the hood. Only then did Dave realize just whose car this was. Only then did he recognize the awful significance of the bumper sticker on the back that read, "I'm Fishing - For Men."

Once again he was rooted to the spot, torn between disappearing before anyone else saw him here and running to the cars to try to help by himself. Looking around, he could see no one else; no one he could yell at to help the boys in the cars. Torn between two huge needs, he was frozen in place. Seconds ticked by, seeming like hours, as he stared at the cars and Jordan's body. He could make out nothing else inside either of the vehicles. It was the sudden increase of smoke coming from the wreckage that finally made him decide to move. The trickle of steam turned to a pouring of smoke within seconds, drawing him to the more urgent need.

Sprinting to the side of the twisted frames, Dave felt for a pulse at Jordan's neck. He found it immediately, but also noticed the blood leaking onto the hood from under the boy's stomach. Thinking about the possibility of a broken neck, he hesitated in moving him, looking into the car instead. There was Chad, collapsed in a heap, held in his place by the seat belt around his chest and hips. The strong smell of gasoline edged past the numbness blanketing his brain, and again he wondered about the smoke and the possibility of fire. Dave raced around the rear of the car to the other side and yanked on the handle. Of course it refused to open, but with the window shattered he easily reached inside and unlocked the door, pulling it partly open against the metallic protests of the bent hinges. He wedged one foot on the door frame and pulled at the door. It resisted and then sprang open all at once, nearly spilling him backward onto the pavement.

He reached across the boy's still form and unlatched the seat belt, holding his chest back against the seat. He was limp as a rag doll, but

Dave had no problem dragging him from the car. He laid Chad's unmoving, quiet body on the grass strip beside the road and felt for his pulse as well. It was strong and regular, and Dave could see no bleeding, although there was a nasty lump on the right side of his forehead.

Dashing back to Jordan, Dave weighed the possibility of fire against the possibility of spinal fracture. Smoke still poured from the hood of the cars, but there was no flame yet. The driver's side door was so compressed into the post, there was no way to pull it open by hand. He felt a prompting to check Jordan's pulse again but hesitated, knowing that he had felt it just moments ago. The prompting persisted, though, and he went ahead and reached across the broken windshield for the point on his neck and under his jaw. This time there was nothing. The fear grew greater, and he rechecked the position of his fingers on the boy's neck - still nothing. In disbelief, he checked his own neck to confirm the positioning, and then felt Jordan again. Nothing. Panic shot through his heart again. The youth pastor had taken first aid as a Boy Scout, but that had been years ago and hadn't prepared him for the harsh reality of feeling for a heart beat that wasn't there in the body of a child who was under his responsibility.

He recognized that he had nothing to lose at this point so he climbed up on the bent hood. He reached under Jordan's arms and, lifting Jordan's weight off the broken, square edged mess of the windshield, he pulled the boy's shoulders forward through the front of the car. He pulled the inert form about four inches before something caught on the top of the dash. Strain as he might he could pull Jordan no further out of the car.

A muffled "WHOOSH" sound pulled his attention to the other car, and icy fingers of fear stabbed through his heart as he saw flames leap up from the back end of the other car and race across the spilled gasoline on the pavement, stopping where the spill had stopped, a scant four feet from where he stood leaning over the windshield. Waves of heat battered at his face and side. He reached farther in through the broken window frame, gashing his own wrist, and pulled the boy's belt buckle loose from the severely bent steering wheel. With the renewed energy released with his fright he dragged Jordan's body out of the window and onto the hood of the car.

It was at this moment that he heard a sound that would stay with him until his dying day. There was a muffled moan which grew louder, and then turned into a scream of pure terror and pain from the other car. He looked over the crumpled hoods, through smoke and flame, and through the other windshield, directly into the eyes of the young man in the driver's seat, who was trapped and helpless in the growing flames. The heat from the flames dancing in the night breeze suddenly leapt higher.

As he watched from a mere four feet away, torn in the anguish of trying to figure out what he could do to help, the flames themselves began to blacken the hood of the other car. He shielded his own face from the heat with his arm, and tried to shield Jordan's inert body with his own. There was absolutely nothing he could do to help the other driver with the flames now engulfing that car, so with a quickly breathed prayer for the man, and thanks for the chance he had to save Chad and Jordan, he turned his back on the screaming man, hopped back down, lifted Jordan across his shoulders and half ran back to the side of the street.

Just then, the book store cashier ran out and shouted that the police were on the way. His eyes then went wide at the sight of the flames, and he dashed back into the store to call the fire department as well.

Again, Dave had to make a decision. Jordan needed CPR, but there was still the person in the other car. Could he be saved? Again he hesitated until a explosive "*WHUMP*" stopped the screaming. Though the man's cries for help had stopped, the echoes of the dying man's screams reverberated in his skull.

Yet another explosion rocked him, and he felt the intense heat of the flames from the second gas tank being touched off by a lick of the flames, and all such decisions were taken from him. Both cars were now completely engulfed in flames intense enough to melt the glass and some of the metal in those doomed cars.

With that option removed, and without taking a second look back at the cars, he rolled Jordan over, lifted his chin, and began breathing for the boy. His mind raced trying to remember the ratio of breaths to heart pumps, and trying to listen for the sound of sirens and rescue, and trying to figure out how he was going to explain all of this mess to Sam and Pastor Miller, the senior pastor at First Evangelical Church. '*What a mess I've made of my life!*' he wailed in the raging silence of his own mind.

After what seemed like ages, the store clerk came back and hovered over his shoulder, but the man knew less about CPR than Dave did, so he couldn't relieve him of any of the work. The man, dithering with fear and anxiety, simply gave a play-by-play, mixed with plenty of foul language and cursing, about the burning of the cars as both were incinerated - and whoever was in the mystery car steadily flaked to ashes.

Gradually, a crowd of about fifteen onlookers gathered, gawking at the burning cars and at the two inert bodies on the grass, and peering into the windows for the shapes of whatever bodies must still remain hidden in the billowing smoke pouring from the second car. None volunteered to help Dave, and he couldn't spare the breath to ask. Sweat poured off him in sheets. *Funny,* he thought, *it doesn't look this hard in the movies.*

Finally, after what was really only about three minutes, though it seemed much longer, Dave heard the sound of approaching sirens, and as though it were a signal that it was okay, Jordan gave a cough and a spasm of his entire body and took his first lungful of air on his own.

Dave nearly fainted with relief, and then found himself with the job of restraining the panicked youngster as he thrashed around trying to get enough air back into his oxygen-starved lungs and to reorient himself to where he was. Jordan seemed to be oblivious to the pain he must have been feeling from the cut on his chest and what were probably broken ribs.

The police pulled up with screeching of wheels and slamming of doors. The fire trucks and ambulance followed in another sixty seconds, and soon after that, Dave was pushed aside by the EMTs - without a job, and temporarily forgotten by all the people now gathered at the scene. While he was anxious to obtain news about the welfare of the boys and the occupants of the other car, he also realized that this was a great opportunity to get away from the scene without having to face awkward questions beyond those he would already have to answer.

He slipped away to his car, kicking the bag of magazines aside as he passed, his anger at himself for being such a spiritual wimp bringing a flush to his face. As unobtrusively as possible, he pulled out and away from the scene, which was still abuzz with arriving police cars, ambulances, fire trucks, uniformed figures and spraying water. He noticed the cashier talking to a police officer and looking around for something that he couldn't spot, and he sank down in his seat just in case it was him they were looking for.

As the adrenaline faded from his system, a whole slew of aches and pains became apparent. The smell of burning oil, gas, and rubber clung to him like a greasy smudge.

Looking at his watch, he noticed the time - 11:43 - and the gash on his wrist, still bleeding from the struggle to pull Jordan from the wreckage. The pain intensified, but he put the discomfort away in the back of his mind as he turned his attention toward the impossible job of explaining to Sam, to Pastor Miller, and to irate parents, just what in the world he had been thinking.

* * *

Gramsting had had his claws full for that twenty minutes. One objective for this scene was accomplished. Dean was gone – gone on to his 'reward,' along with any evidence of his involvement with Marianne's kidnapping. He nodded his acknowledgement to Dean's now-unemployed demon, dismissing him from the scene.

But he still had to make an important tactical decision at this point. Should he keep Dave's pornography involvement in this incident hidden, hoping it was better in the long run for Dave to be able to continue in his sin without anyone knowing? It could be done by diverting attention away from the magazines and the adult bookstore. A puff of wind to hide the pages, a bit of grit in the eye to blur the vision of the neon sign proclaiming the availability of smut, a new flame springing from the wreckage to keep the attention of the reporter away from Dave. Or would it be better in the long run to let the incriminating evidence from the adult bookstore out for public view now, and watch the young pastor's fall from grace over the next few days?

He decided to let it out now, and quickly laid his plans accordingly. Between screeching specific orders to the privates assigned to this phase of the operation, devoting personal attention to keeping Pastor Dave in line, and intercepting the feeble attempts of Aglow to interfere, he was busier than he'd been in ages. Though none of the individual jobs on his immediate to-do list was a big deal by itself, it was quite a brilliant orchestration all told. His team members did their jobs well, and he was proud of them.

Aglow was a third-level angel, but right now he was drained and weakened - made nearly ineffectual by Dave's hidden sin and lack of prayer. There were no other angels of any consequence in the area, so Gramsting hammed it up, calling directions to his crew as though he were a director on a movie set.

By the time things quieted down, Dave had made his escape, oblivious to the fact that he had been caught on tape in front of the bookstore. The demonic crew had thoroughly enjoyed the agonized death of Dean in the second car; death by burning was so delicious to watch. The blackening skin stretching over a screaming face, the inhalation of superheated gases into sensitive lungs; such scenes were rich in agony. Overall it was a stunningly wonderful finish to a phase of operation A-121 that could easily gain Gramsting a long-awaited lowering of rank, though it could have been improved with the death of either Chad or Jordan. The two would survive this encounter, but with continued proper handling, it could easily scar them for the future. And Gramsting would make sure one or the other of them would catch the significance of seeing their youth pastor coming from an adult bookstore. The picture of Pastor Dave Merryl of First Evangelical Church walking in front of the bookstore with its bright neon sign proudly advertising sin, caught on film by the Channel 8 news crew, might even make front page tomorrow.

Things were getting dicey for Dave, and Gramsting intended to make the most of this incriminating situation.

Chapter 6
I'm the one who asked them.

Steve heard sirens, and pulled over to let the police and then fire trucks and an ambulance go by. *Somebody's in trouble tonight. I hope it's no one I know*, he said to himself. *Almost midnight. I guess I thought this search would bear more fruit than this. But I can't give up yet. Marianne is out here somewhere, and she needs me to help her. Somehow.* He drew on the last of his joints, holding the sweet smoke in for several seconds before blowing it out the cracked window.

He held the wrinkled little cigarette up to inspect it. Scowling, he sucked angrily at it once again before throwing the roach out the window. He felt helpless in this habit. "I know it's not right, but somehow I get sucked back into it over and over again." Not knowing if he had spoken to himself or out loud, he groaned, "I'm even talking to myself again!"

Steve pulled the van over into a gas station to refuel and to re-think his approach to this tragedy. As he opened the tank, flipped the pump on, and started filling it up, he lost the focus of his anger again. His ability to concentrate was washed out and eroded by the interference of the drugs in his system. He jumped when the pump snapped, indicating a full tank, and he angrily slammed the pump handle back into its cradle.

He felt a bit embarrassed when the cashier told him that the gas was only a dollar-seventeen. He had apparently not recalled when the last fill-up had been. He counted out his change and turned to leave, but something made him pause and ask, "You haven't seen a new black van come through here lately have you?"

The cashier looked bored, but answered, "Yeah, in fact I did. About forty-five minutes ago. A big, foreign looking guy drove it in. It took almost fifty bucks of gas. Surprised me for just a mini van."

Steve came back to the counter and rested his arms on the stainless steel counter. "Can you tell me anything else about that van?"

The attendant sucked in his cheeks and pursed his lips as he thought.

Steve's excitement was lifting him out of his fog now, and he prompted the cashier, "Like, does he come here often? Which way did he go? Did you get his license number or anything?"

"No, he paid cash, so I didn't need to get any numbers or anything. And I've never seen him before, but he headed that way," pointing to the south, out of town.

"Thanks tons!" Steve blurted as he crashed back out through the door.

He slid into the driver's seat, revved the engine and squealed the front tires heading out onto Hubbardston Road, once again in pursuit of the mysterious van.

Two blocks behind him Pastor Dave's car also pulled out onto Hubbardston, heading in the opposite direction, back toward his own deepening crisis.

Four blocks further south and no more than a block and a half east of the main drag, still well within the city, a shiny black van sat, closed up in the double garage of a boarded up, run down house, engine ticking as its heat dissipated in the night air.

* * *

In the quiet of midnight, in the comfort of the Merryls' living room, three human prayer warriors brought the latest battle to a close and left it in the hands of almighty God, retiring from their foray into the spiritual battlefield. Sam sniffed and wiped a last tear from her cheek. She rose from her knees to help Mr. Caffer up from his frail old knees. Mrs. Caffer had stopped trying to make it to the floor on her creaky, aching old joints a couple of years ago, but they all recognized that the posture of her heart was still one of absolute awe of God's majesty and holiness.

"That's thirsty work," declared Samantha. "Can I get you folks something to drink? We've got lemonade and tea and soda."

"Please, just a small glass of water, dear. We've got to get home and into bed," answered Mrs. Caffer.

"Yes," added her husband, with a mischievous twinkle in his eye, "we're getting too old for this carousing around at all hours of the night."

The tinkle of ice cubes in the glasses and the splash of water from the tap sounded disturbingly normal following two hours of intense concentration and intercession. When the Caffers had arrived at about ten o'clock, they had talked for a short while about what was happening in the city and in their church, and Mr. Caffer had tied it into some of his own concerns regarding spiritual warfare and the spiritual health of the church. He wondered about the expectations of purity in the church itself, and the role that might play in the effectiveness of the church.

Soon, however, the three turned their conversation to the plight of the Fracks and to Dave's recent attitude and behavior. The conversation quickly got to the business at hand, and Mrs. Caffer broke in and suggested that they go right to work, praying rather than merely talking about praying all night.

The three of them joined their hearts together and entered into a time of deep agonizing over their city, their church, their relationships, Marianne's plight, and many other topics. They claimed God's promises where they applied, asked for His mercy over specific aspects of the situation, and sought His wisdom for their own involvements. Now they had done what they could, and though there were still many questions, each of them felt a measure of peace, which they hadn't had earlier.

* * *

These were the kinds of moments angels longed for. The three angels standing around the Caffers and Sam glowed with anticipation as their human charges entered into the presence of the King, bringing their concerns and heartaches, but most of all, bringing their humble hearts. It was another of the great mysteries, but one which the angels were privileged to witness, as these humans, so beloved by the Creator, came and simply spent time in His presence.

Salient lifted himself up into the stream of incense-like prayers flowing toward the throne. Soon, as the Spirit directed, the prayers grew more intense as the three prayer warriors entered into a more interceding mode of prayer, and true spiritual battle was joined with the powers in the heavens. The three saints were strong in their faith, and faithful in standing in the gap for those who were not yet strong enough.

As Sam's and Mr. and Mrs. Caffers' prayers rose to heaven, the battle raged; people's lives were changed, and the heart of God was in some paradoxical way turned to move on behalf of His people.

Elsewhere in the city, Danielle, too, prayed. And though she was less experienced and less mature in her faith, and less aware of the deeper issues, her heart, too, was contrite. She was still in the presence of God. She, too, was investing her time in the only thing that could really help.

As prayers and worship flowed to heaven, power flowed from the throne to the servants of the King, both angelic and human. Though the effects of the battle seemed subtle to human eyes, these prayers truly moved powers in the heavens.

* * *

Ice water seemed so mundane and out of place after spending such focused time assailing evil strongholds and dark powers and demonic principalities, and after being right in the presence of Almighty God.

The Caffers sipped their water and then left within a very few minutes, leaving Sam to listen to the ticking of the clock. The children were all asleep, and after two wonderful hours in the holy of holies, it seemed extremely odd to sit and wonder where Dave was at such a late hour.

She didn't have to wonder long, however, because about fifteen minutes later the garage door opener groaned through its job of lifting and lowering the big door. Sam looked expectantly at the door, and waited for Dave to appear.

It took a bit longer than she expected. But when he came through the door, dirty, bloody and bedraggled, she gasped, jumping up to run over to him and ask, "Are you all right, honey?!"

He stared at her, with no words to say, and yet the force of the emotions pent up within him began to force their way to the surface, and his face screwed up in an effort to keep from breaking down into a babbling wreck right on the kitchen floor. A single tear rolled down his blood-smeared right cheek, finally dripping off his chin and falling to his disheveled, stained shirt.

Sam crossed the last few feet between them with more caution, recognizing that Dave was on the edge of a great gulf of stress and pain. "Honey? What happened?" Her voice remained quiet, though a hint of sharpness came through, because inside she was screaming to find out what had happened to bring her husband home in such a state.

She pulled him gently into a hug, but his taut muscles refused such comfort. He did raise his arms numbly to her shoulders, more out of reflex than out of affection. After a moment of the awkward position, he disengaged from her arms and backed away to arm's length.

"Sam..." he began, but broke off as his voice tightened again to hold in deep sobs of grief and fear. A visible effort of self control brought his body back into submission. "Sam, I blew it big time." Emotion still made his voice tight, but he went on. "I don't know why I did it, and I don't know where to begin, but I need you to understand."

"Come and sit down, honey. I have no idea what's going on, but I love you and I'll do anything I can to help you."

They made their way into the living room, and sat on the front edge of the couch. Sam angled her knees toward Dave, but he was facing square ahead, face rigid, lips set in a tight frown. "There was an accident tonight. Jordan and Chad were hurt. I don't know how bad. But bad."

Sam's hand went to her lips, her eyes wide with concern. "Dave, what happened?"

"I'm the one who asked them to come out and help look for the van that took Marianne." He took a deep breath. Sam held her silence, knowing that nothing she said could help right now.

"I can't imagine what in the world I was thinking. How could I have been so stupid to bring a bunch of kids out to do such a thing. Fortunately I was near..." His voice broke again, as he choked back the reason why he happened to be right there, "when the accident happened. I was the first one there. I had to pull both of the boys from the wreck. Jordan quit breathing. Sam, the cars caught on fire! There was a lot of blood.

I had to do CPR on him. The other driver..." Again he had to stop as the enormity of the trouble he was in sunk another level deeper into his brain. This time tears fell faster and faster.

Again Sam reached for him, and this time he seemed to melt into her arms as sobs racked his body.

* * *

Aglow glanced at Gramsting while maintaining his posture of weakness and subservience. Darting a look at Agrevious, he asked, "Now?"

"Patience. You'll know when it's time. The Spirit is still cultivating the seeds planted in this one. "

"He looks nearly ready."

"Wait," the city's guardian cautioned. "You know better than to rush ahead. Wait on the Lord's timing."

Aglow watched the demon at Dave's side and suppressed a shudder at the evil represented in his bat-faced form. The evil one really had placed a lot of import on keeping Dave bound in his sin, so Aglow knew that he had to balance caution against aggressive strategy very carefully to win. The prayer support was increasing for this operation but was still far less than would be necessary to break the bonds the swarming demons, all under the orders of Bagda, and ultimately Satan himself, had over this city. Both sides had immense plans for these next few days, but Aglow and his team still hoped that the enemy had not caught on to just how big this push was going to be.

Gramsting still appeared at ease, cocky in his over confidence that the city, and Pastor Dave in particular, were firmly under their control.

* * *

Nights last for ever when two thirds of your heart has been ripped out. Pete flopped over on his right side yet again. Molly simply lay still, but he was sure she wasn't asleep either; her eyes were still open last time he looked. Could it only be thirty some odd hours since Marianne had been taken? Just over one full day since this horror had begun? And now Stephen was gone, too. To who knew where?

He lay there in the quiet dark, mind racing, heart dully hammering.

For the thousandth time, he glanced at the clock. For the millionth time, he silently asked God, *Why?! Why did You let this happen? When are You going to do something about it and bring her home?*

***

Badger smirked. Humans blaming the Creator for this stuff! How rich! Once again, he was amazed and full of awe at the mastery of Satan in this battle of the minds. To think that he had somehow brought humans all the way from knowing the Enemy and the depths of His love to the point of thinking that the All-loving One was the one who made tragedy and misery happen. The evil one, Satan himself, had come up with the plan that had evolved human logic to the point where they lost sight of the three factors that really allowed such suffering in the world: their own free will in choosing to say no to God, the accumulation of the sinful decisions of every man, woman and child throughout all of human history, and the plans of Satan.

The hairy, eight-legged demon giggled. The Creator's decision to give mankind the power to say yes or no to Himself was the key to Satan's eventual victory. Every time a human decided that they didn't need God, or that their desires were more important than God's plan, it opened the gate for one of the evil hoards to impact their minds, drawing them farther and farther away from the Enemy.

Pete's despair was a great example of this. Blaming God built one brick after another into the wall that separated the human from the love, forgiveness and protection that the Enemy offered to him.

Badger rubbed his long legs together and then drew them one at a time through his fangs. Though only a private he was very experienced at this level of affliction. Fear was good but often too obvious. Doubt, however, was the tool of a master. Subtlety kept the human heading in the right direction, yet never tipped the scale to actual knowledge of the involvement of the demonic element. And doubt, about any of a number of aspects of the spiritual realm, would keep the human from moving toward the Enemy. Doubt about the Enemy's reality, His interest in the affairs of humans, His goodness, His ability to hear or answer prayers; any of these would suit this situation. Badger considered his options, and then made his choice. Focusing on Pete again, he lightly scratched the surface of Pete's heart, and stirred up doubt.

* * *

If God answered, Pete felt as though he must be on the wrong channel. He rolled heavily from the bed, pulling away from the tangled sheets. He grunted with annoyance at the mess he'd made of the blankets and went around to tug them up and tuck them around his wife's shoulders again. He bent over to kiss her forehead, and her eyes flickered to his for just a moment. The chasm that sat between them was new. Pete didn't know what to do with the silence. He and Molly had always been able to talk through their issues. Now, though, she was unresponsive, and he had no idea how to reach her.

He straightened, turned and shuffled to the window to look out at the front lawn. Nothing moved. The night lacked even the slight motion of the wind in the leaves of the trees. No cars passed. It made him want to hold his breath, thinking that the whole world waited, balanced on an edge, motionless, poised on a razor thin blade - wobbling - wavering before falling to one side or the other. It was a time of decision, but just what the decision was that awaited he had no idea.

The hound in the house two lots down the street suddenly barked and howled. He tried to look down the street in that direction, but the angle was wrong for seeing anything.

The scene before him darkened perceptibly, and still Pete stood, locked in place, waiting for something to happen. A shadow of the fear from earlier last evening sent a chill through his spine, but then the night lightened again and he realized that clouds had merely covered the moon for a moment. The furnace kicked on, and the atmosphere felt normal again, with the usual sounds of the house at night. The fear of the moment passed, and Pete twitched his head as if shaking off the right jab of a boxing opponent. He noticed a tremor in his arms and hands, fading as the memory of the panic attack ebbed. "What was that?" he muttered under his breath. Then, with his lips pressed tightly together, he wondered, *Am I losing my mind? Is this what happens when your life is ripped apart?*

Memories of times with Marianne surfaced from deep in his mind. He sighed as he remembered the first Christmas with Marianne in the house. Steve had been - four? No, five years old, and just adored his new little sister. He had helped her unwrap her presents and was thrilled when she'd been tucked into bed with the stuffed lion they had gotten her.

Pete thought of the day she had gone to school for the first time. He had cried silent tears as the bus pulled away from the curb, his little girl waving and smiling from the side window. It had seemed at the time, as at many times since then, that he was leaving something irretrievably behind. Life passed recklessly fast at times.

He felt drained from these images, yet they continued to come unbidden. The memory of her ice skating for the first time: determined, refusing to stop despite the bruised elbow (and his own aching back). Her grin of triumph when she finally wobbled around the rink by herself for the first time. Then, with far more force and poignancy than the others, the memory of first hearing the news that she had been taken from the mall yesterday.

His knees buckled, and he slid to the bedroom floor with a groan. Slowly he curled into a ball on the carpeted floor, and his breath sighed slowly out, almost in a whine. Like an injured animal, he softly whimpered his pain out in little sounds. Molly was so absorbed in her own misery, she didn't notice his absence from their bed.

It was much later, the first light of dawn showing in through the window over his head, when he finally unfolded and rose to his knees again, grunting and groaning with the aches in his back and his hip and shoulder where they had pressed against the floor for the last hour. Another day to face. Another day without Marianne, without Molly's support, and now without Steve. Even the stress of that relationship in recent months would be missed at this point.

* * *

Lieutenant Lydia Mochek tossed in her own bed, unable to stop the endless circle of probably-unrelated events summarized in files that sat on her desk and ran around and around through her mind. The Frack girl's abduction, the car fire on the south side, the growing list of missing children from the area. How did it all fit together? She was sure it did somehow. There was just a missing piece or two still out there. Pieces that would bring the whole picture together into clear focus. She lay there in the dark in bed. Even her scalp hurt, from laying on her short curly hair wrong. Knowing she would not get any sleep until she turned this complicated case over to God, she focused on Him and prayed through each of the items that weighed so heavily on her heart, handing each one over to the only One who could sort them all out.

As she prayed, a patrolman on duty downtown reconsidered his decision and lifted a complaint form from the dead file and tagged it to be sent to Lieutenant Mochek for further consideration. It was probably nothing, but the woman who had called about the domestic dispute had sounded just upset enough, just sure enough, that Officer Spalding had paid it more than just cursory attention. Maybe the lady really had seen a man treating a young girl abusively. Maybe not, too. But the lieutenant would have to decide tomorrow if it needed to checked out.

Meanwhile, Lieutenant Mochek finished her prayers, kissed her husband on the cheek, got a sleepy groan in response, and inwardly sighed with frustration that she couldn't get to sleep like a normal person.

* * *

Marianne groaned, too. Her hip and shoulder hurt, and so did the rest of her body. Inside and out. She hurt from the treatment she had gotten yesterday during the filming, from the sleep on the hard wooden floor, from the cold pipes against her back, from the shackle rubbing around her wrist, and from missing her family. Early morning light peeped in through the boards covering the window, and she yawned a huge, weary yawn. A single tear slid down her cheek, and she half-heartedly wiped at it with the back of her free hand.

Sleep had come in fits and spurts through the long night - the second of her captivity. Her head felt full of thought-deadening cotton, her mouth had the taste of dirty teeth, and her joints and muscles ached from her uncomfortable position.

She attempted to stretch her arms, but the chains weren't long enough for much of a stretch. She did manage to stretch her legs out and wriggle her toes, and the feeling of pins and needles was actually a welcome relief to the dreadful ache she felt everywhere else. A small smile crept across her face as she thought of how delicious a warm bath and a night in her own bed would feel.

Suddenly the door crashed open and her captor, the man referred to as Art, walked in, wearing a smug smile on his face. His smile deepened to a grimace when he looked at her, "What'er you smilin' about, MiMi?" he sneered. "Are you starting to like this work?" He paused for a minute, but didn't wait for a response from Marianne.

"You know that's going to be your name in your movie, don't you? MiMi." He said the name as if trying it on, and Marianne shivered with revulsion at what he made her feel.

"Yeah, MiMi fits you real good. Your hair. That pretty little face. You're gonna be a star, you know. This flick is gonna sell a million copies. We're gonna get rich from this one."

He walked over to her and set a plate of cold food on the floor in front of her. Then, with his hands freed, he roughly pulled her chin up so she had to look at his face. "Yeah, you're gonna be famous. But you've gotta eat so you can keep your strength up for today's shooting. We've still got a lot to get on film before we're done with you."

Something about the way he said that "done with you" made Marianne shiver, and she cringed back against the wall, pulling her face from his hand with a twist of her neck. The man laughed, and said, "Oh, don't worry. We're not going to really hurt you. Though it might feel like it to you. You have no idea what real pain can be like." His voice took on a kind of wistful tone, as though he were fondly remembering times when he had shown some other innocent victim what 'real pain' could feel like.

Marianne closed her eyes and turned her face to the wall, not wanting to even look at the man. She heard him chuckle, and stole a look as he sauntered out of the room and slammed the door behind himself. The walls shook and a flake of paint fluttered down from the cracked plaster of the wall above her.

She rested her head back against the wall, took a deep breath, and entered into prayer once again, whispering her thoughts heavenward. "Jesus, I don't think I can do this. Will You please get me out of this? Will you please let my family come and get me?" She sighed, and paused, letting His presence fill her with peace again. Then she went on, "Jesus, You know the state of these men's hearts. Can You somehow use this situation - use it to help them find You? You know I don't want to die. I don't even want to be here. But You promised that everything that happens is for a good reason and that You'll use even these kinds of things for good.

"What will be the good out of this, I wonder. Will these horrible men find You? I trust You, but it's so hard to remember it when they are hurting me. Please help me." Again, she felt His arms of love surround her. The aches in her body faded to peaceful comfort. The words of a song her youth group sang came to her;

"Let the river flow, let the river flow.
Holy Spirit come, move in power.
Let the river flow."

Then, another song, a hymn from church came to her. It came in such clarity and beauty, she wasn't sure that she wasn't actually hearing it. It was beautiful, as though sung by angels, angels right next to her, removed from her sight by a mere wisp of a curtain of time.

"When peace like a river attendeth my ways,
When sorrows like sea billows roll.
Whatever my lot, Thou hast taught me to say,
It is well, it is well with my soul."

She sighed again and realized that indeed it was well with her soul. She heard footfalls approaching her room, and calmly lifted her arm as they entered to allow her captors to unshackle her and lead her back to the basement where Art and the "actors" would start the filming again.

Yesterday she had tried to run. She had been willing to bite, scratch their eyes out, anything to get away. The punishment she had received was more than enough to convince her that there was no way she could escape from these men. It had been bad enough that she would surely never try again. There were always two or three of them in the house. They had done things to her that left no marks to interrupt their movie making, hurting her in ways that degraded and embarrassed and hurt so badly she couldn't even draw a breath. Today, she decided, she would watch for a chance to escape, but she knew she would do nothing that would make them hurt her like that again.

Chapter 7
The whole thing falls apart.

Steve was tired. All night he had cruised this part of town, weaving up and down each street, looking for any clues to the whereabouts of the black van. But since the vague tip at the gas station there had been nothing. He had scored a couple joints after midnight from a dealer he knew and had since smoked them up.

His mind sank deeper and deeper into a black hole of depression. He had come across the wrecked shells of two crashed and burned cars a few hours earlier. Crews were cleaning up the wrecks and preparing to haul them away. He gave a sleepy giggle at the thought of the expression 'crashed and burned.' That pretty well described him right now. It could have been the accident that caused the sirens he had heard hours earlier, because the wrecks weren't gone yet. Orange barricades and yellow tape gave some semblance of protection from onlookers. He wondered who had been in the cars and if anyone had died in the accident. It looked that bad.

From there his mind followed the meanderings of a pot smoking junkie, and wandered downhill to wondering if perhaps he wouldn't be better off dead himself. He stopped the van in the parking lot of a convenience store. Looking at his watch he was surprised to see that it was nearly morning, 5:47 a.m. to be exact. The city was slow in rousing on a Sunday morning, but breakfast joints were stirring slowly into action, and traffic was gradually building from the near zero level he'd been part of the last few hours. He felt strung tight like a guitar string.

'Better off dead.' The thought touched a strangely peaceful chord in his heart. "Better off dead," he mumbled, and felt the words roll off his tongue, and let them swirl around in his mind for a few moments. For something that most people seemed to react to in a big way, the idea held out a vaguely enticing promise to Steve, a promise of release and freedom from all this guilt he had been bathing in for the last two days.

He was tired. Physically, mentally, and emotionally tired. Especially, he was tired of dealing with the monotony of living with the conflict between what he had been taught by his folks and in church, and the lifestyle he was caught up in because of his behavior and attitude. He knew that he should love his family and enjoy church and stuff. But he lived in a constant tangle of 'ideals meet reality.' And now his life appeared to be crowned by letting his little sister get kidnapped. What a failure. What a completely disappointing failure he was.

He crashed his bad hand down on the steering wheel, cursing with the pain, and cradling his arm against his chest. Yes, to end it all would be a relief. And it would get him finally out of his parents' hair, too. But how? What did he have that would make the end quick and painless? He certainly had no desire to suffer through a long, painful, drawn-out death.

But try as he might, he couldn't come up with anything that would give him the release he craved. He cursed again and started the motor. It caught immediately and settled into its trustworthy purr. Then it hit him. *Of course! I'll just drive off one of the bluffs along the river! I've always liked roller coasters, and it'll be just like that, but with a sudden quiet oblivion at the bottom. I like that idea!* He nodded decisively, turned the van south onto Hubbardston Road and headed for the river and the end of his torment.

* * *

Twenty minutes before her normal Sunday morning alarm went off, Danielle was lying in bed, wide awake. Steve kept coming to her mind, and having recently heard about a missionary who took such promptings as a nudge from God to pray, she rolled over onto her stomach, folded her hands and said, "Lord, I know this sounds silly, but are You telling me You want me to pray specifically for Steve right now? You know how much I like Steve, but he's dealing with some hard things these days. Would You please take special care of him today? Keep him out of trouble, and help him to find the answers to the stuff he's working through."

She paused, but the feeling of alarm remained. She still couldn't get Steve off her mind, so she prayed again and kept on praying as thoughts of him stubbornly clung to her mind.

* * *

Driving through town was no problem; the fog that had filled his mind seemed clearer now, his thoughts light with the thought of ending his screwed up existence. Within fifteen minutes Steve was at the intersection of Highway 12 and River Road. Traffic was even lighter outside of town here, and so were his emotions. He turned right onto the winding road, heading parallel with the river and rising toward the bluffs. Centering the van in the lane, he stepped on the gas, thinking that 80 miles per hour or so should get him off the road and over the edge. As soon as he straightened the wheel though, the faithful little four-banger sputtered and all but died. He let up on the accelerator and the engine settled out into a smooth idle again. He shook his head, and muttered, "What's up with that? This car always runs perfectly." He pressed the accelerator to the floor again, but the instant he stepped on it, it stuttered and stammered again, giving him a top speed that scarcely moved the needle off the pin of the speedometer.

Coasting along with the engine gasping for breath, he watched a car pull around and pass him. He muttered under his breath, "How can I end it all at this speed?" Indeed, he was going so slowly that he doubted the van could get over the roll-over curb, much less through a guard rail. After limping along for about a mile, nursing the accelerator, he pulled over to the side of the road and prepared to turn around. Filled with frustration, he growled, "I can't even get my own death to work right. What a sorry mess I am."

Not three miles further up the road, yet unseen to Steve, the edge of river valley and the road met at the top of the bluffs, snaking along together through a series of tight curves. The road there was black with rubber from tires belonging to drivers who weren't expecting such tight turns. Steve hadn't made it that far today with his sputtering engine, but within another day he and his whole family would become much more familiar with the area.

Frustrated with the uncooperative performance of the van, and distracted by his fading buzz and growing hunger, he gave up on what he had hoped would be an easy way out. He made it back to Highway 12, and turned back up the road to town. It didn't strike him as unusual that the van ran fine as soon as he turned around and headed back toward town. His hungry stomach crowded out thoughts of suicide, and his pot-steeped brain let the dark thoughts slide away, lost in the search for a restaurant to eat breakfast in.

* * *

Castellain, the angel defending Steve against Furrgstan, relaxed his grip on the electrical system of the van and allowed the engine to resume its normal, carefully engineered and perfectly timed combustion of petroleum products. Furrgstan growled and spat in frustration, driving his claws deeper into the angel's back, but the demon knew that the moment had passed and he had missed a rare opportunity. Suicide is a taboo, that truth ingrained deeply in the human genome by the Enemy. To get Steve to consider it, and to set all the factors up again would take another long, gradual buildup of disappointment and depression. It wouldn't happen today. Perhaps not ever.

Snarling at Castellain, who had surprised him with his sudden leap into the engine of the van, he turned back to Steve. It was time to salvage what he could of the plan which he had hoped would bring an end to the young man's life. It was a major achievement to incite a human to suicide before it could be lost to the demons' great Enemy.

* * *

Looking at his watch against the glare of the newly risen sun, Steve decided that 6:52 was a good time for breakfast. Not a thought of ending his life remained, and he looked around with his new purpose in mind; looking for restaurants rather than black vans, or more pot, or death. His heart was still deep in despair, but hunger spoke louder with each passing moment and he was ready to eat.

His mouth felt like cotton, and his teeth actually felt furry. Cupping his hand over his mouth to smell his breath, he grimaced at the stale smell. He stuck a piece of gum in his mouth in a small attempt to freshen his breath.

In twenty minutes he was back inside the city limits. Two blocks up Hubbardston, the red and yellow sign of Pancake Palace rose up through the forest of other signs clogging the view. He flicked on his turn signal, did a head check and pulled into the right lane. The parking lot was pretty full. The Sunday morning, pre-church rush was in full swing. Walking through the front door, he realized that if he had been with his family he'd have had to wait for quite a while, but alone as he was, he was seated within five minutes.

He ordered and then closed his eyes and sank back into the booth's stiff, slightly oily-feeling vinyl seat, ready to fall asleep if he was left alone for more than a few minutes. He was jarred awake when a gentle voice asked, "Steve Frack? Can we join you for a minute?"

He jerked his head up, and his eyes opened and stared at the age-creased faces of an elderly couple who looked very familiar but whose names he couldn't come up with. Fortunately, he didn't have to. The old man was sensitive enough to let him in on where he knew them from. "We are Mr. and Mrs. Caffer from the church. You probably don't know us, but we've been around there for ages." The old man helped his wife into the seat opposite him and then eased himself into the booth beside her. Mr. Caffer went on, "Why, we've watched you grow up from just a little tyke." The old man rubbed his hand over an imaginary head about three feet off the floor.

"Yes, you were always so cute in the kids' choirs. And you took such pride in your little sister." Mrs. Caffer's voice stopped, and she covered her mouth with the fingers of one hand. "Oh, pardon me, Steve. I'm so sorry! We've heard about your sister, and we've been praying for her and for your whole family all weekend."

"It's all right, Mrs. Caffer," Steve assured the embarrassed woman, though his throat did constrict tightly in his chest.

There was a silence for a moment, and then Mr. Caffer spoke again. "How are you doing with all this, Steve? You look as though you've had better days."

Steve shifted in his seat, feeling a bit embarrassed himself now, and coloring because he knew he was going to have to explain what he was doing here. He was sure they would smell the residual smoke from the marijuana on him. When he didn't speak up to answer, the kindly old man pressed the point further. "What are you doing out at this time on a Sunday morning? We come here for Sunday breakfast 'most every week, and I don't believe you are a regular here." He chuckled and winked to lighten the mood some, and Steve was able to relax a bit.

"Well, sir. Ma'am." He ducked his head, not quite sure what to say. "I've got to admit that I'm not doing all that well right now. Since Friday night, I've been feeling that a lot of what happened is my fault. I should have watched her closer. I should have gotten to her in time. I should have stopped that van." His voice began to shake with emotion, and tears welled up in his eyes, spilling one large drop from his lower eyelashes onto the paper napkin in his lap. For some reason, the emotions that he had been covering up with dope, and stuffing down into his heart, were easier to access here in this booth with these two old people.

The Caffers could see that Steve needed to get a lot off his chest, so they just listened, nodding and encouraging him to let it out.

"I should at least have been able to get my own damned car open to chase them down!" The napkin was now crushed into a ball in his fist.

"So last night, I overheard someone telling my dad that they had spotted the van... er... at least a van like it," he admitted sheepishly, "and I took off to try to find it and track it down." More tears followed the first, and Steve, feeling pretty self-conscious, hid his face in his open hands, sniffling back the sobs that threatened.

"Any luck?" asked Mr. Caffer.

Steve looked at him to see if he was being sarcastic, but the man seemed genuinely interested in what Steve had been able to accomplish. There was no accusation in his tone or his face. "Nah. I thought that I had a lead at one point, but it didn't pan out." His gaze returned to his lap as he went on, "I guess it was pretty stupid to run off like that. I didn't even tell my folks I was going. They must be pretty upset by now."

"Hmm," was all Mrs. Caffer said. She too seemed pretty easy to be with. "What are you going to do now, Steve?"

"I guess I should go on back home. But I sure am not going to church today. I can't imagine sitting through church when God has let all this happen to me... to us."

"Steve," Mr. Caffer spoke softly, "why do you suppose all this has happened?"

Steve held his breath for a moment as all his thoughts, doubts, fears and questions cascaded through his mind. He took a deep, shuddering breath to steady his voice. The circumstances of this weekend had caused the entirety of his worldview to be shaken to its foundational building blocks. All the things he had learned through seventeen years of life in a Christian family were suddenly laid out under the microscope of open evaluation. Part of him was afraid of how those beliefs would hold up under rational scrutiny. So far they didn't seem to measure up very well to the hard questions that were being dropped in his lap.

If God was good, surely He wouldn't approve of Marianne being kidnapped. If He was powerful and loving, surely He wouldn't have allowed some unnamed thug to carry her off to who-knew what kind of treatment. If God was loving toward people who loved Him and who at least attempted to serve Him, surely He would not reward them by ripping their life apart! What possible use could a loving, powerful God have in shredding a family who were some of His own people?

These thoughts surged back and forth from his heart to his mind, swirling around in eddies and currents that he could not control. It took some time to put some order to them, though not nearly as long as it felt. When he focused once again on the faces of the kind-hearted people across from him, they were waiting patiently, expectantly, concern plainly etched on their faces. They appeared willing to let him have whatever time he needed to sort through his thoughts.

Just then his meal arrived, giving him an additional moment to gather his thoughts a bit more cohesively. The waitress placed his hot cakes, milk and juice before him. "Can I get anything for you folks?" she asked the Caffers.

"Just a glass of water, please. We just finished our meal, right over there," indicating a table now occupied by a couple with three young children, "and we spotted our friend here."

"That's just fine. I'll get your water in a jiffy!" and she smiled as she walked away.

"Well. I guess I don't know what to make of it all, sir," Steve started. "I know that I'm to blame for some of this, but I sure don't understand how this great, good, loving God," his voice dripping sarcasm, "I've been taught about all my life could let something like this happen to people who have been Christians all their lives. My sister loves Him and His Bible and is always going on about how loving He is. How could He let her get kidnapped?" *'There, I said it,'* he thought, and glared challengingly at the older couple.

"You know, young man, you've asked a tough question there. But it's not a rare question. In every person's life, some things eventually happen that make us start to question just how this world is put together. In fact it's a question every one of us asks at least once in our lives."

"So you're not alone in your confusion," interjected his wife, and she reached across the formica table top to pat Steve's hand.

"That's right, Steve," Mr. Caffer went on. "You're in good company. In fact everyone from Abraham Lincoln to most of the Bible characters – why, even Jesus Himself has asked questions that are identical in content to yours."

"Jesus?" Steve sounded incredulous.

Mrs. Caffer nodded and said, "Remember when Jesus was about to be arrested, He asked, 'If it is possible, could You take this cup from Me?' And later, 'My God, why have You deserted Me?'"

She went on, "These other questions are really well summarized in your question, but the answers are far from simple."

"You've got that right. I've been banging my head against a wall trying to figure it out."

Steve kept his face buried in his palms so his voice was muffled, but both of the Caffers could still hear the despair behind his simple words.

Mrs. Caffer gently went on, "Son, there is no easy answer, but I think if you put what you already know about God all together in the right order, it'll start to make a little better sense. Maybe not enough to give you all the answers you want, nor as simply as you want, but hopefully enough to live with."

"Let's start with what you already know about God, and about His relationship with mankind."

Steve was silent, trying to decide if it was worth going through this question-and-answer session or not. Heaving a deep sigh, he lowered his hands, lifted his face, grimaced and rolled his eyes, and said, "Alright. God is all powerful, all knowing, all present, and loving." He said it without emotion as though from rote memory.

The old man encouraged him, "That's a fair start, Steve. Let's look at some of those and then go from there. You're right that God is all powerful and loving. In fact, if anything at all in the Bible is true, those two attributes have to be true as well or the whole thing falls apart. Now, remember that God made man for a specific reason. Do you remember what that reason was?"

"Hmm. I guess to talk with him, or to spend time with him," came Steve's half guess.

"That's pretty good, but more specifically, there were two intertwined reasons. First so that man could love God, and second so he could worship God."

"Yeah, but what does this have to do with Marianne?" interrupted Steve, drawn into the discussion in spite of his weariness.

* * *

Furrgstan was growing uneasy. The conversation his host was having was moving into uncomfortable areas. He glared at Castellain, who was still nursing the gashes in his back from their conflict under the hood of Steve's car. The angel looked innocent enough, but had sidled a bit closer than Furrgstan really liked. He bared his teeth and hissed, not really feeling the need to move the angel, but wanting to warn him that he was close enough.

Returning his attention to his host, he missed the slowly increasing glow of power that Castellain was now unable to hide very effectively - power pouring in from the prayers of the Caffers, and of Steve's girlfriend as well.

* * *

"Steve, look at it this way. Right now, we are assembling a building of logic. While the building blocks may look simple, the foundation we are laying is critical if the whole thing is going to stand up under the kind of emotional earth-quakes you've been through this week. God does not expect you to set your faith on a system that falls apart the first time you ask some tough questions of it." He looked at the young man to see if the analogy made sense. Steve nodded slightly, and Mr. Caffer took it as permission to continue. "The next brick in our building is to compare the difference between men and animals. In the creation process, if God had already made animals to please Himself, why did He go further and make mankind? What is the difference between beasts and humans?"

"Well, people have a soul and animals don't. Right?"

"You got it. God had finished making animals, which don't have a soul. And that means that they really don't have the option of obeying or loving God. They may think, but they lack the ability to critically think about what they are thinking. He made them just to be. Now, after He made them, He wanted to make something fundamentally different. He wanted something that could love Him - or not love Him if they chose. He wanted someone not to love Him out of rules and laws, but to love Him because they chose to and wanted to. In order to do that, God had to take a huge risk.

"You see, He could have easily made another animal, one which looked just like people, but which acted loving toward Him because they had to. He could have hard-wired that behavior into them, but then they would have been emotional robots of sorts, with no choice but to act in an obedient and loving way toward God. But God wanted to be loved out of choice. Of course, the only way that could happen is if He actually gave men free choice.

"You see the complexity here? God could have used His power to force men to love and obey; in fact He still could, but where is the love in that?"

Steve nodded, and Mr. Caffer went on. "The choice God had to make in creating human beings was the choice between love and robots. The risk was that if people were really free to choose to love Him, then they could just as easily choose not to love Him. And of course some of them did, and still do."

Steve appeared to be listening intently, hoping to gain something from this old man that would make sense of the mess his life had become. Mr. Caffer went on, ticking points off on his fingers. "So, even though God is strong enough to do it, and even though He loves us so much He would like to do it, the very nature of love itself keeps Him from grabbing hold of people who choose to rebel and forcing them back into line.

"If God reached into history and interfered with our choices by forcing us to do right, He would destroy our ability to freely love Him. And forced love is not love, it's..."

"Slavery," Steve interjected.

"Yes! That's exactly right!" Mrs. Caffer clapped her hands in delight at his understanding.

Steve was less enthusiastic but continued, "Okay. I can see this is leading us somewhere. But, what about people who already love Him? Why can't He save them?"

"Ah, the plot thickens," kidded the old man in a way that continued to draw Steve out of his defensive mental position. "There are several reasons why bad things happen to good people. I'll list them, and then we'll see if any of them fit our situation here.

"First, God will allow seemingly bad things to happen in order to regain His loved ones' attention when they are being led away from Him by things - money, sports, ambition - in the world. Like a father might spank a child to teach him not to run out into a road. He is allowing consequences that feel bad to the child in order to save the child from something that is really bad. This negative consequence, or discipline, is really a greater good in disguise. It can appear that God is doing a bad thing to one of us merely because we don't see it from His perspective."

Steve nodded his understanding, and the old man went on, "Second, a child of God is placed under an umbrella of protection when he or she accepts Christ. This umbrella protects the child from Satan's plans and attacks, much as the authority of olden-day kings would protect the subjects of the kingdom from robbers and neighboring thugs. The problem is that the child can willfully step out from under that umbrella and leave himself open to the attacks of the evil one. Once that happens, the child is effectively fair game for all sorts of bad things to happen that he would have been protected from."

"But how do we step out from that umbrella?" interjected Steve.

"I think you can guess the answer to that one, Steve. But let me share a verse with you so you don't think I'm just making all this up as I go. When you get a chance, look up Jeremiah twenty-nine, verses one and two." He pulled out a pen and wrote the reference on the unused napkin in front of him and handed it to Steve.

Steve pushed his half-eaten breakfast to the side and smoothed out the napkin on the table in front of him.

"Next," the gentle old man went on, "the Bible tells us that, along with blessings of many kinds, we can expect to be persecuted. Do you understand that word?" he asked, looking into Steve's eyes.

Steve nodded solemnly.

"So, you know that in this world, some people just plain hate Christ and His followers. At times in history, and even around the world today, people are being punished and killed just because they love Jesus."

Mr. Caffer held up four fingers and went on, "Finally, bad things can happen to good people when they are in need of character building. You probably remember in the Bible when Paul said that God's purpose was to conform us to the image of Jesus? Here, let me write that verse down too." He reached across to retrieve the napkin again and jotted down, "Romans 8:28."

"This is an important concept, Steve," Mrs. Caffer broke into the conversation while her husband wrote the reference down, "because it's at this point that we can start to look at seemingly bad things as being actually good. In fact, if we really get this point, we can actually look forward to the next refining event in our lives (even the painful ones) and thank God for loving us so much that He is willing to do this work in our lives. James one verse two talks about this, too."

Steve looked a bit skeptical at this. "You mean I should actually look forward to horrible situations like this? I can't see myself doing that after this week."

"Well, give it time, and perhaps your perspective on it will change. But Mrs. Caffer is right. This view of suffering is a key truth that allows suffering to make sense in light of God's love and His power. There are examples in the Bible of God's favorite people suffering and thanking Him for it. Paul is the one that comes to mind first."

"Yeah, I remember his shipwrecks and beatings and prison sentences and stuff. And he didn't deserve any of that either." Steve paused a moment, mulling over what the Caffers had said, and trying to sort his own situation out.

"Yes," added Mrs. Caffer, "and then there's Joseph and Moses. And don't forget John in the New Testament."

As Steve thought of the ramifications of the umbrellas of protection and of God wanting to get his attention, the walls of cold ice in his heart began to melt. The years of rebellion against God and his own family had built layers of guilt frozen around his heart. But somehow, learning that God could be good and powerful, and still allow rough times to happen in a person's life was slowly melting its way through all that cold separation between him and God.

* * *

Furrgstan was now sweating. He knew he was in trouble. Too late, he had seen what Castellain was up to. That slimy, shiny, meddling angel had blind-sided him again, and this time it was going to cost him Steve's soul if Furrgstan didn't start doing some things right.

Castellain was no longer acting hurt, as he had successfully pretended to be. Furrgstan had taken that bait, and had been lulled into a sleepy truce with the sneaky, low-lying angel. But it had all changed. His competition had chosen now of all times, right in the middle of this operation, to come into the fray full tilt. Now was no time to call downstairs for help either. The whole city's network of demons was involved up to their sulphurous snouts with the big operation. So here he was, stuck on his own in a pitched battle with an angel who was suddenly much stronger than he had expected.

Holding tighter onto Steve's heart with his claws, Furrgstan took a swipe at Castellain's hip with a clawed foot and got great satisfaction from seeing the angelic creep wince with pain. But he didn't give up either, but rather took a new grip on his glowing sword, and advanced into the fight again. The battle for Steve's heart raged on in the spiritual realm as Steve continued his conversation with the old couple.

* * *

Tears began to form again, and Steve's chest tightened like a fist squeezing around his lungs as he finally, truly began to understand how much God loved him and how He showed that love. The old Sunday School stories about God and His Son's death took on fresh meaning as Steve inspected his own heart and saw, for what it was, the subtle rebellion that he had fomented over the last few years. The plight of his sister notwithstanding, Steve now realized that he had to get things straight with God himself before he could hope to make any sense of his sister's problem and his own role in it.

Mrs. Caffer could see the inner turmoil and the signs that some walls were cracking inside of Steve's heart. She gently laid her hand on his hand, just beyond the end of his cast once more and said, "Steve? Are you all right? Is there something we can do to help you get things straightened out between you and God?"

Steve muffled his own crying with his free hand, and awkwardly squeezed her hand with the one she held. He couldn't speak for a moment, but when he did, his words were profound. "I… I'm not sure that I ever actually got under that umbrella you were talking about."

His voice was thick with emotion, and his words came slowly as though he were fighting for every one of them. "I think I've been fooling myself all these years about being alright with God."

Both of the Caffers could sense the huge struggle going on within the young man across the table from them. And both of them silently prayed, holding him up in the spiritual world, binding Satan and his minions with the power of Jesus' shed blood. They interceded for him before the Lord who wanted so much for the boy to take this important step. But nobody could do it for him – no matter how much they loved him.

The words came out in a choppy stream as though each word was dragged out over a rock-strewn course. "I know the answers from all those years in Sunday school, but I... I've never really seen my sins for what they are. I know I need to ask forgiveness and to give my life to Him, but it's - it's so hard! I don't want to give up all the things I've gotten into that cover up this mess. I mean, I've done some bad things – drugs, alcohol..." His voice trailed off to silence and tears as his shame and sorrow overcame him. He bit hard on his lip, trying to mask the emotional turmoil with the comparatively solid pain of a bruised lip.

Mrs. Caffer gently squeezed back, and urged him on, "Go on, Steve. Do what you need to do. Give it all up to Him. You'll never regret it, no matter what happens in the future. You'll find that He will forgive all of it, no matter how bad it was."

* * *

The moment of decision had come, but Furrgstan was ready. He had managed to shift his weight around enough to hold Castellain off with his body. Now at just the right moment he would draw his sword and bring it down on the angel's strained neck and end this struggle for good. He was now waiting for just the right moment - Now!

He released Steve's heart with one hand and reached for his sword hilt. The hilt fit perfectly into his palm after thousands of years of use, and the smooth motion of sliding the sword from its scabbard was lovely. He pulled his arm back in the same motion and prepared to slice Castellain's neck in two.

Exquisite pain shot through his shoulder, and he watched in disbelief as his sword arm sailed away, cut clean through by a sword he hadn't seen coming at all. His other arm was severed as well by yet another swordsman. Yellow smoke, mixed with red ichor, shot from the stumps of his arms. With a shriek of pain and rage, he spun away from Castellain and caught sight of his new attackers.

There stood the two angels who guarded the Caffers, swords drawn and eyes blazing. Blue-hot flames licked up and down their razor edged swords, and light blazed from their eyes.

Being so focused on Steve and his guardian, he hadn't even considered them in this conflict! They had sat quietly beside the old saints, biding their time until this moment. Mewling in despair, eyes darting back and forth among the angels, Furrgstan gave up the field of battle to the three glowing heavenly beings, and dissipated into the mists, knowing that he had lost again and that his punishment would likely last a long, long time. His last glimpse of the scene was that of years of work on Steve's heart coming undone. The carefully laced and locked chains of addiction and lies fell away, and the first painfully shining rays of that most hated of all lights, the light that presaged the coming of the Enemy into a new believer's heart.

* * *

Steve looked up at Mrs. Caffer's concerned face, wondering if she referred to Marianne's situation or to the future in general. But then, all the facets of their conversation came into focus at once. There was an almost audible "snap" as he saw in one crystal moment the beauty of God's plan. In that moment, he became a new man. In that instant he accepted the Lordship of the one true God, even with all of its paradoxes, and with all his lack of understanding about the details, and he quietly sobbed out, "Yes. I do trust You, Lord! I need to have You lead me through this mess I've made of my life. And Lord, please save my sister. She doesn't deserve to die - take me instead!" Then his quiet sobbing made it impossible for him to continue, so Mrs. Caffer moved around the end of the table to put her arms around his shaking shoulders, and he responded by turning to her and burying his face in her shoulder.

* * *

Danielle prayed on, compelled to keep bringing Steve to God's mind. Then, oddly, the compelling feeling faded and was replaced by a peace about Steve. She smiled, still not knowing what had happened, but content that he was in God's hands.

* * *

Mrs. Caffer "there, there'd" him and patted his shoulders, very glad to be able to support this young man in such a grandmotherly way. She didn't even seem to mind his tears and runny nose.

After a time, he disentangled himself and, looking a bit embarrassed, blew his nose on his paper napkin. "I guess I needed that. Thanks for being willing to sit with me through this."

Mr. Caffer smiled a huge smile, and said, "There is nothing we love more than helping folk find out that God is big enough to handle all their doubts and questions. And you're more right than you know. You really did need to have this encounter with Him."

"And the cry, dear," added Mrs. Caffer.

Steve blew his nose again and asked, "Well, what now?"

"First things first," said Mr. Caffer past a big smile, and pushing Steve's food back in front of him, commanded, "eat your food. And then I think you probably should go back home and set things straight with your folks."

Steve looked chagrined, "Yeah. I bet they're pretty worried - and upset."

"Oh, I bet they'll see past the anger when you explain what just happened." Mrs. Caffer was smiling, with tears of joy in her eyes.

Steve dug into his food with a gusto that surprised him. Life suddenly seemed to have a new freedom and energy. He wondered about the lightness of heart he felt. *Maybe it's from being so tired,* he thought, but knowing deep inside that it wasn't that. He knew it came from his new relationship with God. When the Caffers got ready to leave, Steve nearly panicked. "Wait! Don't leave me! I need you to go with me! I can't go back there by myself. I'm gonna get killed when I walk back in that house!" The concern showing in his face made the two elderly folks smile.

"You'll do fine, Steve," encouraged Mrs. Caffer. "You're not going back there alone, for heaven's sake."

"That's right, Steve," added Mr. Caffer when they saw the confusion on the boy's face. "First off, you're going home to your family. You'll not be alone there. And secondly, God is going with you."

"*And* before you," his wife interjected. "And you can call us if you think that we can help your folks understand." She took her husband's pen, and bent to write their phone number on the napkin under the three verse references.

Mr. Caffer smiled, nodded, and went on. "God is not going to let anything happen that is not in your best interest. You must only trust Him to do what He will in your life. It may not be easy; in fact, life will undoubtedly become even harder for you now than it has been. It takes much more gumption to say "no" to sin than it does to give in.

"Steve, there are many things that are taking place in your heart right now. Some of them happen instantly, like being forgiven, and like getting a clean heart. But some of them take time, possibly years. Satan wants you to wallow in false guilt, so he'll do his darndest to keep lying to you about things that aren't even your fault. He also wants you to believe that every time you sin from now on, you aren't really saved."

Mr. Caffer went on with great concern in his voice, "When that happens, don't you believe it!"

As he listened, the intensity of Steve's feelings still showed in his expression, and touched their hearts.

"You can call us any time - and I mean any time, and we'll help you remember this morning," soothed Mrs. Caffer.

Steve slowly nodded his understanding. Again the Caffers made as if to leave, and this time Steve smiled and rose with them. Very much out of his character, he awkwardly held out his arms and hugged each of his new friends.

As they walked away, Steve picked up the napkin, folded it with care, and stuck it into his pocket.

***

Castellain grinned a smile that was as broad as the sea. What a wonder! Steve had accepted the gift! Furrgstan was gone, and the coming of the Lord had healed all of his own wounds. What could possibly be better than this? His charge had a new heart and a new set of friends who would begin to tenderly nurture him in his new life.

His wounds were instantly healed when the Captain of the Host of Heaven had appeared, and he stretched his strong shoulders with joy. The tall angel breathed a long prayer of thanks and worship to God, and settled in to watch and guard over this new man of God.

Chapter 8
You should go ahead.

Marianne bit her lip as she was escorted once again down the steep wooden steps to the basement. Two days ago the rough handrail, unfinished walls, and inadequate lighting had not prepared her for what lay on the other side of an uncovered, insulated wall built five feet past the bottom of the steps. The single metal door set in the middle of the wall looked out of place in the dark and dingy, roughly finished, short hall that served as the bottom landing for the stairway.

But once the heavy door had opened on its silent hinges, bright lights set in the middle of dark shadowy areas had assailed her eyes. It had taken a moment to adjust to the glare, but then what she saw made her gasp with surprise. The harsh lighting came from spotlights and photographic equipment hanging from the ceiling and set on stands here and there around the room. Video cameras, microphones, cables, and wires ran across the floor in tangled patterns, which reminded her of the maze puzzles she had played on long car trips with her family. The incongruity added still more confusion to her reeling mind.

That first visit, she had found the set-up intriguing, even fascinating, until she had seen past the lights and cameras and had taken in what finally dawned on her was set up for her filming debut. Some of the set looked almost normal: an overstuffed chair, a couch, a bookshelf, and a large bed. But then her eyes had taken in more details and her mind had registered the shapes of chains, knives, a gun, and a lot of electrical equipment that she hadn't recognized. But she had immediately understood that this was not good, and that her part in whatever was to come next was not going to be a good thing either.

That was when she had made her first serious bid for freedom. And shortly after that she had gained her first-hand experience of how much pain those odd looking machines could cause. She had begged, promised anything to get the men to stop. But nothing she had said had made the least bit of difference. They had gone on twisting dials and pushing buttons and attaching electrodes to her.

It wasn't until much later that she realized that Art and his crew had filmed the whole thing, and that not one thing they had done, despite all the pain, had left a visible mark on her. Visible marks or no, the ordeal had surely left a mark in her mind. The men found her very cooperative from then on.

Today threatened to be more of the same, and she cringed. But then she focused upwardly, and once again felt the soothing, peaceful comfort of the presence and peace of God come over her. As the cameras started to roll, Marianne relaxed in the arms of the Lord, who carried her through another impossible day.

* * *

Pete had finally coaxed Molly to get up and to take a shower, promising to stay by the phone, and then he encouraged her to have a cup of coffee and a piece of toast. It was now about ten o'clock, and Molly was back at her post, sitting on the couch in the living room within reach of the phone, once again staring far away and moving nothing but her hands in her lap.

Pete was worn out; completely drained. There was not much left of whatever it took inside his heart to try to help a wife who acted like someone had pushed her power button off, or a son who had now been missing for almost twenty-four hours with no explanation, or a daughter who had been kidnapped. His tidy, well-planned, predictable life was truly messed up.

His whole life felt misplaced, shuffled. Even missing church in order to be home this morning felt like another hole in his heart. For Pete, church was a comfortable place to do his time for God. There didn't seem to be much of importance in what he heard or did at church, but as a father, he figured it was good for the kids to hear it. It was little enough to do if that's what God really wanted from him. Amidst everything else that was screwed up this morning, it was odd that missing church today felt so important.

As it was, his whole life felt like one huge irritation, exhausting every ounce of energy he could muster just to go on breathing. So when he heard a car pull up and the garage door open, he stayed put on the sofa next to Molly until his son walked in through the door. It seemed so normal that at first he didn't react. Then, all his anger and frustration reached the boiling point, and Steve became the target at which he aimed his release valve.

"Who do you think you are, boy? Don't you realize that your mom and I have plenty enough to worry about without you running off with no word to us at all?" There was a small portion of his mind that felt guilty for venting at

Steve, but mostly it just felt good to finally unleash some of the pent up pressure and venom he had been holding in for so long now. Pete was enjoying the feeling so much that he failed to notice the calm look of joy on Steve's face.

Steve's expression wavered at his dad's onslaught, but then he set his chin square and settled in to take his punishment. He knew he deserved his dad's shots after having left without permission and it looked as though his dad could use the target practice.

"What were you thinking? Since when are you all grown up enough to just take off with my car?" Pete's tone became more and more venomous, and finally the words Steve was inwardly dreading came out, too.

"You know, if you hadn't been screwing around instead of watching your sister, none of this..." and then he stopped. His eyes grew wide, and his hand flew to cover his mouth as he realized what he had just accused his son of.

This got through even to Molly, so lost within her protective shell. She reacted to this attack by gasping, and half rising and reaching out with her hand to stop Pete's tirade. Both of his parents stared at Steve, then at one another, and then Steve again as they all realized just how far Pete had gone with his accusing words. But

Steve simply stood there, battling against anger, pride and guilt. His face reflected each emotion briefly, and after a few moments the words of the Caffers returned to him. *Remember, Steve, Satan will try to convince you that this never happened, but you're a new person now. You're forgiven and you're a child of the King.*

Steve wondered how a forgiven child of the King would handle this situation. The moment stretched, awkward and silent as Steve sorted through the options of response. Pete stammered, "Steve, I – I..."

Steve lifted his hand to stop his dad. He looked at the floor as he chose his words, and said, "Dad, it's okay. I know what happened, and I'm trying to deal with my part in it. I've beat myself up over what happened and what I did, and what I should've done. I'm sorry for my part in this mess, and I know I deserve some punishment. But Dad, Mom, I've got to talk to you for a few minutes."

Pete felt his virulent, pent up anger fizzle away into shame. "I'm sorry Steve. I had no right to say that to you." Pete's voice shook with fatigue and emotion. He was truly at the end of his reserves. "But dog-gone it, I can't take any more. I'm stretched too thin here, and your leaving in the car yesterday was just another thing to deal with in the middle of an impossible couple of days."

"I know, Dad, and I'm really sorry. I spent the night looking for that van that was sighted."

"You what?" his dad exploded again. "That is the dumbest thing I've ever heard of. You could have been killed. Or you could have gotten Marianne killed! What were you thinking?!"

"That's just it Dad. I wasn't thinking at all. I just overheard you on the phone with Ted's dad and took off." Steve's voice got quieter as he spoke, and as he realized just how stupid what he had done really was. "I know now that it was dumb, but I wasn't thinking at the time.

"But Dad, I've had some time to think this through, and I met up with Mr. and Mrs. Caffer this morning. You know. That old couple from church?" The words tumbled out in a stream. "And they helped get me straightened out with God. I finally realized how much I've been hiding from Him, and how much I need Him. And this morning I gave my heart to Him again.

"Dad, Mom, I've got a fresh start today. And I know - I know with all of my heart that God will bring about good even in this rotten situation."

Steve's enthusiasm did nothing to help Pete's anger, in fact it grated on his already raw nerves. He spat out, "Well that's great. Your sister is God-only-knows where, and you're out getting religion. Well, Steve, that doesn't fix anything. You're grounded. Get in your room and stay there until I figure out what we're going to do about this."

"Okay, Dad. I'll go. I know I deserve it. But I just want you and Mom to know that I'm sorry for how I've been acting lately, and for Marianne, and for last night. I promise I will do anything I can to make up for it."

Where Steve's words hadn't gotten through to his dad's heart, his son's quiet acceptance of his punishment started to. Unlike their usual pattern of escalating verbiage, this 'non-argument' was a one-sided non-starter. No matter how much Pete tried to push Steve's buttons, his son just stayed calm and humble. Pete stared at Steve, and took in his sincere expression and the apparently honest way he had bared his heart. This was so out of character for Steve that he was forced to slow his words and control his anger. His own heart softened a bit, and he sent his son away with, "Thank you. I'll be in later to talk this over some more," more muttered than spoken.

Steve nodded and slowly walked down the hall to his bedroom.

* * *

Pastor Dave was a sight, both outwardly and inwardly. He had stayed in the living room all night slouched in the easy chair, clothes still a mess from his exertions at the car wreck. *Interesting,* he thought, *how my life-saving efforts have probably resulted in my own life being wrecked.* He truly did look and smell like a wreck, with his hair tousled and his clothes all smoky, wrinkled, bloody, and stale. He had washed his hands, but otherwise he still bore the smudges and soot from his exertions at the accident scene late last night.

Sam woke, yawned, stretched, and rubbed her pretty but tired face. The events of the previous evening didn't register until she swung her legs off the couch and sat up, gathering in the sight of Dave in his chair. Then it all came crashing back in on her, and she scooted over to sit on the floor by his knee.

The last of her fatigue fled as she shook her head. "Dave? Honey? Are you all right?" She placed her hand on his knee and gazed fearfully up at his face. "Dave, did you sleep at all last night?"

He responded by running his hand through his dirty, unkempt hair and grunting. She felt that she needed to remind him, "Hon, do you know what time it is? Church starts in less than an hour."

He responded with a worn sounding voice, "I can't do it, Sam. I can't go and teach today. You know what I've done? Do you know how badly I've messed up?"

"But you can't hide here. You've got to face the people of the church sooner or later. And I'll help you. They'll understand."

"Not today I don't. And they won't understand either, not while this fiasco with the youth group is so fresh on their minds. I'm telling you I can't go in there today. I can't. I just can't do it."

Sam bit her lip, exasperated and confused. Dave had talked all around what had happened last night. But though she had called the hospital to find out that Chad and Jordan were still critical but stable, and though she had called their folks to begin salvaging what she could from this catastrophe, she knew that there was something more to Dave's dilemma than simply the use of poor judgment in calling out the youth group and the accident involving Jordan and Chad. Something was eating away at Dave, and now, in hind-sight, she realized that it had been for months. Some slow and subtle changes had been eating away at her husband and at their marriage for many weeks. Her concern for her husband, deep enough already, grew deeper yet with the realization.

Earlier she had fallen asleep on the couch while staring at Dave, who sat in his chair and stared at the floor refusing to say anything more. Sighing, she went to the kitchen and called the church to let Pastor Miller know that Dave would not be in today, and then thought through her mental list of youth staff to see who could fill in teaching the teens on a moment's notice.

Twenty minutes later, having arranged for a teacher for the senior highers, she went back to the living room, finding Dave unmoved. "I called the church, and I got Harold Geoffry to teach the class this morning. I also checked at the hospital. Chad is stabilized and serious, but Jarod is still in critical care. At least he's not getting any worse. Are you ready to talk any more about whatever it is that's bothering you?" She paused to let her words have what effect they could. Dave still made no response. "I'll be here if you want to talk, hon."

Eyes still on the floor between his feet, he mumbled, "You should go ahead and go to church, Sam. I just need some time to think through this."

"I think you have thought long enough, and it's time to talk. But I'll wait. As long as it takes, I'll wait." To her it was a solemn promise, a renewed vow. Some of the intensity of her intent must have broken through to him, because after a pause Dave finally raised his head and looked at her. Their eyes met, and Sam was deeply troubled at what she saw there. Not a glimmer of the joy and hope that had filled those eyes just a very few months earlier. Not a trace of life - only despair. Dark, hopeless despair.

Chapter 9
That's not the worst news.

Lydia Mochek eased into the dark oaken pew next to her husband, having said hello to the pastor and gotten through the drop-the-kids-off-to-their-classes process in decent order. Mercy Seat Sanctuary was a small and very close church family. Though the leadership and choir were all black, there were three white families who attended regularly. Lydia felt very much at home here, and found Sunday morning service to be one of the very few times she could really relax. Her husband put his arm around her shoulders, and felt some of the tension leave – at least for now.

The Fracks' situation had occupied Lydia's mind even away from her office, and even now she wondered how much of the situation she could share in the prayer time at the close of the service. The organ and piano began playing, and soon she was singing along with the choir, enjoying the atmosphere of praise and worship. Soon enough though, she was again distracted from the worship, and her mind pictured the face of Marianne as depicted in the picture her folks had given the officers who responded to their first call.

***

The eleven o'clock service at First Evangelical was the largest of the weekend. There was much talk about Marianne's abduction, gossip, to be more accurate, ramped up another notch when Pastor Dave didn't show up to teach the youth group at nine forty-five. Most of the members had heard of the kidnapping, but few had any facts concerning her status or the posse the youth pastor had pulled together. The grapevine hadn't had enough time to do a thorough job yet, but by the time the second service started, it wasn't only the families with kids in the youth group who were aware of the dumb fool thing he had done in calling the youth group out to search for the black van.

Word of the accident in which Jordan and Chad had been so badly injured was also making the rounds of gossip - in the thinly disguised form of the prayer chain. Of course it was Fred Hatch, while talking to John Stirming, who put the data together, and boy did the dirt fly then!

"I want an emergency meeting of the elders, and I want it now!" Fred's tightly controlled voice reflected his barely contained rage. He went on in his forced whisper, "I'm telling you, John, that guy has pulled his last stunt at this church."

John tried to slow him down a bit with, "Relax Fred." But the angry elder was having none of it.

"Relax? Are you nuts? We could be sued into next Easter by those two families. Don't you see what's at stake here?"

"I see it all right, but I don't think we should be having this conversation in the middle of the hallway. Let's split up and gather as many elders as we can and meet in the boardroom in fifteen minutes."

"Okay, let's do it. And grab Pastor Miller, too. He should be there, even if it means Toby has to do the announcements and the offering by himself today." Toby Wallace was the minister of worship for First Evangelical and was only twenty-seven years old. He was inexperienced enough to be thrown by the disruption of the Sunday morning schedule, and Fred was concerned about what the young man might do if left on his own for too long.

"I'll make sure Toby knows that Mark will be in there in time for the message," John added, still thinking clearly even though Fred wasn't yet.

The two went their separate ways in search of elders, quickly finding well over the eleven required for a quorum. They gathered in the church library, where board meetings usually took place.

"Gentlemen, we haven't got much time. So I'd like to bring you all up to date on the situation which we face." Fred took charge of the meeting because he was the chairman of the official board. Even Pastor Miller deferred to Fred at board meetings. "I assume all of you have heard the news about Marianne Frack being kidnapped." He paused and looked around for any blank looks from the members. Each of the members acknowledged their awareness of that news. "Yesterday afternoon, young Pastor Dave Merryl took it upon himself to deputize his youth group and send them out in cars to patrol Hubbardston Road in search of the van that was involved in Marianne's abduction." Several gasped at this news. Others had already heard, and looked around with grim faces for the reaction of the others.

Fred held up his hand to forestall any talking, and went on, "Wait. That's not the worst news. Late last night, one of the cars involved in this posse," he nearly spat the word out, "ran into another car, seriously injuring Jordan Tesch and Chad Buchanon. They are both in the hospital, Jordan still in critical condition, and Chad doing little better. The driver of the other car was killed in the accident." Again he paused to allow the weight of his words fall on the shoulders of those around the table. The men now sat in shocked silence, waiting for him to tell them what they should do next.

"I've asked you to come to this meeting to make a decision about what we should do to keep this disaster from getting any worse. Anybody have anything to offer for insight here?" The opening music could just be heard echoing through the now empty hallways leading to the main sanctuary.

Mr. Caffer raised his head to meet Fred's eyes and then raised his hand for recognition. "Yes Al?"

"I think we should pray about the situation."

Fred sighed, rolled his eyes, and said, "Yes, of course, we will, but first let's get our action steps formulated here." Fred punctuated his answer with a chop of his hand, but the old gentleman was not to be put off. In fact he barely waited for Fred to finish speaking before adding. "No, I think we should pray *first*."

Again Fred waved him off, vexation beginning to show in his eyes. "Yes, Al, I know we need to pray, but we've only got about five minutes to put some controls around this, and then we're going to have to go out there ready with answers for the people. We'll pray when we get some breathing room."

Very much unlike the Al Caffer that everyone was used to, the oldest of the elders rose to his feet, planted his hands on the table in front of himself, and went on as though Fred hadn't said a thing. "In fact I think we should ask Pastor Miller here, to go out to the service and explain the problem and ask everyone to set aside their expectations for this morning and have the whole congregation pray right now. If there was ever a time when this church needed to seek God on its knees - it is now."

Though he spoke no louder, his voice and face filled with such passion that every person present sat up and listened with new intensity. Even Fred Hatch was speechless for a moment.

The most gentle member of the Board of Elders went on firmly, "Gentlemen, I beg you. Quiet your hearts, swallow your pride, lay aside your plans, and seek God. Pastor Miller, I leave it to you to do what your heart knows is right. Lead your people, not with words, not with plans, not with sermons, but in prayer."

All eyes turned silently and expectantly to Pastor Miller's, nd waited for him to speak. His head was tipped down as though he were reading or in deep thought. None of the waiting board members could read his face, and none could guess what his reaction to Al Caffer's comments would be. In fact, he did not seem to react to Al's challenge at all. Several thought that he hadn't heard, and Fred cleared his throat as if he were about to take charge of the meeting once again.

But Pastor Miller raised his head and caught Fred's attention with an uplifted finger, bringing him back to silence with a pointed stare. Fred closed his mouth and slowly exhaled, but his blood pressure rose as his anger surged. He was entirely unaccustomed to being silenced like some young whelp fresh on the board. Inwardly he told himself that he would have to have a talk with Pastor Miller about his treatment of board members - without mentioning any names, of course.

Still the senior pastor waited, now slowly looking each man square in the eyes - taking the measure of what he saw there. Some looked calmly back. A few, held his gaze for a moment, and then looked away as they saw the sadness and the sincerity of his heart. Some of them sensed that this was a moment of decision; a point in time in which eternal choices were being made. Consciously or not, every one of the men gathered around that table recognized deep in his heart, that they were at a cusp, that they were about to make a decision from which there would be no going back or second guessing. What they decided now, in this room would affect the course of this church, the life of each member, with eternal consequences. For this was a pivotal moment in deciding whether this church body would seek to answer their needs with their own human resources, or seek God and His answers.

* * *

Lieutenant Crimnog, the demon in charge of First Evangelical Church glared at Maniroff, the level-three angel who had opposed him since the founding of this church sixty-two years ago. Their eyes met across the room full of elders, pastors and assorted private class demons and level-one and level-two angels. Both of these mid-level spiritual beings, one godly, and the other as dark and evil as the darkest night, realized the importance of this decision. Like the ancient King Asa in the land of Judah, the men gathered in this room, over whom the spirit-beings hovered, had a choice between acting on their own best abilities or seeking God and His wisdom. The option the humans chose in the next thirty seconds would pivot this specific battle in the millennia-long war in crucial ways.

Both of the beings had surprises in store for the other, and each hoped to pull the other off balance with the use of feints and misleading battles elsewhere across the city. Maniroff, his armor glowing ever more brightly, however, was in ascendancy with new prayer warriors coming into the fray every hour, and hadn't enjoyed this much fresh spiritual energy in years.

For the first time in more than a decade, the forces of righteousness had an opportunity to tip the scales in a decisive battle rather than scraping by with an occasional individual victory here and there. For the first time in just as long, there was an opportunity for the balance to swing, for the tide to shift - in a word, here was a chance for revival to sweep this city, and it would begin with one decision. Here in this room. At this moment. In the decision of this middle-aged senior pastor. The outcome rested precariously on a cusp, with a fall to deeper darkness and increased depravity on one side, and a fresh taste of freedom, light and truth on the other. A city waited: the spoils of victory for the demon hordes, or the fresh, full fruit of the Spirit.

Maniroff, assigned to protect the church, and Pastor Miller's personal angelic guardian, Freely, knew the importance of this moment. They both knew that Pastor Miller was at his own personal pivot point, and that the decision he made right now would throw great weight into the balance, either for trusting God or for a continued reliance on human abilities.

Both of these angels waited for the sign from Agrevious that would signal the diversionary action that was to occur at the healing meeting on the south side of town at Mercy Seat Sanctuary. That church was becoming more and more effective in evangelism, and was meeting this morning to culminate the week's meetings.

At the prearranged moment, the two angels noted Crimnog's look of aggravation as he received news of the need for support for frustrating the efforts of the church across town. Several of the demons, three privates, a couple of nasty corporals and one evil sergeant disappeared from the boardroom of First Evangelical, but the two angels waited a few moments more to allow Crimnog to relax again.

* * *

Near the end of the Mercy Seat service, Deacon Windsor stood to ask for prayer for the big Evangelical church across town. Lydia Mochek's eyes widened in surprise. She had no idea that anyone else had any interest in what was happening in that congregation, but she was grateful that Mr. Windsor had spoken out. As the deacon explained the situation and the need of that church, several people volunteered to uphold the people and pastors of First Evangelical in prayer. Then the people prayed together, and again, new power for the battle was infused into the forces of righteousness.

* * *

Maniroff felt the fresh influx of spiritual energy resulting from the Mercy Seat prayers. It was what he had been waiting for, and finally he gave a slight nod, and all the angels present launched into full combat mode, each with his assigned job.

Maniroff rocketed across the few feet separating himself from Crimnog, knocking the ugly, blister-skinned demon from his perch on the table in front of Pastor Miller. At the same moment, Freely pointed his lance at the head of Schmelledorf, and a blue hot spear of focused laser light skewered the lopsided head of the demon resting on Pastor Miller's head. The head exploded, leaving a grisly, steaming stump on top of the sinewy shoulders. The body of the demon slumped, as though collapsing in upon itself, and then fell to the floor, though the whole thing dissolved into greenish yellow smoke before it landed on the carpet. The smoke settled down into, and then through, the floor into the unseen place where Schmellendorf had come from originally.

The advantage of the moment was won, and within a few heartbeats the angels had subdued all of the demons present, other than the two whose human hosts had never accepted the gift, and therefore were able to hold their hosts almost totally unopposed by any angelic guardian.

* * *

Mark Miller, the pastor of a church that was thriving, at least as far as the rest of Alagonic could see, was a man who had come to appreciate the importance of give and take. He was very savvy in the arena of righteous compromise, as he liked to put it. He knew how important it was to keep from alienating any of the people of his church, especially the members who donated consistently and generously. And because of this, it had been years since he had gone out on a limb for any cause that anyone could get upset about.

Right at this moment, however, Pastor Miller surprised himself by straightening in his chair, as though a weight had been lifted, and as though he had arrived at a new source of strength and resolve. He looked at each man again, and again measured what he saw. Most of the men appeared to rise to the spiritual challenge that old Mr. Caffer had dropped in their laps. But a couple of them, and those were some of the most powerful of the group, seemed to brace themselves, as though they, too, saw what was at stake and instinctively steeled themselves to do battle. Sadly, they were on the wrong side of the battle.

The silence drifted past the comfortable stage, and John Stirming cleared his throat. Pastor Miller looked at him, too, and quietly quoted, "Be still and know that I am God." Looking around the table one last time in the tense silence, he said, "Al is right. It is high time we left our own wisdom behind, and spent some time seeking God's council on matters that are far beyond our ability to control."

"Gentlemen," he began, and then shaking his head, "Friends. I ask for your patience. I ask for your understanding. But most of all I ask that each of us set aside our own personal thoughts, plans, and agendas, and that we take whatever time is needed to seek God and His answers to the circumstances which we now face."

With new determination and resolve, he went on, "As I see it, there are three major problems that we need to deal with." He held up his hand and ticked the items off, one by one. "The predicament of Marianne Frack and her family. The injuries that Chad and Jordan are fighting back from. And the mess Dave has gotten himself into." He watched as most of those gathered nodded their understanding, and then went on.

"I am asking each of you to sacrifice whatever plans you had for today, and to stay right here, silently in prayer, until God leads us to His answers. I intend to go out to the service, deliver the shortest message I've ever given, ask the congregation for their prayers, and then return here to spend whatever time is necessary with you to seek and find God's leading through this valley of darkness." Several nodded their approval, most simply looked on, speechless. Only Fred Hatch and John Stirming showed their resistance and disapproval by glaring back at their senior pastor.

Pastor Miller nodded, picked up his Bible, and turned from the table. As he walked along the hall leading to the door to the platform, he was torn between hurrying to get there before Toby ran out of songs, and slowing down to delay the moment he had to put into what words he could, the spiritual battle that was facing this church.

* * *

Toby knew there was something major going on. During the three years he had been Minister of Worship at First Evangelical Church, he had never once had to cover for Pastor Miller. The man was always on time, come holidays, anniversaries, birthdays - whatever - if the man was in town, he was on the platform when the service began.

Then today happened. Just before the service began, John Stirming, one of the 'power broker' elders of the church, had grabbed him and told him that Pastor M. was going to be a bit late getting to the platform, but to go on and start

- that he would be there before it was time for the sermon. Toby's shock must have shown on his face, because John had turned to leave, but then had come back to reassure him that Mark wasn't ill. He tried to look calm, but his tone belied his words as he told Toby that something had come up that Pastor Miller had to attend to before the service.

Well, that was far from reassuring, but Toby was convinced that even though Pastor Miller tended to get caught up in the power plays and politics that happen in a large church, the man was definitely a man of God. So, Toby opened the service as usual, with a hymn, leading with passion and enthusiasm. In fact he almost lost himself in the moment as he usually did - worshipping the Creator in spirit and in truth - except, he kept noticing the congregation looking around, whispering to one another, not quite entering into the worship as much as they usually did. He knew they had noticed the lack of Pastor Miller. How could they not? The man was always on the platform by this time.

By the end of the third song, a chorus that had become sort of a theme song for the church through the last year or so, he realized that he was going to have to say something to get the people's minds back on track. At the end of the song, he had them sit, and before the announcements, said, "I suppose you've noticed that Pastor Miller is not here yet. Well, I want to inform you that he is here, he is fine, and he will be with us in just a few moments. Something came up that required his attention, and he will be with us shortly.

"If you will look in your bulletin this morning..." and he went on with his announcements. Though the sense of tension had lowered in the sanctuary, he could tell that the people still had half their mind on Pastor Miller's absence.

* * *

"You're my guardian angel, aren't you," Marianne's words were a statement more than a question, but Ajourney nodded his confirmation anyway. He was glad the Master had approved of his appearing to Marianne now. He was glad that he had been able to take so much of her suffering on himself, and that she was so filled with the assurance and presence of the Lord.

Her eyes narrowed as she took in his condition, however. "Are you all right?" she asked with concern. He chuckled at the irony of this child, so abused by her captors, asking him if he was all right. How like a true child of the King. What an awesome mystery, that the Creator had worked so much of His own nature into these human creatures. "I'll be fine sweetheart. I just want you to know that you are very much loved by your heavenly Father, and by your family."

"Will I be going home soon?" she asked, and Ajourney knew by her tone, that she wasn't referring to her home here on earth.

"Marianne, that's one of the things I can't tell you. But you can be sure that I'll be here with you, and the Lord will be too. You'll be fine. Just keep on as you have been, and you'll be just fine." He hugged her gently, and she sighed as she relaxed against his strong chest.

"I don't know if I can keep on, but I know that I believe you. I'll do my best, just don't leave me alone here. Okay?" And she looked back up at him, measuring him, and looking for assurance.

His deep brown eyes looked unwaveringly back at her. "I'll be right here," he promised.

She stared at his kind, ageless face for a few moments as he held her to his chest and stroked her hair. Her eyes grew heavy and then closed, but a soft smile stayed on her face. The two-day-old wrinkles on her twelve-year-old face smoothed and disappeared as her helper, her guardian, eased her heart of its burden.

* * *

Halfway through that Sunday afternoon the phone at the Frack's house rang.

When Pete heard that Mr. Caffer was on the phone, he couldn't quite put together that the older man wanted to talk to Steve. Then he recalled that Steve had told him about meeting Mr. and Mrs. Caffer at the restaurant that morning, and it clicked. "Oh! Sure, Al, I'll get him for you. Just a minute."

He laid the receiver on the counter, and walked down the hall to Steve's room. Knocking, and not waiting for a response, he said in a voice that would carry through the door, "Steve? Mr. Caffer is on the phone for you. Do you want it in there?"

"Thanks, Dad. Yeah, if you don't mind," came the uncharacteristically polite response. Last week at this point, there would have been harsh words from Steve over any invasion of 'his space.' Pete shook his head, wondering again just what was going on in his son's head.

He tossed the phone to Steve on his bed, and closed the door as he turned away. The old man had apparently taken quite an interest in his son, which was fine with him. Lord knows, Steve needed some kind of new and positive input in his life. He listened from the doorway as Steve said, "Hello Mr. Caffer," and then thought, *Man, since when does he act so respectful to his elders. Maybe he really is changing.*

Then Steve answered whatever it was that Al was saying with, "Well, I'm grounded, but I'll ask my dad if it's okay. Hold on just a minute." Steve cupped the receiver in the palm of his hand, muffling Mr. Caffer's ability to hear what he was going to ask his dad before calling out, "Dad, Mr. Caffer is having a prayer time tonight for Marianne, and he's asking if I can come. Would it be okay, or should I say I can't?"

Immediately Pete's mind went into "hurt mode" and asked himself why Al hadn't asked him to come rather than his rebellious son. Then he felt his anger rise even further with the injustice of the position he had been put in - what could he say other than "yes" without looking like an idiot? "No, my son can't come and pray with you?" What kind of dad would refuse to let his son go pray with an elder from the church?

Barely holding his anger in check as fear piled on top of frustration on top of misunderstanding, he muttered through clenched teeth, "Go ahead and go. But be home before -" and he checked his watch to see the time, "- before ten o'clock." Then he turned on his heel, not giving Steve a chance to speak, and headed down the hall again.

As he walked away, he could hear Steve's voice telling Al Caffer that he would be there at seven o'clock.

Chapter 10
Fade to black.

Art, the man in charge of the child-abduction and filming business, was none too happy. Standing behind the camera, telling the others what needed to be done next, directing the filming, and watching firsthand what had to be done in this basement; these things usually fed and seemed to satisfy a gnawing, and growing hunger inside him, at least for a while. Now, however, the frustrations of the last day or two were quickly coming to an explosive head.

Normally the things they did to the young girls they took would result in first their screams, then their begging for mercy, and then a strange state of dependence or reciprocal addiction. Capturing that transition on film was the pinnacle of what he considered to be his filming artistry.

Marianne, however, wasn't cooperating. Oh, she had begged him for release, but only once, after she had nearly escaped prior to her first filming. Since then, she had reacted to Art's thorough and harsh techniques with a peaceful detachment that was totally unusable on film. It was odd. No matter what they did to her, no matter how they pushed her, she failed to react in any way. Nothing seemed to hurt her all that much, nothing got through her calm determination to wait them out. Art had never seen such an attitude from one of his 'stars,' much less one as young as Marianne. It was driving him nuts, and he was taking it out on his crew as much as on Marianne. In turn, the camera man snapped back some nasty comments, and ended up ruining a seven minute clip that had shown some promise. The sound man kept missing his cues. The light guy was somewhere in a world of his own, and everyone was yelling at him all at once. Art was convinced that MiMi was just bad luck for his studio, and he could hardly wait till he was through with her and could get rid of her.

In fact, this very morning, she had begun to preach at Art - some crap about 'God is love,' and Jesus, and forgiveness. She wouldn't shut up about it until he lost his temper and smacked her across her face. That was something he never did to his little starlets. He never marked them where the camera would see it until he was through with them, but this kid was getting to him. So then they had the expense and time for new makeup to cover the angry red splotch on MiMi's face. On top of that incident was the whole list of technical glitches that were costing him an arm and a leg, both in time and in money to fix. A superstitious guy would think MiMi was jinxing the whole set up.

The latest of these snafus was a supposedly fool-proof filter for the number one camera designed to give a whole bunch of soft focus effects that had gotten gummed up somehow. *Geeze,* he thought, *What next?* He slammed his palm on the side of the camera, earning yet another angry look and sharp retort from the camera man. Art gave an exasperated snort, and ordered the crew to set up for the final day's filming, working around the loss of that filter. "Let's just get this done with, and get it in the can." Art loved to use terms that he thought made him sound like a big time producer.

Nope, this film was definitely not going according to plan. Much of the stuff they had on film was pretty low quality, thanks to Marianne's imperturbable, unshakable, un-normal calm. And here she was, now. Still dry eyed, calm, not even nervous. *What was with this kid?* Art thought, *This girl has got to go.*

Well, today will be different. Today is the final shooting, the final act, and the last day I'll have to put up with her Jesus crap. He was glad he had set up her buyer, the man who would pay thirty-thousand dollars in cold cash for a healthy, untraceable young girl, for today. Normally he liked to hold on to the kids for a few days for his own entertainment, but for some reason, the guy who was taking Marianne insisted that he pick her up today. Now Art was glad to get her off his hands. He didn't know, and really didn't care, what his buyers did with the kids once they were out the door, but the buyer coming today gave him the creeps. There was something about this guy, something so cold and hard and dark, and yet velvety smooth, that even Art shivered when he looked in his eyes.

The filming began. Marianne put in her usual unaffected performance, which made the other "actors'" performance flat and uninspired as well. When the last scene was ended, and the last tape marked and filed, he sent Marianne back to her room to be shackled to the pipe and to await the man known only as Henry, who would pay thirty grand for any living, reasonably attractive, and untraceable young girl that Art could get for him.

An hour later, Henry showed up right on time, as always. Art brought Marianne, collected his envelope without even taking the time to look inside to count the money, and ushered Henry and his new property out the side door into the garage as quickly as he could. There weren't many people who scared Art, but Henry absolutely terrified him. To Art, Henry represented a whole new level of inhumanity - a quantum leap in evil.

Henry noticed his discomfort, though he usually paid as little attention to Art as he probably would have paid to an alley cat. Today, for some reason, was different. As he entered the garage, he turned back to face the door, where Art was waiting by the garage door opener button, and smiled at him. Art cringed and then froze, finger on the button, poised to open the door, hoping to hurry these two out of his life.

Then, with no warning, but making sure Art was watching, Henry reached into his immaculate suit coat pocket, pulled out a small pocket knife and flipped the blade open with a "click" that sounded as sharp as the blade looked. He smiled, still locking eyes with Art, took a hand full of Marianne's hair and pulled her head around so that she faced him. The edge of the blade gleamed with a scalpel bright edge, and with the cool precision of an experienced artist, he pressed the blade against the side of her sweet face, drawing a trickle of blood that immediately welled up and dripped down her neck to be absorbed in the cloth of her shirt.

Marianne's face remained calm even at this, and Henry said, "This is not normal, Art. You've gotten yourself involved in *forces* this time." The way he said "forces," made Art's face blanch even more than the cold hearted way he had cut Marianne's face. Henry went on, "Forces and conflicts that you don't understand and that you can't control. But don't let it fret you. It's my problem now. And I *do* understand." With that he propelled Marianne into the back seat of the silver colored and mirror-windowed Mercedes, calmly closing the door behind her.

Henry walked around to the driver's side, and as he climbed into the seat behind the wheel, he added through the open door, "She'll be no trouble to you after tonight. Sleep well, little man."

Art was still shaking later that afternoon as he ate his dinner of greasy fried chicken and beer. The rest of the crew had been paid and sent home. It was quiet after the rush and business of the production schedule. When the doorbell rang, he jumped a foot out of his chair, and had just settled back down into his seat intending to ignore the caller, when the back door crashed open, smashing glass all across the floor of the kitchen with the force of the blow.

Art jumped to the side, tipping his chair up onto two legs. Then, the legs still in contact with the floor skidded to the other side sending him crashing to the floor. His neck cracked with a whipping motion, and his head smacked into the cheap, stained vinyl floor sending stars shooting across his vision.

When his sight cleared he was still dazed and staring sideways across the dirty floor. A pair of shiny black dress shoes – fancy, high-dollar jobs - stepped into his vision. He heard a familiar "click" that he couldn't quite place for a moment. The pounding in his brain resulting from the crack he had taken to the side of his head pushed everything else out of focus. Then he recalled that it sounded just like the noise Henry's knife had made when it snicked open before cutting MiMi's face.

The next scene registering in his brain, and the last thing he ever saw, included the legs from the thighs down. These, dressed in expensive, sharply creased slacks, bent nearer, and then a fountain of his own bright red blood sprayed across the floor, followed instantly by a sharp bite of pain across his throat. In horror at the reality of his own plight, he clutched at his gaping throat, but was unable to staunch the flow. The pain slowly faded, graying as his vision did, his brain losing the blood pressure and oxygen needed to sustain those functions.

With darkness came the blessed cessation of, not only the pain from the cold blade across his neck, but the deeper, soul filling ache that had followed him, filling his heart for as far back into his cold, worthless, loathsome life as he could remember. It felt good to have that subtle ache finally fade away. He felt relieved that the end was just like a filmed 'fade to black.' No more pain, no struggle, just let go and be gone.

Finally, he formed what he felt must surely be his last thought ever, the thought that he was glad that his long, worthless life was over, and that he would gladly sink into this blackness forever. But then he sensed an approaching presence. This presence was not a good thing at all. But though he struggled to flee the evil that drew closer with each weakening beat of his heart, the evil presence approached as if he wasn't moving at all.

Art's body struggled to push the presence away with the last frantic neural release before its physical death. But his soul merely cringed in helplessness as the awful being in front of him sank its claws and then its fangs into him and effortlessly lifted him. The beast carried Art down into darkness and heat to torment him with pain far beyond anything he had been allowed to inflict while he was still alive. Art's last gurgled scream was from a fear far greater than any he had inflicted on his victims throughout his sordid career.

Henry watched Art's final spasms, little comprehending the horror Art was experiencing. He only knew that Art's death severed the last connection the police could have drawn leading them to Henry.

* * *

Sam watched Dave from the corner of her eye while she cleared the dishes from the table. Dave normally helped with the dishes, but he was so caught up in whatever was eating him away from the inside, he was scarcely aware dinner was over.

As she moved from table to counter and back to the table again, her heart was in her throat. Through the clink of dishes and silverware, she prayed silently and fervently, knowing that Dave was on the edge of a precipice, and that eternity was in the balance. She could clearly sense the battle being waged: the battle in and for his mind - for his very soul. She knew without a doubt that he was struggling for balance, teetering on the narrow ledge between a long, dark fall on one side, and the loving arms of the Lord on the other. She knew that seven o'clock was approaching, and she didn't know what to do. She knew that the Caffers were expecting her to join them for prayer, but that she couldn't leave Dave like this.

After the last dish was placed on the stack in the cupboard, she walked back through the dining room, running her hand along her husband's shoulders. He hardly acknowledged her touch, barely raised his hand in an aborted effort to catch hers. She murmured, "I love you, hon," as she left the room to call the Caffers.

"We understand, dear," came the sweet old woman's voice, and Sam was sure that she did, and that she had done the right thing in choosing to stay home with her husband. "The good Lord knows that you need to be there with him, and that our hearts and prayers are together, even when our bodies aren't."

"Thank you, Mrs. Caffer. I surely am grateful for your prayers. I think Dave is right at the moment of decision. Whatever is gnawing at him is at the point of either being fixed, or destroying him. Please pray hard for him!" New tears filled her eyes, and she dabbed at the corners of her eyes with her fingers in a futile effort to stop them.

She could say no more for a moment, and Mrs. Caffer's understanding voice was a balm from heaven to her weary heart. "You know we'll be praying, and you know that our God is a loving God, and that He will do whatever He can to save your Dave."

Sam swallowed and spoke past the lump in her throat, "Th - thank you. I'll call you in the morning. And, I'll be praying for you all, too."

The two ladies - the two warriors: one wise and old but still vital, the other weary though still relatively new to the battle - hung up and returned to the fray, battling for the souls of those whom they loved, and whom the Lord loved as well.

* * *

People showed up at the Caffers' home pretty much on time. It seemed that those who came were very serious about the task they faced. They knew that the responsibility they shouldered was an important one. By five after seven, eight people of widely differing backgrounds had gathered. Their ages varied from Steve's seventeen years to the Caffer's eight-plus decades. Some were new to their faith, while others had been walking with the Lord for many years. But all knew Him, not just as Savior, but as Lord as well. All of them had at least some grasp on the reality of the battle going on in the spiritual realm and the part they played in it with prayer.

By a quarter after seven they were up to date on the events of the last two days, and were on their knees assailing the heavenlies with their heart-felt requests - pleading the blood of the Savior, and lifting up by name those who were involved in this climactic spiritual battle.

Some of those present had prepared for this evening by fasting; all had spent some time before assembling by cleansing their own hearts with confession of all known sin. The temple of their hearts made ready and knit together in purpose and in spirit, was then filled with the incense of prayer rising into the holy of holies. And the heavens shook as battle was joined.

* * *

In the unseen skies over Alagonic the forces of light and truth were fully engaged with the forces of darkness. The battle raged, swords clashed, sending sparks of incandescent brilliance in countless directions. These sparks often shot off to sputter into nothingness. But other times they would light on the skin of one of the hordes from hell. At these moments the white spark would set fire to the skin of that unlucky fiend, sending him into paroxysms of pain. This distraction would often give his angelic opponent opening enough to dispatch him.

At still other times the spark would last only a microsecond before encountering some of the darkness which shot from the blades of the evil ones. This darkness was not simply the absence of light, but was the very antithesis of light, and was accompanied by a yellowish smoke that constantly leaked from their dark and crimson blades. Sulphurous smoke puffed as well from their grimacing, gaping mouths and noses as they gasped for air, laboring against the forces of righteousness. Spiritual muscles and sheer will strained against opposing, evil strength and will. Energies beyond the senses of humanity launched across space, shimmering within and across dimensions that men consider but cannot know this side of eternity.

The battle seemed hopeless at one moment, darkness swallowing up light step by desperately defended step, but suddenly the feverish pitch of the battle hesitated and every head lifted for a moment. Each of those engaged on this field of battle felt the change, as though a fresh breeze had made its first cool effect felt against a stifling heat. Cool fingers of renewing, enervating energy ran through the ranks of the heavenly host, lifting discouraged heads, strengthening weary arms, and bringing hope to despairing hearts.

Immediately, the tide of the battle swung against the hellish company, as the weight of the prayers lifted at the Caffers' home were thrown into the battle. Though the demonic horde fought on, there was little doubt that the battle had indeed turned. The rays of darkness striking from their blades delivered less power with each sword stroke. The advance of the sickly yellow smoke was halted and even blown back an initial step or two. Though the battle was not won, though evil still claimed victims both in the heavenlies and on earth, the forces of heaven had finally begun to claim back some of the ground lost to Satan and his minions over the last few decades in the city of Algonic.

* * *

Lieutenant Lydia Mochek wiped her forehead with the sweat dampened sleeve of her shirt. Today, her 'day off,' had turned into a weary day. It had started well with church, but had gone bad with a mid lunch phone call, a call that jarred her out of her mental meanderings and roused a small comment of displeasure from her husband. *You would think we'd get used to these interruptions, after all these years,* she thought.

The call had been from the department, of course. They had received an anonymous call, tipping them to a possible homicide on the south end of town. A black and white had gone to the address, and had found a body, lifeless, bloody, throat neatly slit. Once again, a good tip, a whole lot too late. The fact that the tip coincided with the otherwise insignificant domestic disturbance complaint sitting on her desk went a long way toward making her mood foul and the bad day even worse.

The officer responding to the homicide had called back in to headquarters, where somebody was actually paying attention, and had seen a possible connection to Lydia's line of investigation with missing persons, and particularly the latest string of young teens taken from the mid-state area. So here she was, sweating as much from the onslaught of the stink of the corpse as from the heat. Whoever had done this guy had thought it a cute trick to turn the thermostat in the house all the way up, and it hadn't cooled off a lot in the hour since the first officer had arrived on the scene. The heat, in turn, had hurried the downhill slide that the stiff was on, and the stink from this partially cooked corpse was far worse than most corpses created in the few hours since his death.

Tom Barrington, the first officer to show up, hadn't gotten any farther than the back door of the kitchen before calling in a report, and then had waited for Lydia to show. He had thoughtfully left the door open to air out the heat and the dead meat stench, but if it had made much difference, she hated to think of how bad it had been before.

Danielle stepped over the coagulated blood and the corpse, noting the grisly, bloody, mouth-shaped slit across its neck, and moved on into the living room to turn the heat down. The quieting of the furnace blower made the squelched exchanges on the officers' radios seem very loud. Lydia wandered from room to room on the ground floor taking note of items to refer to the photographer when he showed up. The handcuffs on the pipe in one of the empty bedrooms caught her eye, as did the pile of wrinkled, dirty clothing - make that women's clothing - piled in a dead-end corner of the hallway.

The case became truly disturbing, however, when she walked down the steep, dark basement steps, carefully flipping on the lights with the end of her pen. The steps ended in a short hallway with one heavy, metal door set in an unfinished but heavily insulated wall. In the next room, on the other side of the wall was a complete recording and film studio, with several cameras, lots of lights, and wires draped hither and yon, and a stage set up for pornographic filming. Imagining the horrors that were enacted and filmed in this hellish place made her heart melt and her anger rage, threatening to send her blood pressure through the roof.

The scene was set as a bedroom with all sorts of perverted apparatus sitting around, ready for use, yet hastily abandoned. The implications of the set up made her head spin, and she clutched for support at the wall. She managed to pull herself together and turned from the wall knowing that she had stumbled onto something much bigger than just the simple death of another small-time punk.

A hunch nagged at her mind, though she didn't normally pay much attention to hunches. Contrary to the popular movie lore, hunches usually led to nothing. But this one wouldn't let her go no matter how firmly she ignored it. Marianne's name and picture kept leaping to the front of her mind, and finally she gave in and scribbled a note to look this scene over, carefully cross checking for any tie in to Marianne's case.

She focused her attention back to the routine aspects of gathering information and sifting it for clues. Turning back to the gathered patrolmen and the just-arrived photographer, she began issuing orders.

Chapter 11
The end of all their best efforts.

Pete stared out through their bedroom window. Evening was leaching the daylight from the sky in a slow, fade-to-gray process, much like slowly turning the color tuning control on the television down from color to black and white. The process put Pete in mind of smearing a subtle shade of death across everything in sight. Even the air itself appeared to lose its ability to give life, and as the light and color faded from the scene outside the window, what little peace and courage he possessed faded from his heart.

It was still. No wind moved the leaves. No dogs barked. No traffic motored past.

He could feel the somnolence, which held Molly in its grip, creep slowly into his own soul, gradually stealing his energy, his will, his hope. At first he fought it, knowing that he didn't want to end up like Molly, but bit-by-bit the desire to fight drained away.

He heard Molly get up from the couch and head down the hall, coming to get ready for the night he assumed, though it was only seven-thirty in the evening. Moments later, he heard the bathroom sink shut off, and then the bed gave its old familiar squeak, as her slight weight settled onto the edge of the mattress.

He turned to watch her, wondering anew at the changes that had affected them in only three days. Only three days had passed since the time when Molly would not have thought of going to bed without coming to hug him and give him a loving kiss. She looked the same, yet different. Her hair, pulled back out of her face, was the same. Yet her smile was gone. He sighed, having no idea what could be done to help her deal with their loss – a loss which had completely overwhelmed them.

Then a new thought entered his mind. If their whole world could be turned upside down in such a little time, perhaps there was something wrong with what they were building their life upon. Since it was the loss of Marianne that had capsized their life, didn't that mean that they were, in effect, building their entire life on their kids? A question that should not have needed an answer - perhaps not ever - suddenly demanded satisfaction now.

For years he had heard the words about "building his life on the Rock," meaning Jesus. All along he had mouthed the words that he trusted Him as his Lord and Savior, that he was not idolizing money, or his job, or his family. But the wreck of his life over the loss of his daughter, perhaps this showed something very different. Perhaps this signified that one of the props for his very life had just been jerked out from under him, and only a very basic foundation could have such devastating effects on his life. Had they been putting their children in a place that should have been reserved for God alone?

These new thoughts swirled through the gathering gray in his mind, stirring a fresh breeze in his heart. He decided that he had to talk to someone about this. *But who?* he wondered. *Who would hear him out without judging and condemning.*

As he puzzled it over in his mind, he slowly got up from where he was and moved toward the door and into the hall, heading for the family room and the telephone. As he turned the corner into the hall, the now-familiar, yet still unexplained fear came upon him once again. The same sourceless fear, quickly building to a panic, that had assailed him last night as he walked down this hall. He tried to use reason to push the fear back, but as he entered the usually-welcoming den, panic seemed to wash over him in waves, each wave reaching deeper into his heart, quickly eroding his will, beating him backward and away from the telephone.

He gulped at the air, clenched his fists, and glared around for a physical reason for the fear, but everything he saw and heard appeared normal in the dimly lit room. In the silence of the sleeping house, his heart thudded wildly in his ears. There was nothing here but the couch and chairs. Outside, seen through the windows, was the same unthreatening back yard scene he had looked at every day for years. Yet everything was different. The shadows that had welcomed him into this warm place over the years had come to life, exuding menace from every dark corner. Again the fear washed over him, inundating his reason, and with his will broken, he forgot why he had even come to this room.

Wheeling from the room, he retreated back in the direction he had come, until, as he passed Marianne's empty room, the fear suddenly disappeared. He stopped dead in his tracks. The incongruity of the sudden calm caught his attention and brought sanity back. Waiting and listening as his heartbeat and breathing slowed, he felt chilled as the panic-induced sweat evaporated from his neck and bare arms. His sweat-dampened shirt stuck to his back, but now he could think again.

What is going on here? He looked back up the hall toward the kitchen and family room and the hair on his arms prickled. He looked at the door to Marianne's room next to his right shoulder, paused, and then reached for the handle. As the door swung open, he saw the same kind of lighting he had seen in the family room; deep shadows broken only dimly by light from various sources outside glowing gently through her window. But here there was no sense of fear, no feeling of imminent danger. The shadows were not menacing. There was no lurking danger here. It was merely Marianne's room. Empty of all but memories, but not frightening at all.

As he walked slowly into the room, the last of the fear melted from his heart, and looking around, he saw that little had been moved by the police. Before they had learned of Marianne's kidnapping, Molly had picked up the clothes that usually lay all over the floor and had stacked Marianne's magazines and school books in a corner. Otherwise all appeared as a normal, teenaged, American girl's room.

There were pictures of various Christian groups and singers on several walls, a dresser covered with knick-knacks and mementoes, its mirror edged with taped-on pictures of friends. The door to the closet was slightly ajar, but what finally caught his eye was a gleam of white in the center of Marianne's bed, brightened by a beam of light from outside.

Lying there on the comforter, pages spread open, was Marianne's Bible. At the sight, grief engulfed him and a sob broke from his throat. He edged closer to the book, and leaning onto the mattress, he bent closer to look at the pages.

Of anyone in the family, Marianne was the most 'into' church life. Of course, they all went regularly to church. But it was clear that for Marianne, Jesus was a close and very real, minute-to-minute friend. It seemed that she referred to Him with every decision she made, and she loved to spend time reading her Bible or in worship.

The book lay open to the book of Romans, and as he scanned the open pages, his eyes were drawn to an underlined area at the bottom of the right hand page. "We know that all things work together for good for those who love God, for those who are called according to His purpose." He traced the words with one finger.

He recalled that this was one of Marianne's favorite passages. He groaned and slowly lowered himself onto the bed next to the Bible. *God! How could You? Go ahead, try to explain this one! How does Marianne's abduction work into your wonderful plan?* He cried silently, and then, as his cascading thoughts slowed, he listened.

Any question dragged up from such a deep part of someone sincerely seeking truth warranted an answer from a caring God. *Does He care? Does He listen? Does He even exist?*

Lying there with these thoughts running around and around in his head, he felt a heaviness creep over himself. He closed his eyes, giving in to the weariness that seemed to seep up from the warm comforter on Marianne's bed. Not sleeping, yet not fully awake, his angry, accusatory thoughts toward God gradually faded. He found himself dreaming, yet still not really dreaming. A scene formed in his mind that was much more real than a dream, and he found himself wholly immersed in a different place and time, as though it was as real as the bed beneath him.

His dream placed him in a castle hall, and suddenly he was immersed in this dream in a very un-dreamlike way. The lights were dim. Flickering candles augmented the fading, stained sunlight that seemed to be barely able to force its way through the thin slit windows. Smoke from fires in the courtyard seeped into the room on the fitful breeze. The heat was oppressive, though the day was nearly over. The smell of sweat, blood, smoke, and despair filled the air. Those crowded into the stone-walled room hoped for more from the wind than an occasional teasing touch of cool.

It was quiet. Only muted sounds entered the hall. Outside, from whence only minutes previously came the crushing cacophony of battle and violent death, it was now still. The moans of the wounded and dying did not enter through the proud, thick, stone walls and oaken doors. In his dream Pete simply knew these things. The dream was as real to him as the book in his hands had been before he entered this dream place. His right hand rested, blistered on the hilt of his sword. He forced himself to let his hand fall to his side. His left hand, clenched in a fist, grated against the stone wall behind him.

Within the hall were gathered, in that moment of respite, a group of weary, nearly-defeated knights meeting with the enemy to hear his terms for surrender. Pete's fellow knights were bone-tired warriors. They were surrounded, out-numbered and at the end of their strength. The previous eight days had been a nearly non-ending string of battles, attacks and defeats. The enemy, through treachery and sheer weight of numbers, had systematically cut the heart out of their strength, and he was nearly sure, out of their leader's will to resist.

Sir Thomas, the leader of the enemy, a haughty and proud man, and evil to his very heart, stood before Pete's captain with a smirk on his face and a sneer in his voice. "All you must do to ensure the lives of you, your men, and all of your people is sign this proclamation and lay down your arms. I promise that if you will but deny your king, you shall live." He paused, looked at the fingernails on his left hand, and added, "Your king is not going to arrive in time to save you."

Pete's captain, Sir Marlby, a good, brave, and honorable man, listened to the terms of surrender with head bowed. In all his days, Pete had never seen a man so poised at the limits of his strength as his weary captain. His ability to endure the weight of his responsibilities had been, over the previous days and weeks of battle, stretched to the point where he would surely break if he moved from his dejected posture. It appeared that he couldn't even muster the strength to raise his head to meet the eyes of Sir Thomas. Weakly, he sighed, "Sign?" His agonized breath filled the silence. "Deny?" A groan like a torn heart, escaped from the depths of his torment. "Give it to me."

All of them in the great hall stared, holding their breath, knowing in their hearts that Sir Marlby would sign. Pete started to push away from the wall, desperate to stop Sir Marlby from signing any treaty with this man. His captain caught his eye and slowly shook his head. There was no other way, there was no escape, no hope of rescue or reinforcement. This was the end of all their best efforts in their service for their King.

But then – there was a change, a shift in the air in this place of defeat. Pete could have sworn that he could hear at that moment, faintly, yet ringing clearly in the air, the sound of a trumpet. Others must have heard it too, for each, in varying degrees, responded to that call. Even the timid breeze strengthened, bringing fresh air to their leaden lungs, and clarity to their weary minds.

Sir Marlby, too, responded to the distant trumpet call. He squared his shoulders, stood from his chair, and said, with slowly growing strength, "Deny the king? You could as well command the earth to deny its roundness. As well deny water its wetness, or deny a bird the sky. I would as easily, with my words alone, deny gravity its ability to hold us to the ground. Deny my king?! NEVER!" His last words rang in the close air of the castle keep. Those waiting outside could even hear as he finished his response. "The king's man is what I am! I cannot deny who I am!"

And with that, Sir Marlby, Pete, and all those within the hearing of his bold proclamation were renewed. Their ragged cheer crescendoed to a mighty roar. Sir Thomas, face paling with anger, left the castle followed by the sound of shouted orders, growing faith and renewed hope. Within the hour, his forces were swept away in terror before the wind of the newly energized knights, and defeat was turned into glorious victory, born of faith, born of honor, and born of obedience to the highest call - the service to their King.

Pete heard a new voice calling out as the scene faded from his subconscious, "This is what it means to BE TRUE! To become what we are meant to become, no matter what the cost. This is what it means to be more than conquerors. This is the heritage of the children of the King! Know this! After being stricken, after losing everything, know that death is far from being the end, but only a step into forever."

Pete jerked awake from his dream. He thought of Pastor Dave, the youth pastor. Sitting up, he looked at the clock on Marianne's headboard. 9:32, it announced silently in large pink numbers. He had lain there for over an hour. He hesitated, but then got up and once more headed resolutely for the kitchen and the telephone there.

He didn't even think of the fear he had noticed before, but marched past the family room, around the corner, and into the kitchen. He flipped on the lights, and rummaged in the drawer for the church directory, coming up with several other books before finding the right one. He quickly thumbed through to the M's, and then found the Merryls' home number.

* * *

Peter Frack's guardian angel, Brilliantly, sighed and sat back against the wall under the window, wiping the blood from his forehead where the demon's talons had raked him. That had been tough. Pete had been nearly lost in his own shell of helplessness, but God had won a victory here. Small as that victory seemed, Brilliantly had beaten the demon - Badger was his name - beaten him at his own game.

The demon had made a mistake in pushing so hard at Pete. The fear he had poured into that room while Brilliantly feigned weakness, had been enough to sensitize Pete, and when Brilliantly suddenly surged against the demon's hold, he had temporarily gained the upper hand, enough to feed the emotions that had directed Pete into Marianne's room, to the Bible, to the vision, to the phone, and to make the call.

Now Brilliantly was exhausted and hurt, but Badger was gone; summoned back to his master to answer for this loss, and for a sound beating probably. He wished Pete would wake up enough to enter into a proper relationship with the Lord. Then his power would be multiplied; then he could help Pete in greater ways. And, he thought a bit selfishly, he could wipe the smug grin off the face of Furrgstan.

Up until tonight the only prayer support had been from an elderly couple in the church who prayed for the kids in the youth group by name, and from Sam, Pastor Dave's wife. The angel smiled at the thought of those three, three who had little idea how critical their work was, yet who kept at it month after weary month.

But now Brilliantly could still feel the lingering glow from the fresh support those dedicated few had lent with their unofficial prayer meeting tonight, along with Danielle and the few others who were responding to the call. Prayer support had come from the elders of Marianne's church, as well. Certainly without that support he could not have taken Furrgstan, not even temporarily as he had tonight. As it was, what was done was enough for now. A new, though admittedly small, chink in the enemy's armor had been found and used. Hopefully, with the same suffusion of spiritual energy, Agrevious and Aglow would be able to break through with their assignments as well.

As amazing as the gift of free will was, it was just as great an act of the Master's creative will to give humans the authority to do battle backed by the power and authority of His name, His blood, and His will. His will was clearly stated in the written Word, and humans had been given the authority to enforce His will to be done on the earth as it is in heaven.

Though things had gotten too far out of hand to retrieve the Frack family back into God's original perfect plan - Pete and Molly had stepped out from under their proper umbrellas of protection for too long - still, even this seeming chaos was going to work for good for each of the Lord's human children. A chill spun up Brilliantly's back as he wondered anew at the amazing immensity of the Lord's wisdom and power. How He could spin and weave the lives of these humans and all of His angels so intricately was nothing short of miraculous - divine, you might even say.

He chuckled to himself, ruefully rubbing his aching muscles and bruises. Turning his attention back to his charge, he watched with satisfaction as Pete dialed the number and waited while the phone rang. Brilliantly knew that, if other parts of the plan were proceeding as they were meant to, Pastor Dave would not be answering the phone for a couple of hours yet. But with Furrgstan away licking his wounds, Brilliantly he felt sure that he could keep Pete focused long enough to keep trying until the time was right, and all the ground work was prepared for that conversation.

Picking himself up from the floor, he moved closer to Pete, hovering protectively over his soul, watching for the slightest sign of any returning enemy demons.

* * *

At about nine-thirty the group of prayer warriors gathered in the Caffers' home agreed that they had done all they could for now. Steve looked at the clock and stifled a gasp. He was amazed that two and a half hours had gone by so quickly - while praying at that! This was a truly amazing turn in his life, one he would have laughed at had someone told him, even three days ago, that he would be here in the home of this older couple praying for two hours - and enjoying it.

These people really brought prayer to life. He felt as if he had just spent the last couple of hours talking face to face with God! Never in his life had he had any clue that his religion, his faith, could be so invigorating. He knew now, more than ever, that he wanted more of this.

Mr. Caffer caught his eye, winked, and waved him over. "Well, young man, what are you thinking now?" The smile on the old man's face made Steve realize that Mr. Caffer must have a pretty good idea what Steve was thinking. Perhaps the expression on his face gave him away. Certainly he couldn't have kept the feelings of joy and awe from his face, even if he had desired to.

"Sir, I don't know what to say. This has been a great time! Thank you for inviting me, and for putting up with my weak prayers."

The elderly man's face went serious in a heartbeat. "Don't you even think that way, Steve. Your prayers are obviously from your heart, and no matter what words you use, God is big enough to know what your heart is saying. You just keep on baring your heart to Him, claiming what He has promised in his Word, and He will take care of the rest, never mind how fancy or stumbling your words are."

Steve grinned ruefully, "Thanks, Mr. Caffer. I guess I'd better get going. My dad wants me home by ten."

"I understand. You keep on obeying your folks, even when it doesn't seem fair. God will honor that, too. And who knows, you may yet have a big part to play in resolving your family's crisis. I've a feeling God's gonna use you in big ways before this is all over."

Several of the people had already left by the time the two of them had finished talking. So Steve said some slightly awkward goodbyes and headed for home.

The twenty minute drive home gave him some time for thinking through his family's situation from the new perspective that becoming a Christian allowed him. What Mr. Caffer had told him made an awful lot of sense. What if all this had happened because of his willful, and frankly sinful, lifestyle? What if God had allowed Marianne to be abducted because of Steve's own refusal to listen to God speaking to him in more gentle ways? What if his family had allowed Satan to have a foothold, an open back door into their lives because they were willfully stepping out from under the protection of God? How could he live with such guilt?

The feelings washed over him in waves, as he thought through his own guilt, his anger at his parents, and then his sorrow for not listening to them when they did try to lead him rightly in the past. At one point he was forced to pull into a darkened and quiet parking lot, because his eyes were blurred with tears. He sobbed out his renewed confession to God - not from fear, but secure in the new knowledge of His love and forgiveness. He also came to the decision that he would see his parents in a new light as well. They, too, struggled to make life in an imperfect world fit together with their need for God. And they, like Steve, were learning the hard way how difficult that could be.

After a few moments, he dried his eyes on the sleeve of his shirt, put the van back into gear, and started out for home once more. He realized with joy that the anger and bitterness and apathy that he had held for his parents was gone, replaced somewhere in the past twelve hours or so with love and concern and gratitude for their love - even though they didn't show it in the best ways at all times. Suddenly he found himself looking forward to being home with his parents, looking forward to just being with them, supporting them through another long and lonely night without his sister.

* * *

On the fourth ring, and just as Pete was seriously second guessing himself for calling so late, he heard the phone on the other end lift and a feminine voice clearly said, "Merryls'."

Pete still hesitated, but before Samantha could speak again, forced out, "Samantha Merryl?"

"Yes, this is Sam. What can I do for you?" Her voice was now hesitant, and Pete felt bad for worrying her for no reason.

"Listen, I'm sorry for calling so late, but could I speak to Pastor Dave, please?"

"Mr. Frack? Is that you?" Pete could hear the relief in her voice, now that she knew it was no prankster on the phone in the middle of the night. "Mr. Frack, Dave can't come to the phone right now, but is there anything I can help you with?"

Pete hesitated once again, feeling a little funny about sharing his thoughts with her instead of with the youth pastor himself. "I'm not sure I should. Is there a time when I could get ahold of him?"

This time it was her turn to hesitate, and he wondered if she had heard him. In reality, Sam was looking into the darkened living room, trying to decide if Dave would ever be able to pull himself out of the pit into which he had fallen. "Samantha? Is there a better time when I could call back and speak with Dave?"

Finally deciding that she should speak freely with Pete, that there was no point in hiding her situation from the people in the church, and that this man of all people could not be kept waiting for Dave to return to normal function, she lowered her voice and answered, "Pete, Dave may not be returning to work for some time. He's had a really rough time of it last night, and he's in a really difficult place right now. I think he could use your prayers as much as you need his right now."

Pete was surprised. He hadn't heard about the events that had occurred with the youth group last night, so he had no idea what Samantha was talking about. "What's wrong, Sam? Is Dave all right?" Even from the depths of Pete's personal crisis, a desire to help the Meryls surfaced. "Is there something I can do to help?"

Silence hummed across the phone lines as each of them fought emotions and tears, emotions wrought of stress, of weariness, of fear, of the impending loss of something that each of them held very dear.

Pete regained control of his voice first, and swallowed a couple of times before managing to say, "Listen, Samantha, if you need some help, Molly and I can come over, but neither of us is in much shape to be of real use. What would you like us to do?"

Sam swallowed the lump in her throat and forced herself to answer. "No. No, Mr. Frack, we'll be alright. I'm convinced of that, even though there is a lot of what seems to be real bad going on right now," her voice gained strength as she reminded herself what she believed to be true about her God. "Even though it seems hopeless, God is going to use all of this horrible tragedy to bring about a greater good for each one of His children. I'm certain, even though I don't see right now how it can possibly work out, that He is working, orchestrating all of this into a way for each of us to be drawn closer to Himself."

Pete caught his breath as what she was saying registered in his weary mind. The very thoughts he had called to clarify, and here she was answering his questions even before he asked. "But, - but, - how…"

"What is it Mr. Frack?"

"How did you know what I was going to ask Dave about?" His voice was hesitant and almost fearful. "How did you know?" he demanded. For some reason this was an important point to him. Somehow the fact that she knew what he was thinking got deep into the heart of the battle going on within him.

She sensed it too, and realized, even through her own turmoil, that she needed to tread carefully here. Silently she prayed, *'Lord, this man needs Your help here, not mine. I don't understand what is going on here. But You've placed me in this position, so use me, and guide me.'*

Out loud, she went on, "Mr. Frack, I think it's pretty obvious that there is more going on here than we can see. I have no idea why God placed that verse in my mind right now, other than the fact that it sums up what we both need to know right now. I think you know what the Word says about God working in our lives, but maybe it's not getting through your head and into your heart."

Pete listened carefully, weighing each word.

Samantha went on, "Mr. Frack, I don't want to be insulting, but I also don't want to assume anything that might not be true, either. Can you tell me, was there ever a time in your life when you asked Christ to be your Savior - and here's the important part - your Lord?"

Again Pete was silent, pondering her words and feeling emotions wash back and forth in his heart. Part of him was indeed insulted at this young lady casting doubt on his religion. But the other part of him was alert and eager, knowing that she was on to something here, something that he had never really resolved in his heart. Indeed, he realized that he never had felt any peace about his relationship with God, never had known the assurance that others, including Marianne, had known and shown about their eternal destiny.

His silence stretched on for a moment or two, but Sam respected it for more measured heartbeats, again somehow knowing that he needed this time to sort through his own inner dialogue. After another silent moment she went on, gently, "Mr. Frack, I want you to know that I'll be praying for you. And please pray for us. We're struggling with some stuff here, too. And if there is anything I can help you with, please know that you can call here anytime."

"Thank you." His voice faltered, filled with emotion. "You've been more helpful than you can know. And you've given me an awful lot to think about here. Thank you again."

"Good bye, Mr. Frack."

As he hung up the phone, he heard the garage door closing, and turned to watch as his son walked into the house. He hurriedly dried his eyes, and grabbed a tissue to blow his nose.

Steve was smiling as he entered the house, and just seeing him so happy lifted a weight from Pete's shoulders and a shadow from his heart.

Then Steve did something that he hadn't done in years. Without hesitation, he walked right up to his dad and wrapped his arms around him in a great hug. Pete was so startled that all he could think of at first was how tall his son had gotten since the last time they had hugged like this. Then all sorts of dams inside fell all at once, and with silent tears of loss mixed with love, he encircled his boy in a hug of his own. After a few moments, they relaxed their hold on one another, and Steve said, "Dad, could we talk?"

Pete held him at arms length, and then nodded and led the way into the family room, a room which had held fear and threat an hour earlier, but was now a warm and welcoming room, seemingly custom made for just such conversations as they were about to have.

* * *

Steve's angelic guardian, Castellain, was ecstatic - thoroughly pumped for this confrontation. His sword fairly hummed in its scabbard, and his powerful hand itched to draw it and send it singing through the air separating him from that foul denizen, Furrgstan, newly back from his whipping in the pits of hell. It hadn't taken long, as humans measured time, but Furrgstan showed welts and scars where his supervisors had viciously dressed him down for making the ultimate mistake for his kind. He had slipped up and let his charge, Steve, accept the matchless gift of salvation from the Creator, and there was no greater setback for one of the hell hounds. An angry, sullen fire burned in Furrgstan's eyes, a smoky, glowing yellow that could not be masked even though the little amoeboid devil knew he was way outmatched at this point in the ages-long struggle.

Right now, Castellain's job was only partly to guard his newly saved charge. He was also assigned to support the forces of righteousness in their assault on the ground defended by Satan's forces in Pete's heart. For now was the appointed time for the spiritual showdown for salvation for Peter Frack. The confluence of many forces – the Father's will, the prayers of the saints, and the circumstances that focused such emotional stress on Pete's heart – meant that this was the prime moment for Pete to choose truth and life over Satan's misdirections, lies and death.

Angels of various ranks were on guard for the duration of this conflict. Badger clung to Pete's heart like a leach. The demonic horde had gathered their forces and marshaled their resources as well, for they, too, knew that something big was brewing. Castellain felt confident in the Master's plan that today would indeed be the day that Pete would see the truth and the Son of God would claim another child as His own.

Without any warning, Badger pulled his clawed hand from a fold in his skin and threw a glowing powder into the faces of Castellain, Brilliantly, and two other angels who were gathered to assist. The powder burst into flame as it struck their skin, but thanks to the increased prayer support over the last few hours, the powder quickly fell off and dropped harmlessly to the ground.

Badger was not finished with his tricks, however. He knew what was at stake here. He had seen what Furrgstan had just experienced and wanted nothing of the sort to befall himself. He followed the powder with a cloud of enveloping smoke, smelling of sulfur and rot. This clouded his enemies' angelic eyes and hindered their ability to defend against his wicked scimitar, which spun in a blur in its sudden attack against the angelic host.

Both Castellain and Brilliantly fell back in surprise at the ferocity of the attack. Other demons joined the fray, preventing support from rallying to the side of God's servants. Stumbling, barely able to keep the fearsome black blade from his skin, Castellain reeled back from the attacking demon. Sparks flew at the clashing of their blades, and all around he could hear the shrieks of attacking demons, as well as the grunts of exertion from the angels.

Pete's heart clenched shut once more on the tightly held but false beliefs of his skewed world view. The lengths of chain and strands of lies and deceit drew tightly about his soul once more.

* * *

Pete moved to sit in the easy chair and motioned Steve over on the couch to his right. The room was still, the television quiet and dark. Though the rest of the city probably watched America's Funniest something or other with rapt attention, there was no pull toward that for these two. They both sensed that there was a breakthrough about to happen here. Pete looked at his son as he settled himself into the sofa's cushions. *Curious,* he thought, *he has grown so much, and so quickly. But those changes don't seem as apparent as the inner changes that have occurred in the last two days.*

Steve grinned as though he could hear his dad's thoughts, and said, "Dad, I have so much that I want to talk to you about. First, I want you to know that I meant what I said earlier about being sorry for the way I've been acting lately."

Pete nodded his understanding but kept silent, allowing his son the room to take this conversation where he wanted for now.

"This morning - sheesh, it seems like days ago, now - this morning I gave my heart to Jesus, and asked Him to be the Lord of my life from now on. It was pretty hard to do, because I felt like I had already been a Christian forever. You know? I mean we've always gone to church and stuff. But I finally realized that it wasn't enough."

Pete nodded again, interested that someone else's thoughts could so closely follow his own. He thought through his brief conversation with Samantha Merryl moments earlier, light beginning to dawn on the fact that maybe these conversations weren't just coincidence. Maybe God was throwing these people and topics in his face to get him to realize that his situation was just exactly as Steve was describing here.

"Dad, think over your own life and your own decisions about God and Jesus. Consider if you really are a child of God or if you've been as deceived as I was, thinking you were saved when maybe you weren't." He stopped here as he saw a frown cross his father's face.

Pete had been open to this exchange, and had taken the insinuations from Samantha fairly easily - after all, she was a pastor's wife; a guy could take advice like this from her. But now it was just a kid, his own son, only sixteen years old who was accusing him of this kind of confusion and delusion. His back stiffened, and he started to form words that would put his boy in his place.

* * *

Having bashed Castellain on the side of his head with the hilt of his sword. His backswing sliced deeply into the upper arm of Brilliantly, and Badger felt that he had freedom to return his full attention to Pete once again. The chains that locked the door of Pete's heart still held strong, keeping truth, light and love out. The man's heart remained firmly under the control of death and deception. Jabbing rudely at the man's pride with his bony finger, he turned his host's attention to the humiliating fact that a mere teenager was telling him how to run his life. It was so deliciously simple to divert this human's focus to negative, harmful directions, thus insuring that nothing of positive, eternal value ever got through to his heart.

The battle that had involved several dozen of his fellows and a like number of the bright ones from the Enemy, still went on. But the numbers had dwindled, and the heat of the fight had shifted away from Badger, allowing him this time for some defensive work. While he was focused on his host's mind, however, Brilliantly had snuck around his back and subtly caused a slight lightening in the room, a brightening that focused attention on Steve's face. Before he knew it, his host was drawn out from himself and his own misery and pride to focus instead on his son's expression, an expression of obvious love and hope.

Now Badger's attention wavered. In that critical moment, Brilliantly jumped back into the fray with Castellain right behind him. Brilliantly grappled to control Badger's arms, and finally gripped and held on, muscles straining to keep the demon out of the way. By the time Badger had fought back out of Brilliantly's grip, Castellain had gifted Pete with a special moment of spiritual vision, vision which saw beyond his own pride and showed him the selfless love with which his son was opening his heart to him.

* * *

Pete seemed to rouse from a daze, and shook himself mentally to refocus on what Steve was saying to him. Then he saw Steve's face - hopeful, even vulnerable - and saw the look of almost fear that crossed it when the boy saw his dad's reaction begin. He saw it and knew that if he allowed his anger to rule his reaction he could lose his relationship with his son forever. He wasn't sure how he knew it, but he was sure that if he didn't stay open and calm in the face of this conversation, he would be taking an irreversible step down the wrong path for the remainder of his life.

So he swallowed, closed his eyes, took a deep breath and slowly let it out. Placing one hand over his chin and mouth, and leaning on that elbow, he focused his thoughts away from reacting to his boy's words and onto the state of his own heart.

Steve watched the struggle in his dad's face, and then, summoning his courage, he asked, "Dad, have you ever really asked God to forgive you? Asked Jesus to be your Savior, and given your life to Him to lead and rule?"

Pete thought back through all his years of growing up in a Christian home, going to church, teaching Sunday school, working on committees, always doing the right things. He thought through some of the sacrifices he had made for the church - tithing, often sacrificing his vacations to help with church ministries, leaving his family at home in order to be at board meetings. He thought about his time reading the Word and praying, and how dry and forced that had always been.

And like a light coming on in a fog-filled room, he realized that Steve was right. Samantha Merryl was right. And at this moment his heart was right - he had never really made Jesus his own Lord. He knew that Jesus had died for everyone's sins. He knew that believing that was the only way to be forgiven and to get to heaven. But Pete had left it at that - mere knowledge. And from then on, he had held onto his own efforts to please God. Afraid that he was about to break down in tears, he lowered his face to his hands and shook his head - still silent, but now knowing what he had to do.

"Dad," Steve's voice was soft and full of emotion as he reached out a hand and placed it on his father's shoulder. Misinterpreting his dad's silence, he went on, "I know this is hard; it was for me, so I'm sure it is for you, too. But, Dad, you can see the difference between what we've been doing, and what Marianne believes, can't you? We have to come to the point where we realize that we can't possibly pay for God's forgiveness. We have to accept His gift, His free gift, and then ask Him to be our friend, our leader – 'our Lord' is the term that Mr. Caffer used."

His father shook his head, further confusing Steve, who assumed his dad was rejecting the whole discussion. "But Dad, it all makes such clear sense now."

Pete held up his hand to forestall further intrusion on the process that was taking place inside his heart.

* * *

Still unseen to Steve, was the continuing battle on the spiritual plane, a battle over the final threads of resistance to God's grace. Castellain swung his gleaming sword again, and again sparks flew as Badger parried the stroke. But the tide had turned; each blow fell harder, and the harried demon grew weaker. Each time, the razo-sharp edge drew closer to the dark band of doubt and the dull metallic band of traditional trust in salvation by works that wound about the door to Pete's heart. Badger guarded it jealously, as though fighting for his very life, but knew that he was losing.

With a cry of despair, Badger threw his nicked and blood-crusted blade at the increasingly empowered, attacking angel and fled into the roiling clouds of his domain. Castellain easily parried that last desperate bit of defiance and drew his blade across and through the years-old shackles. They were so ingrown into the man's heart that Castellain could not help but draw some blood. But the pain was a small price to pay, for at that moment Pete's heart opened wide, letting waves of old resistance flow out. Simultaneously, shimmering beams of gold, silver, and incandescent light shined upon the opening within. From heaven's very throne, the Son of God stepped into that dead and vacant place for the first time.

Castellain fell to his knees before the Prince of Gory, and in his heart, so did Pete, both physically and spiritually, as he finally surrendered himself to his Maker. For the first time in his life, the lies and misdirections of Satan were revealed and replaced by the Light and the Truth. Another child of God was born into eternal relationship with his King.

***

Pete still didn't cry. There were so many recent wounds, he didn't dare to let go of his precarious grip on his emotions for fear of totally losing control. But he *knew* he was a different man. He *knew* that something fundamental had totally changed deep inside him.

What Steve saw was that his dad had slipped forward out of his chair onto his knees. His dad stopped shaking his head, loosened his shoulders, and his hands drooped loosely between his knees. He knelt on the carpeted floor, leaning forward in front of the chair. Steve wasn't as sure of the inward changes, and had to wonder what was going on in his dad's mind. He had given up trying to talk his dad into this when his father had raised his hand imploring his son to stop. But the silence had gone on for another several minutes, and the boy had no way to know what inner conflicts his dad had resolved in that silent time. He merely prayed for his father and waited, hoping to be a comforting presence at his father's side.

He watched as his father slowly raised his face and looked at his son again. What Steve saw there made his heart soar with joy, for in his father's eyes he saw hope. There was still a mixture of pain and fear, yet the sparks of hope and the unmistakable beginnings of joy shown through. Steve knew from the bottom of his heart that the corner had been turned. The Lord had visited his father's heart as He had his own only that morning. He sensed that his father was now headed for healing.

Steve practically leaped from his seat and grabbed his dad's shoulders, hugging him and pounding him on the back. Pete gasped for air, but managed to say, "You know? You know what I just did?"

Steve pulled back from his dad and crowed, "It shows in your eyes, Dad! You can't meet the Lord and hope to hide it. Not from me!"

Pete glanced toward the dark hallway, and Steve immediately hushed himself, realizing that his mom was still trying to get some sleep. "Steve, I..." his voice faltered, thick with all the emotions welling and warring within him. "I want to thank you for helping me through all of this."

"Dad, thank the Lord. He reached into a deep pit to pull me out, and He wants to do the same with all of us. We need to start praying for Mom now. She's having a tough time with all this, too."

"Yeah, you're right. She is struggling, and Son, I feel as though I'm losing her. I don't know what to do." Again, he wavered on the brink of tears, choking back the flood of fear and despair that threatened to carry him away.

Steve, too, was filled with grief for his mom and for his sister. He swallowed the lump in his throat, and suggested, "Well, let's pray right now, and then maybe we can call and ask the Caffers to pray with us tomorrow. They've been great through this whole thing. Did you know they've been praying for us since Marianne first disappeared?"

Dad and son bowed their heads together, and for the first time together entered the presence of the King of Kings, humbly seeking

His intervention on behalf of Marianne and Molly.

Chapter 12
Twin pools of light.

Henry smiled, but it was a tight, forced smile that spoke volumes about how unhappy he was with his latest purchase. The girl in the back seat was very different from his previous projects. He had treated her with a casual roughness that came from the evil center of his heart, but she had never once asked him for mercy. He loved it when they begged for mercy. She had not once shown fear, no matter what he threatened her with, and no matter what he did to her.

His own fear came from an idea that he couldn't shake, the idea that this little girl was somehow much more than just a little girl irredeemably caught in his cruel grip. Somehow this little girl, MiMi, Art had called her, though he knew that wasn't her real name, somehow she was more. And it was this unidentified 'something more' that had him scared. He had spoken to Art as though he had it all under control, but now he knew only frustration and fear. The more he thought about it, the more sure he was that for the first time in his wanton and selfish career, he was in over his head.

He steered his car north along a dark, deserted stretch of the river drive, curving gently along the winding turns of the river bank. The lights of his Mercedes splashed on the road, the rock wall to his right, the guardrail unspooling on his left. The dark, smooth surface of the river, fifty feet or so below the embankment, reflected the stars and the moon, noticeable only when he took his eyes off the road ahead to look at the dark beauty there. He didn't look often.

He pressed his foot into the accelerator and the tightly engineered engine growled. His speedometer crawled up over sixty, seventy, eighty miles per hour, and the tires began to squeal on the pavement with each turn in the road. Past ninety miles per hour and the car started to poach into the oncoming lane with each right hand curve. He glanced in the mirror and saw Marianne's pale and marred face looking at him, just awakened by his fast driving. There was still no fear there. He tore his eyes from the mirror, hating what he saw: calm eyes holding wisdom and peace that had no right being on the face of a child who had experienced what she had in the last few days.

He pushed his foot harder onto the floor, fleeing invisible demons that flapped black wings in the back of his mind. The low-slung Mercedes swayed through each turn, hugging the pavement but slipping further out of the intended path with each turn. Henry wiped sweat from his forehead before it could drip into his eyes.

A new fear pushed its way into his thoughts, and he imagined what would happen if he were to lose control and drive through the guardrail and into the river. He lifted his foot off the accelerator, but rather than slowing, he heard the finely tuned engine's R.P.M.s whine. The tachometer wound up even further into the red zone. He kicked at the accelerator to try to free it, but the engine raced even faster. The speedometer crossed the three-digit red numbers - one hundred miles per hour. Panic began to fill his mind with inchoate thoughts of escape and flight. The speed of his car was completely out of his control! Pressing his foot to the brake pedal did nothing but burn away the pads in a streak of smoke and red-hot discs. Crossing the pavement at the rate of nearly nine thousand feet every minute, he frantically pumped the accelerator attempting to free it, but each time he stomped on it the engine only raced faster.

* * *

Marianne felt no fear at this point. As real as the shirt on her back, she felt Jesus' arms of love and protective comfort around her, holding her in safety and security even in this new and dangerous situation. She sighed and smiled and snuggled a bit deeper into his arms. His breath was warm and comforting on the top of her head, just as her dad's had been after a childhood nightmare.

As the car accelerated and careened around each corner, faster and faster, and nearer to losing control, Jesus lifted her from the seat with his strong arms. "It's time to go home. You can come with Me now, My child," He murmured into her ear, and there was nothing in the world she wanted more than to do just that.

Had she looked back, she would have seen her earthly body relax in the back seat of the speeding Mercedes. She didn't look back. Her gaze was entirely focused on her Friend and Lord, her King who had come to take her home, leaving a tired and aching body behind. She was soon distracted from that, however, by a growing light that emerged seemingly from nowhere, right in the middle of the starry sky. The glow was a golden, warm light that built into a vision as breathtakingly beautiful as anything she had ever seen or imagined. In fact, it struck her that what she was seeing was so far beyond her imagination, that the verse about all He had prepared for her went through her mind. "Eye has not seen, and ear has not heard, nor has it entered into the heart of man, what God has prepared for those who love Him." That verse had always felt like an understatement, but finally made perfect sense as she stepped out of time and entered the wondrous reality of that place hand-in-hand with Jesus.

She looked into the face of the One who had died for her, and whispered, "Thank you! Oh, thank you!" She wrapped her arms around His neck, pulled herself up and planted a kiss on His cheek as they entered heaven together.

* * *

Henry glanced into the mirror again just in time to see a sourceless glow cover MiMi's bruised face. She smiled peacefully, closed her eyes, and fell to the side as though all the strings holding her upright had been cut at once. His eyes were frozen on the now empty rear-view mirror, but his attention was jerked back to where the road should have been by the sound of an impact like an explosion.

Where there should have been black pavement and yellow painted lines there were only twin pools of light shining across the swirling, muddy water of the Mississippi River. He screamed as the nose of his beautiful car split the still surface of the water, setting off the air bag and slamming his body into the shoulder restraint and his head into the shockingly hard air bag. He felt his ribs and clavicle snap, he bounced back into his seat, and blinked tears and dust out of his eyes.

He shook his head to clear it and began to laugh at how he had foiled death again. Then he stopped in cold shock as he went to unlock his seat belt. There was water pooling in around his feet! The car was dark save the glow of the dash lights, so he flicked on the roof lights and saw to his horror that the car was filling rapidly with water. Without a sound, all the lights went out as water shorted out the electrical systems, and he grabbed at the door handle - locked. In the dark, he jabbed a finger at the electric locks and missed, jabbed again and again, only to realize that they, too, had succumbed to the water and weren't working.

He reached back to manually pull up the button and felt a wave of relief as it moved easily into the unlocked position – until he pulled again on the door handle and pushed to open the door. The water on the outside of the car pushed inward with far more pressure than he could, and try as he might, he could not budge the door. His ears popped with the increasing pressure, and he felt the rising water now almost to the top of his shins.

His lungs panted for air, though it was surely too soon for him to have used up the oxygen in the car. Completely unthinking now, he clawed for the window buttons, ripping off four finger nails in his panic. The water in the car swirled around his waist now, and if he had been still enough he would have felt the car finally settle to a rest on the muddy bottom of the river, about forty feet below the surface.

He screamed, beating his fists against the window, but to no avail. The darkened safety glass refused to budge. As the water rose to his chin, he finally released his seat belt and raised his feet to try to kick out the front window. But the water dragged at his legs, robbing them of any impact or leverage that he might have hoped to use.

The silty, brown water filled his mouth as he gasped for one last breath, and he coughed out his last precious taste of air in bubbles that rose to the roof of the car. The only thing left for him to inhale in his eighty-thousand-dollar death-trap was water. His lungs filled with water, forcing a gag reflex, which in turn, closed down his breathing passages completely. His struggles weakened, and finally stopped. His body floated to the top of the compartment, and his staring eyes never saw the door gently swing open in the current as the pressure equalized from the inside to the outside of the car. A curious catfish swam into the car and past Henry's sightless eyes, his feelers swaying around in the eddies of current.

Chapter 13
More of his own strength.

By Sunday evening, rumors flew like chaff in a rising wind. Before the evening service, at the prompting of the swarming, crawling, slithering, poking demonic minions, people talked all about the teens' fiery accident. They hashed over Dave's poor judgment in calling out the "posse," as everyone now called it, and about the poor Frack family. In the name of 'getting information for prayer requests,' both men and women spilled everything they knew about anything pertaining to the situation into which Pastor Dave had gotten himself. Demons specializing in gossip had nearly free rein as they dug deeper and deeper into folks' minds for gossip fodder. Discernment was a rare commodity as folk shared truth mixed with guesses, and the story changed and got more injurious with each retelling.

It wasn't too long before some bright soul thought to question the location of the accident and Dave's fortunate arrival on the scene so quickly. What was Dave doing there in the parking lot of the adult bookstore anyway? The rumor mill churned into an even higher level of activity, and soon Dave was accused, in hushed tones and in his absence, of course, of being everything from a drug addict to a child molester. Most rejected these ideas out of hand, but a few doubts were planted, his credibility was tarnished, and the demons were satisfied with a good night's work.

The church board called another meeting and selected a delegation to visit Dave the next day. They desired to find out what the situation was with the young pastor - he still had not been heard from, though Samantha had called that morning to say that he wouldn't be in.

Pastor Miller did what he could to control the snowballing circulation of inaccurate information about the youth pastor, the injured boys, and Marianne. By the time the evening service started, he had decided that this, too, would have to be a special meeting. A meeting designed to seek God's heart for this congregation, and for the future of this church.

Opening the service with no music was enough to make everyone in the congregation sit up and take notice. But what their pastor did next shot straight through their complacency into the deepest part of their hearts. "My dear friends!" he cried out. With anguish that now filled his soul to overflowing, and tears trickling from his eyes, he went on, "I beg you! I plead with you! We have come to a point in our church life where we need to pull together stronger – as a team – than at any time in our history. We have family members who are hurting with loss. Pastor Dave Merryl is in a situation that is troubling, though we know almost no details of what he is dealing with. This is not the time to share empty words about this. Now is the time for us to grieve with, to pray for, and to intercede for these family members. And it's time for each of us to get right in our own hearts as well."

Tears rolled from the eyes of their pastor, a man who had been seen as in complete control for twenty-five years. Yet now, here he was, on his knees, crying out in front of a full auditorium of six-hundred people. And each one of them knew - this was no act. The Spirit of the living God filled that place. Starting at the front and sweeping to the back of this sanctuary, people began to cry as well. As the Spirit illuminated the hearts of these people, they were able to see, many for the first time, the depraved condition of their own hearts. Now more than just a large room in another pretty building, one which had been called a sanctuary for years, was finally a sanctuary indeed. For the presence of God came and filled that place and filled each heart there. And as they confessed, these people were made clean once again. The sins of each repentant heart were swept away in the truth of the Word, and the blazing, cleansing fire of the Holy Spirit.

There were only a very few who clenched their hearts and fought the moving of the Spirit that night. John Stirming and Fred Hatch caught each other's eye across the room and slipped quietly to the back of the room. "What in the world is going on here, Fred?" asked John. "Has this whole church gone mad?"

They watched as many in the crowded auditorium moved out from their pew seats, found space at the front or in the aisles, and knelt, opening their hearts to the Lord's loving, cleansing touch. Some wept quietly, some raised their hands in silent acknowledgement of the presence of the King. "I guess Mark has found a new way to get through to the people. He has been worried about the offering levels lately," Fred murmured into John's ear.

"I don't think so, Fred. There's something strange going on here, and I get the feeling that it's not just an act. We're going to have to get to Mark after the service and get him to come clean on this. This is way out of control."

"Yeah, look at him up there."

They both watched Pastor Miller as he went on in an obviously broken-hearted way, sharing hope, and inviting any who wanted to repent to come forward. And to the shock and disgust of the two elders, people all over the place got up from their seats and began walking forward to the edge of the platform.

Pastor Miller met them at the altar with open arms, "Let the Lord have His way with you. Don't hold anything back from Him. He already knows your heart. He's simply waiting for you to give it up to Him." And still more people came until the aisles and the space around the piano and organ were filled with people, some kneeling, some quietly waiting on the Lord; all convinced that now was a major turning point in their lives and in their relationship with their God.

An hour later, Pastor Miller quieted the people once again, "I know this is highly irregular for our church. But I don't think anyone here will argue that God has done a work in our midst. We are renewed." Spontaneous applause broke out, and went on for several moments. "We are renewed," he went on, "and I feel that God is asking us to go on now. To go on and to hold the ground taken back from the enemy. To go on and continue taking more ground from his evil grip.

To go on and support those who need our help right now: the Fracks, the Merryls, the Buchannons, the Tesches. And I feel that He is granting us a window of opportunity to take new ground back from the enemy. I feel He is with us now in a way we haven't allowed Him to be before because of our hard hearts. I feel He is calling us to prayer, to wage war in the heavenlies against the likes of Satan and his evil minions. I feel that we have a unique opportunity to take this city for the Lord."

"But we must do our part. We must turn our backs firmly on our selfish, fleshly ways. We must humble ourselves. We must continue to seek God. We must arm ourselves fully with His armor. And we must pray. We must pray. We must pray."

And with that, Pastor Miller sat down. Toby came from his seat, drying his eyes, and sang in a quiet voice. "Create in me a clean heart, oh, God. And renew a right spirit within me." The hushed voices in the building gradually added to the heartfelt plea. "Cast me not away from Thy presence, oh, Lord. And take not Thy Holy Spirit from me. Restore unto me, the joy of Thy salvation." The crystal clear notes rang into the night air, and the purity of the moment sent demons fleeing for miles in all directions. "And renew a right spirit within me." And God, the Healer, was faithful to do just that. Heart after heart was washed clean, renewed, and born again.

The last note stilled, hearts knelt, open before the throne of God, and His people stayed, drawn by the need of the moment: the need to pray and uphold their church, their brothers and sisters, their city in that hour of violent battle.

* * *

Around the church was an area of calm. The angelic host held the area with a cordon of sentries. From there on out into the rest of the city, however, the fiends of darkness still fought open battles in some areas, walked with impunity in others, and slunk around in covert operations in still others. This area was now the headquarters of the forces of righteousness, and no demon dared come close. The explosion of righteous power that had cleared the area, had empowered the angels to maintain control of this part of the city with no problem.

Inside the church, angelic messengers came and went, sifting through the ascending prayers of the saints still gathered within. Some of the congregation left to attend to duties that could not be postponed, but several hundred still gathered, huddled in hushed groups, or silently and alone. But each in their own way continued the spiritual prayer support that was so sorely needed in Alagonic.

* * *

The next battle, and the last important step in sweeping this area free of demonic stranglehold for the first time in decades, was still tilting on the scale with the outcome far from sure. Each angelic warrior, from the weary, battle-hardened veteran to the greenest of the newcomers, had to do his or her job with purity and selflessness, or all could still be lost.

Aggrevious conferred with Freely who was standing behind Pastor Miller, who knelt once again at the altar, leading a small group of prayer warriors in intercession for the welfare of Pastor Dave. "What is next, Captain?"

"We need to hold and reinforce the work He has accomplished," came the hushed reply from the commander of the city's angelic host.

Freely's wings feathered the air, soothing the anguish of Mark Miller's heart. "And then?"

Aggrevious went on, "Then we fight on. The Lord is using all of this to break through the darkness of Dave's heart. And the hardness of his resolve to hide this from Samantha is weakening. But Aglow and Gramsting are still matched toe-to-toe over his soul. Remember how long and how fiercely the battle was fought over Daniel's plea for help these three thousand years ago?"

Freely nodded, thinking back three millennia ago to the faith of that prophet, and Aggrevious clarified, "This battle is not long in the eternal scheme of things. Don't let the impatience of these humans rub off on you. We must keep a proper perspective."

Freely agreed, "I know. It just hurts to watch them struggle so. If they would only take their eyes off the world and look to the Father and His Word with their hearts."

"They have made great progress this day. With our help, and the guidance and power of the Creator, they will continue the process, being transformed day by day, closer and closer to the image of the Son."

Freely murmured his agreement, and Agrevious drifted from the room to prepare for the final battle. One for which he was sure the enemy had prepared just as thoroughly. He could sense a gathering darkness out there beyond their clear territory, a growing tension – a dark pressure that he had felt before, at times presaging the arrival of great spiritual powers gathering to wage war over strategically important strongholds. He held his breath for a moment, recalling one such battle fought over western France in the years known to the humans as the Dark Ages. Then he released the pent-up air, gratefully and fully surrendering again to the flow of the work of the Father.

* * *

Aglow nodded at the angel who hovered over Sam's kneeling form, and then turned to Dave once again. Moving gently, yet powerfully, he reached into Dave's heart and expended yet more of his own strength in attempting to bring the young pastor to a fresh sense of resolve to get right with God.

Aglow had been waiting for this day for months. Now all the pieces were in place; the stage was set; with the help of the revival at First Evangelical and the new prayer warriors in the city, he had managed to overcome Gramsting - however temporarily - and sent him packing. Sam was right where she needed to be, praying for the Fracks and for Dave; this was the moment ordained by the Almighty - the moment that Dave would come back to His Lordship or be buried yet another layer deeper in his sin and helplessness.

Applying just the right amount of pressure Aglow tweaked Dave's memory, calling back a clear memory of Sam and Dave praying with passion for a fellow student back when they were in school. This he followed with a clear picture of Dave's hiding a magazine in his desk just the day before, and then a recall of the frustration he had been feeling with his prayer life lately. Then he stood back, watching Dave's reaction, and standing guard to make sure that none of the evil ones would come to interfere. With thanks to the Creator, he noted Dave's surprised jerk, and he drew a deep shuddering breath. Aglow held his own figurative breath as Dave teetered on the brink of denial.

Suddenly Aglow was thrown forward past Dave by a brutal attack from behind. Turning as he fell, he reached for his sword, but his arms were pinned to his sides by the demonic monster who had struck him. He was borne back by the weight of the demon, his strength already depleted by the fight with Gramsting.

As he sank back he noted with a surge of trepidation that this monster had four arms, and with the two free hands, the beast was reaching for Dave ready to rend the fragile work of repentance and healing that had begun to grow in his heart. This framework of renewal appeared much like a crystal lattice-work on this spiritual plane - very fine - very fragile. Just as the beast prepared to slice through the new growth, a bright light glared all around them, and even without looking, both of the combatants knew what had happened.

Glancing at Dave from the corner of his eye, even with the demon's talons raking him across the back, Aglow began to weep with joy at the sight of the man on his knees - both physically, and at last, in his heart as well, crying, repenting and turning back to his Lord and God.

That was when, accompanied by the overwhelming light of righteousness, the Son Himself had arrived on the scene. With a mere glance at the demon, the Son of God banished the hideous caricature of a creature – all that was left of the once-angel that God had created in beauty and truth eons before – banished him light years away into a confusion of screaming and wailing and slashing itself with its own talons. In a micro-second he was gone. The walls in Dave's heart - dark, stony, dirty, steel reinforced walls - crashed down with a single word from the Son. Light streamed in, and a heavenly breeze blew with freshening, cleansing scents through the dust and cobwebs of Dave's heart.

With another glance from the Son, Aglow's wounds were healed and strength flowed back into his tired and aching limbs. Then all his attention was on the sobbing form of Dave, kneeling on the tile of the dining room floor. With infinite tenderness, Jesus reached His arms around his heart, forgiving, healing and cleansing his now tender heart as clean as purity itself.

Dave could be seen to relax as the weight of all that hidden sin was lifted from his soul, and the wounds underneath began to heal.

* * *

"Dave, are you all..." Sam stopped short when she saw him sobbing on the floor. She knelt beside him and wrapped him in a hug. "What is it honey?"

He responded with a hug in return, but it was some time before he could speak clearly. When he could, he poured out his heart to her, including the sin, the frustration, and the desperate acts of the last few months – especially over the last day or so – with which he had tried to cover up his real need: the need to open the darkened corners of his heart to the Lord once again. He also described to her the confession and repentance that he had just experienced.

As he spoke, her tears of joy, though mixed with much pain, joined his, and together they celebrated his new lease on life. Yes, there was pain in both the confession and in the hearing, but there was also healing. Samantha had known they had problems, but she had no idea that he had fallen so far into his sin. It was just the way her mind worked, but there was very real hurt in imagining that somehow she had disappointed him so much that he had to seek help in pornography. It was difficult for her to understand that his sin had nothing to do with her, but was a result of his failure to say "no" to temptation at an early age.

As they talked through the evening, healing began. For the first time in more than a year, they went to the living room together, knelt and joined in a prayer that rose and mingled into a symphony, flowing together to the Father's ears, and moving heaven to help on earth.

In closing, Dave offered, "Father, thank You for rescuing me. Now we ask for healing for us. We lift up the Fracks, and ask You for protection for Marianne and peace for the rest of their family. We don't understand, but we know that You've promised that all things will work for good for Your children. Now we trust You with her, and wait to see how Your kingdom will be furthered in this situation. We pray these things in Your Son's perfect name, Amen."

Sam murmured "Amen" as well, and then both simply knelt there in silence for a time of bathing in the presence of their loving and tender Father, and soaking up the feeling of having the tremendous weight of sin lifted from the shoulders of their relationship. After a time, they both stirred. Sam shivered and looked at her husband. An odd chill made her shiver, and she noticed Dave looking around as though he were looking for something that had just gone wrong.

"What is it, honey?" she asked.

"I don't know. I thought I felt something, or heard something. But I don't know. I guess it was nothing." He sat still for a moment, thinking, and then said, "I think I need to go to the Fracks' house tonight. I can't just let them sit through another night alone."

"You're right, hon. And you can bet they won't be sleeping. Not with all this on their minds. Can we go together?"

Chapter 14
We've lost his dad, too.

Lieutenant Mochek drove the final miles along River Road 25 miles north of Highway 12, winding along the river. She should have enjoyed the drive; it was a beautiful day, and the drive brought back memories of when she used to drive this route with her husband Anthony back when they were dating. They used to come up here with the gang to a quiet spot in a bend in the river and swim and picnic on warm summer Saturdays.

But today was different. The sun warming her only added to her growing uneasiness, and she reached to turn on the air conditioning even though it was only 68 degrees outside. The report from downtown had said that some observant motorist had noticed a new break in the guardrail halfway between Highway 12 and LaCross, and the responding officer had found clear evidence that a car had driven through the rail and into the water. The river was deep enough there that he couldn't see anything in the water, but he was sure that it would be there.

The lieutenant's growing inner discomfort was not a result of simply another accident, but seemed to stem from the way the Marianne case was showing up in more and more intricate patterns. The pile of clothes at that studio house where the punk, one Art Malgiddo, had been found dead with his throat slashed, had included clothing that matched the description of what Marianne had been wearing the day of her abduction. Lieutenant Mochek hadn't gone to the Fracks with that information yet, but would have to eventually, probably tomorrow. Right now she had to deal with this accident and the mounting conviction that this was another piece to the Marianne puzzle.

She saw the flashing lights around the next curve, and slowed to find a place to park along the now crowded shoulder. Two black and whites, an ambulance, two large wreckers, and a police diving team truck were already there. The divers were just making their way down the embankment to the edge of the river, tanks on their backs, ropes looped over their shoulders and flippers in their hands. They looked like strange crabs inching over the rocks and around the stunted shrubs that grew amongst them.

The area was located at the tip of a sharp curve that jutted into the river and dropped abruptly, at least forty feet into the Mississippi, which curled lazily along below. The surface was flat and deceptively smooth. Lydia knew that the currents below the surface had ended many a confident swimmer's life. She didn't envy the divers having to fight that current, dragging ropes and then heavy towing cables with them. They were good men, though, and she knew that they had done this drill many times without a mishap.

Again she wondered how this would tie in to Marianne's disappearance. What would they find in the automobile, hidden but sure to be found, below the surface? It would be a while before they returned to report anything, so Lydia parked, flipped on the flashers, and walked over to the waiting group of police officers and emergency medical personnel. "Anything new here?" she asked, knowing that there was nothing that she wasn't already aware of.

Paul Timmons, the Sergeant on the scene, pointed out the break in the guardrail, and said, "The car had to be doing at least eighty to break through so cleanly and miss the whole slope down to the river."

One of the divers concurred, "Yeah. The river goes deep right away here, but still, he had to clear twenty feet horizontal to get out to where we can't see anything at all." The younger of the officers looked a bit anxious, waiting to see the grizzly remains that no doubt awaited them when they brought the car to the surface.

Lydia nodded, acknowledging one of the divers, who had happened to see her drive up. Tony was the man's name, and he had nearly ten years' experience diving for the department. She watched as the two waded carefully into the current, playing out the ropes they had attached to the sturdiest of the shrubs well up the shore, and twenty or thirty feet upstream from the likely site of the wreck. Two other officers stood on the shore tending the lines as well. The bottom dropped quickly away, and with a final thumbs-up signal, they ducked under the water and disappeared, their bubbles tugged away downstream, and their ripples flowed away in dissipating rings.

Lydia leaned against the side of the wrecker, feeling the vibration of the motor as the operator paid out cable, running it down to the edge of the river. Sergeant Timmons had the young patrolman, Officer Spalding, flagging traffic with a lit flare as the other wrecker backed around to a better angle for pulling the car from the river. It was liable to tax one machine alone to hoist the car from the river and over the jutting rocks along the small cliff. Lydia carefully clambered down to the riverbank, unwilling to wait up on the roadside for delayed information.

After twenty minutes or so, the divers returned to the shore and explained what they had found. Tony spoke, having raised his face mask up to his forehead. "It's a Mercedes. Silver. Two occupants: one adult male and one younger female, both Caucasian. We won't have much trouble rigging the cables, but we'll bring the bodies up first."

Lydia felt the heat rush to her face as she felt - no, knew - who the female would turn out to be. Again, she felt her head spin, and sat down heavily on a rock. Tony looked at her, "Are you okay, Lieutenant?"

Lydia nodded and waved him back to his work. The diver gathered two black bags and laid them out on the shore, then grabbed two more ropes and asked one of the other officers to go up to the ambulance to get a body basket and call for another ambulance. Recovering bodies from a river required more equipment than the casual onlooker would expect.

Moments later, the divers were back in the water and working on the unpleasant task of pulling two dead bodies from the muddy Mississippi River.

* * *

Bagda was in no mood for more bad news. This city was coming apart around his head, and no matter what he did, no matter that he sent his very best operatives to support different portions of operation A-121, he was being thwarted at every turn. Growling savagely at the frightened, cowering demon crouched at his feet, he spat, "What is it now, Fellon? It had better be good news this time."

Fellon choked back a squeal of fear, and croaked out, "Y-Y-Your lowness," he bowed himself from his crouched posture, abasing himself before this potent demon lord. "Your lowness, we are seeing some encouraging successes."

Bagda stopped his pacing and turned toward the messenger with greedy eyes, hoping yet to snatch victory from this debacle. He hated the thought of calling down to headquarters to beg for help. That would be an ugly situation indeed, yet one to which he would have to bend if things went much worse. He had already been forced to send two of his operations demons to Rehab and Discipline for losing their cases to the Enemy.

Fellon went on with shaking voice, "Yes, sir. We confirmed two deaths that we were hoping for, and drug use is still up from last year." He grew more confident when Bagda remained silent. He went on with more enthusiasm, "There were five new teenage pregnancies this week, and abortion continues with lovely regularity."

Bagda's eyes narrowed, and steaming breath hissed from his nostrils. "What are you hiding from me, you sniveling, snot catcher? I know all of that! And you know what news I'm after today! What is the situation?" His last question was bellowed with hot rage, right into the face of Fellon. The smaller demon backed away a step or two before Bagda stomped on his foot, halting him in his tracks. "Report, demon slime!"

"I- I- I- I- "

"You, you, you what?" the demon lord sneered.

"I think we've got a problem, sir."

"Well? Out with it! I haven't got time to waste on waiting for you to spill your guts. What news have you brought?"

"We've lost the Frack boy to the Enemy." The messenger cringed, waiting for his boss to explode.

"That's old news. I've known that for over a day."

"We've lost his dad, too."

"Yeah, yeah. Go on."

"The daughter was taken from our control by the Enemy before we could do all we wanted to with her."

"I found that out hours ago, you worthless twit." Bagda was feeling less threatened now, thinking that he had a grip on how bad the situation had gotten.

"The youth pastor, Dave Merryl, has also been lost to the Enemy." This time Fellon held his breath, because he knew that this was the news that Bagda didn't have yet and that Bagda was going to go ballistic over it. He was not disappointed.

Bagda stopped in mid smirk, choking off his inhaled breath. His motion froze in mid gesture. He turned slowly to face Fellon, his already dark face threatening and mottled with fury. Rage shot from his nostrils in yellow jets of hot steam, and as what passed for his blood pressure built, vessels burst and greenish red ichor oozed from his nose and leaked between his compressed lips.

He stalked closer to the cowering smaller demon. Fellon was small in stature, but just as large in his evil nature as his boss. The runt snarled at Bagda, knowing that he had nothing to lose now. He snapped at the hand that reached out to grab his neck, sinking his fangs into the side of the thumb. Bagda seemed not to notice this at all, but simply shook his hand free in order to get ahold of the terrified messenger's neck. He lifted the demon up, wrapped his other hand around his waist and thighs and began wringing him out, immensely energized by his rage. The torment that Bagda inflicted on the smaller demon was excruciating, but he only squeezed harder, choking Fellon's screams off like a needle scraped across the surface of a record.

"We lost who?" he shrieked into the contorted face of Fellon. "We lost who?" There was no answer possible from Fellon's contorted position, and Bagda was in no state to wait for one. With a final wrench he tore the demon messily in two, green gore splashing in all directions, and furiously threw the parts into the pit of darkness which suddenly yawned open at his feet.

Panting as he tried to recover his composure, Bagda gathered his thoughts and knew that it was time to call for help. This was not a good thing at all. Calling for help was admitting that he needed help, and he would be seriously disciplined for that. But to let this go further down the road to a major screw-up, why... that would be the end for him. He would be busted back up to licking the hooves of gloating sergeants in the blink of Lucifer's eye. The risk was now too great. He had already let this get too far out of hand. He quieted his mind, dusted off his hands, and sent a carefully worded request for help down the chain of command.

Seconds later, Bagda got his answer and knew what action he was to take. The hierarchy was that organized. Of the great principalities including Baal, Asteroth, Molech and a half dozen others of that exalted rank, Molech was his favorite. He was, in appearance, a huge skeleton, sheathed in armor, hideous in strength, impossible to be satiated in evil. Bagda thought back to the years in the Middle East, and recalled with fondness the rich humor and artistic touch of Molech's leading thousands of loving parents into burning their own children alive in a futile attempt to gain the mock-god's approval. And then, to watch the Enemy's own chosen people mimic such a hideous parody of proper sacrifices. What a disgusting and lovely joke on Him.

Molech had also played instrumental roles in leading Stalin and Lenin down the paths they walked in building Communism into the world force it had become, resulting in the very real murder and butchering of millions of humans in the name of Communism.

His Lowness was sending Molech himself, one of the ten most potent demon lords in all of creation, to Alagonic. Bagda shivered with fear and anticipation. Fear, because he knew that Molech would not miss the opportunity to grind Bagda's face in this debacle. Anticipation, because he relished watching and helping Molech wipe this city clean of all signs of light and hope and righteousness. He was grimly satisfied that His Lowness was sending such a potent demon to clean up this screwed up operation. A regional principality with all his attendant support demons was on his way, and there was nothing that the Enemy had in this town that could stand up to that kind of power.

Glimmer of hope sparked in him as he considered a new possibility. The fact that they had ordered in such power could be interpreted that he had been under-supported to begin with. Maybe he wouldn't be punished so harshly after all once His Lowness saw how badly their intelligence had underestimated the Enemy here.

In spite of his recent failures, he actually grinned, thinking more about the punishment about to be meted out on the Enemy's warriors than on his own impending situation. They were going to pay now. Oh yeah, they were going to be hurting in a huge way before the next day was over.

* * *

Lieutenant Mochek sat in her office contemplating the convolutions in the way this case was developing. The car had been extracted from the river with a minimum of fuss. The sleek silver Mercedes had been registered to a certain Charles Henry Farrier, a shadowy character with little recorded history, much mystery, and now no life. He had driven his own car into the river and drowned. The forensic report stated that he had been conscious when the car entered the water - not a pleasant way to go.

The other passenger in the car, the younger female, had matched the description of Marianne Frack. Preliminary reports made it clear that she had not been treated delicately while she had been missing. As messy as her case appeared on paper, the interesting thing was that even in death, and in spite of what she had been through, there was something different about her. Something quiet in her still face. *Reading peace on the face of a dead teenager whose body had spent several hours under water. What would she be thinking next?* Yet there was something there. Somehow that girl had maintained a center of calm that was visible even after her death. The coroner had reported that she had been dead prior to entering the water, but had not yet concluded what the exact cause of death was.

The phone call to the Frack family could not be put off any longer, and now the lieutenant had more to report than simply some clothing. The body they had was undoubtedly that of their daughter.

Lydia was thankful that the family was a church-going family. They had a better chance of dealing with this loss than most families did. She knew that God offered a real and supernatural peace, and a hope that looked beyond this world to a future of healing. As horrible as it was, at least this family would have an end to this nightmare. All too often the missing child was never seen or heard from again, leaving their family in a never-ending quagmire, a miserable paradox of hopelessness and never-say-die kind of hope. She said a silent prayer for the family, and reached for the phone.

Chapter 15
Loud in the silence.

At six thirty on Monday evening, the police telephoned to say that the body of a twelve-year-old girl had been found. There was no identification with the body, but the description matched that of their daughter: four feet, seven inches tall, blond shoulder-length hair dyed with several colors, brown eyes, ninety-three pounds. They asked if they could come to identify the body, and, numb from four days of grief, worry and shock, they drove through the bright sunshine of early May.

Odd, thought Pete, how even the weather could lie. What an intense paradox; his new peace with God's forgiveness, his heart rending grief over the loss of Marianne, and this impossibly cheerful weather. How could the sun possibly shine while there was so much hurt inside his heart? Surely God knew that this was no time for seventy-three sunny degrees with a light breeze. This was no time for happy people to be out walking their dog, or riding a bike, or flying a kite on a sun drenched hillside in the park. This was a time for wailing, for grief, for drowning in a whirlpool of sadness.

But that didn't happen, not yet. Now there was only numbness and a deep resentment that life should go on around him when his world had lurched, and then rudely, sickeningly stopped in its tracks.

Silence reigned in the plush interior of their Pontiac 6000, the comfort of the seats denied by the absolute stiffness of Molly's posture. Her back scarcely touched the seat, and her hands twisted and gripped one another. Four days of this unconscious wringing had reddened and cracked the once soft skin of her delicate hands.

Pete looked at her, and the anger deep inside moved a little closer to the still surface of the numbness. His love, his bride, the joy of his life had been hurt so badly. And there seemed to be nothing that he could do to take away her pain. He reached across to place his hand on the back of her neck, lifting her hair with his fingers so that he could touch her skin; trying to break through to her; to let her know that he was with her.

She didn't respond at all. Her eyes stayed unfocused, staring through the dashboard, through the passenger-side air bag, through the engine block, through everything. What she did see, she hadn't shared with him. But he knew it wasn't anything good from the look on her face and the creases around her eyes and across her forehead. Pete sighed, and dropped his hand back to his lap.

The sun glinted off the hand rail in front of the police department as he pulled into the angled parking slot at the curb. He shifted into park, shut off the engine, and pulled the keys from the ignition.

The warmth of the sun failed to reach through the icy shell that encased him as he slid from the seat. Locking the doors shut, he walked around the front of the car to coax Molly into motion, up the stairs, and into the lobby of the dull, gray tiled building.

The uniformed woman at the desk must have been alerted to watch for them, because he saw her place the phone back into the cradle and smile in an oddly forced manner as she waved them toward a row of beat-up, vinyl seats. "Lieutenant Mochek will be with you in just a moment," she metronomed, and then returned to her computer without giving them any further attention.

Pete and Molly stood there, all of their forward momentum stolen by the disinterested, nameless figure behind the counter, who hadn't even asked for their names. They stared at the woman, who then hesitated when they failed to obey her signal to sit down and wait. No longer disinterested - someone was falling outside her plans for an orderly waiting room - a cross look began to transform her face from professional politeness to impatient displeasure. Fortunately she was distracted from correcting their infraction by crisp footsteps approaching from the elevators across the room.

"Mr. and Mrs. Frack?" came a voice that they dreaded, since they knew what she was going to tell them, yet which drew their reluctant attention. Looking at the lieutenant for the second time in two days, they saw a sharp black woman in her forties, with short black hair and a middle-aged, used-to-be-trim waist line. Even in the depths of their pain, they sensed that this woman did care. Her kind eyes and concerned expression underscored a voice that was professional, yet empathetic.

"Thank you for coming so promptly." She carefully shook each of their hands. "Are you alright?" They both looked much worse for wear than they had only a day earlier. At their small, automatic nods of affirmation, she went on, "If you folks could step this way, I'll take you to a room where I'll give you some idea of what to expect."

They wordlessly followed her back to the elevator, and as the doors slid shut, their sense of foreboding increased yet again. Lieutenant Mochek was a woman who had seen it all. Twenty years on the force, starting with five on foot patrol and seven more in a black and white patrol car, had given her ample opportunity to witness mankind at its very worst, and more rarely at its best. Riding in this silent, tension filled elevator was familiar to her, but no easier for having taken this walk with dozens of parents just like the Fracks. They knew that the body in some unknown, other room was going to be their daughter. They knew.

Lieutenant Mochek surreptitiously observed the couple standing to her right and slightly in front of her. She took in their stiffness, and the almost visible wall standing between them. She knew they were hanging on to their ability to go on by their fingernails. Only her own faith in God allowed her to go on doing this job, offering what she could to help these people through this impossible time; a time that no parent should ever have to go through. She silently prayed for wisdom and for the Fracks, asking God to somehow use even this situation to draw the Fracks closer to Him.

The steel doors slid open, and with Pete holding Molly's elbow and guiding her along, they walked down an echoing corridor, the air so cold it seemed that they should have been able to see their breath. When Lieutenant Mochek opened a solid looking metal door, they held their breath, afraid of what they would see on the other side. But it was only a small room crowded with a table surrounded by five more of the same dilapidated chairs, haphazardly set around it, that they had seen upstairs.

They let out their breath in a sigh that seemed loud in the silence that hung thick in the air.

"Please, be seated," suggested Lieutenant Mochek, and the three of them bent stiffly into the seats. There was no easing of the tension from the change in posture, however. It seemed that they rested no weight on the seats – the taut springs of their leg muscles would lift them again, instantly upright on command.

"The body you are about to see could be your daughter," the lieutenant plunged into the matter, knowing there was no way to make it easy or pleasant. "I need you to be prepared, because the body is not in good shape. I'll tell you now that the victim was murdered, and not quickly. She was not treated gently before her death, though the forensic report is not final yet."

Molly's face grew even more pale, while Pete sat tense and resolute.

"It might be helpful if only one of you were to go in – perhaps, you, Mr. Frack. Mrs. Frack, you could wait here while we go in?" The question was a suggestion revealed by the detective's tone.

Molly set her chin and shook her head. In a fragile, yet determined voice, she said, "I'm going with Pete."

Lieutenant Mochek nodded, and went on, "There is no way to make this any easier, so unless either of you has a question, we will go in now."

They paused, but after looking at Molly, Pete gave a twitch that Lieutenant Mochek took as permission to proceed.

She rose to her feet and extended her hand toward the door. Pete followed suit, rising to his feet and turning to help his wife up. She paused, her stare still elsewhere, but then took his offered hand, stood, and slowly straightened as well.

Again they filed out of the room, and silently followed the officer down the echoing hallway. Their shoes marked their progress with three different tones of tapping and squeaking and shuffling. They made their way along the hall and around a corner to the right. They stopped before a set of large, stainless double doors with small, square windows set in them. Lieutenant Mochek paused and looked at the distraught couple, her own face calm, but her heart mirroring their distress, and then pushed the right-hand door open.

Colder air and the septic stink of chemicals flowed out over them. Pete and Molly entered hand-in-hand, and followed the lieutenant across the room, past a row of ten or twelve tables, four of which had black, rubber covered body bags on them. The last table, placed under a set of harsh lights, had on it a smaller form covered with a heavy white drape. A man in a long, dingy white apron stood by it, speaking quietly into a microphone suspended from overhead by a long, angled arm. He paused as they approached and stepped on a floor pedal to stop the recording.

"Ted, this is Mr. and Mrs. Frack, here to I.D. this body."

Ted looked at the couple, and said, "I'm sorry. This won't be easy. Or pretty. She was treated pretty badly, and I haven't had time to clean her up very well."

Pete now noticed the brownish wet spots on the covering over the still form on the table. Molly's eyes were locked on Ted's face just as her hands were locked on Pete's arm. She refused to even glance at the table.

Ted moved around to the other side of the table, and reached for the edge of the drape. But he paused when Molly moaned and covered her mouth with one hand. His look shifted to Lieutenant Mochek, who hesitated, but when she nodded to go ahead he reached for the sheet again. Pete's arm went around Molly's waist, and he too nodded.

The material rustled as Ted pulled it down over the forehead, face and then shoulders of the young girl on the table. He appeared to change his mind when he remembered who was in the room, and pulled the sheet back up to the child's neck. Pete thought of the hundreds of times he had made just that same motion in tucking his little girl in at night just before saying prayers together.

The rustling sound of the covering pulled Molly's eyes finally from Ted's face to the face of the form lying so absolutely still on the cold metal of the table. Her breath all but left her, and her legs turned to rubber as she saw her baby's bruised face.

A sob escaped Pete's mouth, straight from his heart. Marianne lay there, her skin a waxen bluish color where it was not blackened with bruises or white at the edge of the single razor straight cut on her cheek.

He and Molly turned to one another and locked their arms around each other. Pete opened his eyes for a moment to give a jerky nod to Lieutenant Mochek, and then clenched them together again as if to lock back the hot tears that threatened to spill from them. His body spasmed with sobs that he refused to let loose, knowing that once they started he would never - never - stop weeping.

Molly and Pete held each other tightly, as though the only thing in the whole world that held them from flying into individual quivering atoms was the rigid strength of their own arms. Tears poured from her eyes, absorbed into the blue oxford material of his shirt.

Her lungs - her whole body - ached from the sobs that racked her to her soul, and that had kept her from breathing for at least a lifetime, measured in the few moments since she had seen what had happened to her little girl.

Pete stood as still as a rock, feet spread for stability, eyes clenched tightly shut against the horror and his own tears; clenched, and refusing the sight, as if he could erase the memory and stop his imagination of how this could have happened. Or could have been prevented.

They wanted their little girl back. They wanted to see Marianne take that last little hop off the bus step onto the shoulder of the road in front of their house. They wished for the smile and joyful laugh that would never again lighten the face that lay completely immobile and lifeless on the table in front of them.

They would have given anything - anything - to be able to go back four days and say "No" when Marianne had asked to be dropped off at the mall to spend a couple hours shopping with her friends. Just a simple "No" would have made all of this go away. *Is there anything that can change time? Please! Just this once!* Pete's cries were silent, yet echoed in his mind.

But time is set in cement, a matrix that will never change. And no one will ever have the chance to change what is past. And Marianne will never smile her smile on earth again.

Ted covered the small, still form again and reached for a clipboard to add Marianne's name to the form on top of the stack of papers. The Lieutenant shepherded the distraught couple from the room.

* * *

Four dark and shadow-cloaked figures watched the scene from a darkened corner at the ceiling of the room. Each of them silently drinking in the horror and hopelessness that filled the room. Though there was light in this room, light which these four hated, the fresh waves of emotional darkness were a sweet taste to Bagda, the demonic overseer of this city, as well as the three privates who were active in this part of the operation.

Skallum, the demon private assigned to Molly Frack for this operation, spoke softly, "Isn't it sweet to be able to see this dear family falling apart like this?"

Bagda glared at him, and the private shrank under his baleful gaze. "You fool! This is far from a sealed victory for us. Haven't you been reading your updates?" he demanded. The demon cowered lower still, giving the chief all the answer he needed. "Make sure you do your part here or you're finished. We've already lost enough on this operation."

Bagda turned his blazing eyes on the other two, who were enjoying not only the ambiance of this room, but the dressing down of their fellow. The more Skallum got reamed out, the less attention was paid to their own shortcomings. "You! Badger! You've got nothing to grin about. Sure, this is a beautiful moment, and one we are privileged to savor. But you've got some explaining to do downstairs. And we're going to go deal with that right now!"

The air shimmered ever so slightly as two of the demons disappeared into the lower regions of hell. The remaining two breathed a sigh of relief to have their boss gone, and turned their attention back to the scene of grief playing out in the room below them.

Chapter 16
They knew fear, too.

The skies over Alagonic were clear of any clouds, yet a darkness that didn't effect the sparkle of the evening sun on water or the blaze of the waning light on the pavement, dimmed the spiritual realm and was noticed by few other than angels and demons.

Angels in the area felt the chill and drew closer to their charges, knowing that powers, marshaled but as yet unchallenged in this city, were about to be unleashed. Demons froze in their tracks, simultaneously hoping to go unnoticed and yet inwardly cheering as their champion, a huge and hideous, monstrously strong lord of demons by the name of Molech drew close to the city. They knew that their failing plan had just received a boost that would throw righteousness out of this city once and for all.

* * *

Gentle, old Mr. and Mrs. Caffer sat drinking their evening tea. Mrs. Caffer shivered, pulled her sweater from the back of her chair and wrapped it around her shoulders. She looked up to see her husband sitting quietly with his eyes closed, in a posture that she recognized. He was praying, and something inside her called her to prayer as well.

Just then the phone rang, and she jumped, startled more than a simple ringing telephone should have startled her. She gave Al a chagrined grimace and got to her feet to answer the phone. "Hello?"

"Mrs. Caffer? It's Samantha." Sam could hardly contain the excitement she felt, and it sounded in her voice.

"Yes dear?"

"Oh, Mrs. Caffer! I can't believe what happened just a couple of hours ago. Dave has opened his heart back up, and God has brought him to repentance. He's answered our prayers!"

Mrs. Caffer's voice was warm and gentle with feeling, "I'm so glad, dear. God is so good to us, isn't He?"

"Yes He is. But it's quite painful, too. Some of the things he's done are so painful." Her voice tightened with sorrow and pain.

"Even healing can be very painful and difficult, Samantha." The older woman's voice sounded like a warm hug, even through her own emotional distress.

"Mrs. Caffer, Dave and I got the feeling that God is asking us to go over to the Fracks' to pray and to see if there's anything else we can do to support them. I was wondering if you and Mr. Caffer would like to go with us."

"Why certainly, dear. That would be a good thing to do."

"We will pick you up in twenty minutes. Alright?"

"Yes, we'll be ready."

Mrs. Caffer hung up and looked into the kitchen again. Mr. Caffer looked up from praying and said, "I think now would be a good time for us to be praying with our brothers and sisters. I don't know what it is, but there is something big going on in the heavenlies right now. The Lord is telling me that we need to be praying right now."

* * *

The momentum of prayer, repentance and spiritual healing at First Evangelical Church had faltered late Sunday evening. Tired parents took their more-tired children home. Now the Monday morning working people had gone to work, students attended classes, moms took care of the daily needs of their families. It seemed, to the casual observer, that life's routine had imposed itself over anything that had changed in their hearts. But there was a difference. Many hearts were swept clean, and come Monday evening, a renewed call, silent but still compelling, was sensed and memories were prodded, encouraging one to call another, friends to call friends, and couples to call other couples. Across the city, alone or in small groups, face-to-face or by phone, the church responded by inviting one another to come together again in the still unfinished battle to uphold their families, their church, and their city before the Lord.

In a way that hadn't been seen in Alagonic in decades, scores of members from several unrelated churches gathered around the city. By eight o'clock that evening, God's people had settled to their knees or in their seats and were interceding once again, doing battle in the only way they knew how. Assisted by the Holy Spirit, they confronted potent, evil powers in the name of Jesus.

The hordes from hell responded with growing anger. They knew fear, too, but at first they nursed a growing fury that a handful of pitiful humans would dare to come against them in battle. They swarmed together, gathering around Molech, their newly arrived and awesome leader. This leader, whip, sword, and talons at the ready, and flashing with a deadly glow that somehow underscored the darkness that accompanied him, walked among his minions. His armor clanked over his skeletal form with every motion. He growled a word and all the demons fell back, leaving Bagda standing near - and alone.

Molech's whip sang as he struck at Bagda. It looped around Bagda's neck, scoring into the skin, and Molech's hideously strong arm pulled the ogre close. He whispered into the cowering city-lord's ear, and the skin on the side of his face blistered and boiled with the heat of his master's breath. "You have failed me," hissed the master, his voice sibilant as it issued from his skeletal chest, then ringing harmonically with his armor. "You have turned our plans into a mockery."

Even if he had come up with any words to say, Bagda couldn't respond with the whip tightly coiled around his windpipe. Molech released the swollen-faced ogre to fall in a humiliated heap at his feet, and turned to address the watching demonic horde.

"We shall still be victorious in this city," his voice rumbled like gigantic boulders grinding together deep beneath the surface of the earth.

"We shall not disappoint the master. The Enemy has left us a huge weakness to exploit. Their free will," and he sneered the words in mockery of the one part of the human mystery that even he could not comprehend. "Their free will shall be our point of attack. We go now to the Frack home to finish this once and for all."

The assembled demons sent raucous and obscene victory chants into the evening sky, and Bagda crawled between their massed bodies to a quieter spot, absorbing many kicks and blows along the way. When he found a quieter corner in which to hide, he curled into a pitiful ball to recuperate from his humiliation. Alone and angry, he nursed that anger, loving the sour poison of rejection and hatred.

* * *

Night had fallen by the time the Fracks got home from the morgue. But even in the dark, a deeper gloom gathered as Pete drove slowly up his driveway, throat still tight, lips pressed together, anger, fear and grief warring for supremacy in devastating waves in his mind and heart. Molly still wept, the sobs having given way to a piteous whimpering that wrenched at his heart almost as much as Marianne's end had. His new faith had faltered on seeing Marianne's innocent, lifeless face, motionless on the morgue table.

As he drove into the garage, parking next to the van, the feelings roiled, and fear began to take the upper hand in a way very similar to the way fear had gripped him the night before. The sense of panic grew like a dark force just as when he had walked down the hall just 24 hours earlier. Knowing that – and even recognizing the fact that something un-normal was happening – he did nothing to control the strange and overpowering emotions. He shifted into park, killed the engine and head lights, and quickly got out of the car, needing to get Molly into the house as fast as possible.

She was feeling the oppression too. Even through her grief, he could see that she was scared, though they could not tell of what. The house was dark, save the light coming from under the door to Steve's room. Flipping on the entry light didn't help, and they made their way down the dimly lit hall to their own room. Pete decided to get Molly to their bedroom before telling Steve that his sister had been found dead.

As they entered the bedroom, Pete let go of Molly's arm to flip the light switch, but with an eerily empty-sounding click, the light failed to light. Pete's skin crawled across his neck and back, and he felt the hairs on his arms and neck standing on end. Molly's breath came in short pants, and she asked with a quavering voice, "What is it, Pete? What's wrong?"

"Nothing, hon," came his unconvincing reply. "The bulb must be burned out is all." But the fear continued to build in him, and Pete had no idea which way to turn to try to fix whatever was wrong. They sat on the edge of the bed, Pete's arm around Molly's shoulder, feeling her sniffing back her tears. But the quiet in the house built behind her quiet crying, and the feeling of something nearby and very wrong built in his heart. As they sat there, Molly's crying quieted, and the strange silence filling the house grew to a palpable feeling of dark evil. A sound startled Pete, and he jumped.

"What is it?" Molly asked again.

"Shh," he hushed her, and got up from the bed to listen at the door to the hall. All was silent, but then he heard it again, the sound of a carpet-muffled footstep coming from the living end of the house. He peeked down the hall and saw Steve's door still shut and a line of light seeping from under it.

In the other direction all was dark except for the dim light from the garage seen through the entry door that now silently hung open. *Didn't I leave the hall light on?* he asked himself. As he watched, the light on the garage door opener went off, leaving pitch darkness, broken only by a ghost of light coming from the street lights out in front of the house. The eerie feeling of fear, of having an intruder in the house, grew stronger. As he listened he thought he again heard the sound of someone moving quietly around in the living room.

Fear-induced sweat dripped from his forehead and down his neck. He stood rooted to the spot, wanting to retreat into the room and close the door on whatever waited in the house, but knowing that he couldn't simply hide from this, whatever it was. He felt completely unprepared for this. Completely weak in the face of this nameless, faceless threat.

The sounds moved from the living room to the kitchen from where he heard a piece of paper slide on the counter. A spoon or something clanged jarringly into the sink.

"Is Steve up?" Molly asked from her huddled position on the edge of the bed.

Again, Pete motioned for her to be silent, and then tip toed over to her. He whispered into her ear, "Call the police and tell them that we've got someone in the house. I'll be back in a minute."

"Where are you going?!" she asked in a pinched voice. "You can't go out there. What if there's someone out there?" Her harsh whisper cut through the silent house like a whip, and Pete froze at the door. More scared than he'd ever been in his life, and not sure why he was doing this, he motioned at Molly and at the phone, and slowly poked his head out into the hallway.

* * *

Steve lay on his bed reading a magazine, but couldn't concentrate. His mind repeatedly wandered to the situation of his sister his parents. He was new enough in his faith that he didn't recognize the Spirit's prompting to pray for these people.

After a time, he flipped on his MP3 player, but a few moments of skipping through his music list brought no release from the growing worry for his parents. And below that concern was a nagging, dank, nameless fear that started in his guts and wormed its way up his spine into his brain. A headache grew along with it, and he couldn't find a comfortable position on his bed no matter what way he contorted himself, and no matter how he bunched up his pillow. The house was quiet, completely still since his folks had left in such a hurry. He knew their strange behavior had to be about Marianne. But they had been in such a hurry, he hadn't asked what the deal was, but simply hollered, "I'll be praying for you!" at their backs as the door closed behind them.

Hm. Maybe I should be praying for them. I did say that I would, after all. He recalled the joy he had found in praying with the Caffers, and sat up in his bed to better position his body and his mind for talking with God. Crossing his legs Indian style, he whispered, "Dear God. I hope you are taking good care of my sister and my mom and dad. Our whole family is torn up right now, but God, I trust You to do what's right. Help my mom to trust You like Dad and Marianne and I have done. And help them not to worry so much. Amen."

He relaxed a bit, and opened his eyes. Nothing had changed, and the fear in his heart was greater than ever. He sniffed, thinking he smelled something burning, but then decided that it was just old smoke smell from the ashes of his old joints which he apparently hadn't been so clever at hiding after all.

Still the fear grew, and he sat up further toward the head of his bed, grabbed his Bible from his dresser, hugging it to his pulled-up knees and chest. He thought of the joints he used to smoke and how comforting a joint might be right now. He began to wonder if he had any more stashed in the back of his drawer.

* * *

The air over eastern Alagonic grew heavy with wind whipped clouds. The starlight was cut off again and again by the scudding wisps. But the heaviness was something more than simply moisture-ladened air, for Molech had arrived and was leading his minions to battle for the city of Alagonic.

Before him Fear, Doubt, and Confusion winged their way across the town, preparing the way for their master. Below him lights dimmed and hearts grew cold and heavy. Those who already held a proclivity to hate and anger gave vent to those feelings which were normally held in check by society's rules and the faint glimmers of truth which lingered in their hearts. But tonight fear combined with coveting in hearts that were already prone to violence, and in a wide swath across the town mayhem and brutality broke out. The police department was swamped with calls demanding help and protection. Officers on call were summoned hurriedly in to duty, but their resources were overwhelmed by nine o'clock.

Fear entered the Frack home, and those living there felt it in an almost palpable way. Demons whipped through the house with glee, slashing at the hearts of the Fracks with abandon. Doubt concentrated on the son, working in conjunction with Furrgstan, though he was not much help, newly defeated and chastised as he was. Just the same, Doubt did a fair job of keeping the boy distracted, and Furrgstan was able to begin new inroads to making Steve's new life worthless for eternal matters. Old habits were brought to the surface in the form of temptations. They dangled in front of Steve's eyes as guilt assailed him; guilt over past failures that had already been washed away by the blood of his Savior. The young man's faith, too, faltered.

Fear was having a heyday with the adults in the house. He gloried in the gasping breath of the mother, and the sweating, tight-chested attempts of the father to muster the courage to search the house for intruders.

And all the while Molech drew closer. The horde of demons savored the moment, watching as the angels in residence collected their all too pitiful strength in an effort to resist the demon lord. They were brave, thought Molech, but he would simply enjoy squashing their puny strength and sending them running, broken and bleeding, back to their lair.

Bagda, at the rear of the mob, left behind and forgotten when the demon horde rushed off, noticed an isolated island of light approaching from the north side of town and peered intently to find out what was coming. Noticing the car with the four Christ-followers in it, he hurried to rejoin the forces from hell, forcing his way through the mobs of demons, and tugged on the wing of the hugely muscled Molech.

"What do you want?" the demon Lord thundered, backhanding the disgraced city-lord across the face. The watching horde laughed at the humiliated Bagda.

Bagda, in turn wavered. He knew that the approaching Christians formed a threat to the powerful demon lord in spite of his great strength. But after the way Molech had treated him, embarrassing and shaming him in front of his overlings, he was sorely tempted to let Molech face his own challenges without the benefit of Bagda's help.

"What is it, you has-been?" rumbled Molech's voice like thunder from a threatening storm. "I thought I had dealt with you already; that I had taught you your place." His sword snaked out of its scabbard, and quick as striking lightening, the barbed tip snagged the skin at Bagda's shoulder, and he drew the squirming demon in close to his face. "Do you have anything to say to me before I get really tired of you? You've already screwed up here. Do you think you can do a better job of fixing this than I can? Hmm?"

Bagda's throat choked with fear, and with a final twist and a ripping of the flesh at his shoulder, he tore free and fled to the rear of the demonic company, not daring to completely desert the operation for fear of even greater discipline. The hoots and laughs of the soldier demons that used to be under his command followed him all the way back. He looked again at the approaching concentration of light, and thought, *We'll see how prepared you are for this conflict. We'll see.*

Molech thundered to them all, "Now hear me. We are going to clear this city of all signs of the Enemy. We hold the upper hand here, and the forces of You-Know-Who have nothing to match our strength in this area." The listening demons whistled and cheered, cavorting in jubilation that Bagda considered a bit premature.

"Even so," their lord went on, "we will take nothing for granted. I didn't get to where I am by losing easy battles. I've sent Fear and his ilk on ahead to loosen up the territory. I want all of you on the alert, and be sure to report anything new to me at once."

The mob cheered again and moved across the sky once more, eagerly closing in on the target.

* * *

Dave Merryl drove cautiously through the dark streets. There was a darkness gathering in this city, a darkness greater than simply that of the sun gone down. Each of the four in the car felt it, and though few words were spoken on this trip across town, they all knew that they were doing the right thing in going to the Frack's house for prayer. When they turned onto the Frack's street, Dave was the first to note that the lights were out in the house. The garage door stood open. The van and car both sat inside. It seemed odd to have the house so dark at nine in the evening.

He pulled into the drive, and from where they sat with the headlights shining into the garage, they could all see the door into the house was standing open as well. "There's something wrong here, you guys." Dave's voice reflected the fear that they all felt.

Samantha asked in a small voice. "What do you think we should do?" Even as they sat debating, the fear grew stronger, though none could figure out what caused it.

* * *

Pete saw nothing down the dark hallway, but paused anyway before heading down the hall. He thought for a moment, and then quietly went back to their bedroom closet to rummage around and find the old hunting shotgun that he kept there, unused for at least ten years. Though he tried to be quiet about it, the noise of shifting shoes and boxes sounded loud in the silent house. He unzipped the musty case and awkwardly pulled the gun out by the barrel. There were some shells in the bottom of the case, though he didn't know if they would still be good after sitting in the closet for years. He felt much better with the cool, solid weight of the weapon in his hands. He looked again at Molly, who was trying to get the phone to work. "What's wrong?" he whispered.

"I don't know! I dialed, it rang once, and then it started hissing and the connection cut off. Now all I get is static. I can't dial out at all." She looked very frightened sitting there in the near total darkness, and Pete walked around the end of the bed to give her another hug.

"Try your cell phone, and I'll be right back. It's probably nothing." Though fear tightened the muscles of his face into a mask.

"Then why are you taking that thing with you?" She pointed at the gun with a slight shudder. "Please be careful."

He gave her another squeeze. "I couldn't bear to lose you, too," she added with passion in her whispered words. He had to pry her arms away to go back to the hall door.

He inched into the hall, shotgun held in a ready position, pointing down the hall and to the left, toward the family room, his finger on the trigger.

* * *

This is so delicious! thought Fear. *With a little luck, I'll get old Petie to shoot his wife or his son. That would be a notch on my grip.* But then he realized that any glory would go to his boss, Molech, because just then, the demon Lord, Molech himself, entered the house. Fear went on working over the nerves of Molly, Pete and Steve, but the presence of Molech made Fear's part almost insignificant in comparison.

The guardian angels of Steve and Pete were far outmatched in this confrontation, but they stood there just the same, waiting for any demon to come within reach of their shining swords. They acted as though they were assured of victory even though there were dozens of demons waiting for either of them to fight, and Molech alone could have dealt with both of them single-handedly. The little demon, Fear, checked his antics and settled into his work. He certainly didn't want to screw up in front of Molech. Even if the Master Demon was busy as he dispatched these two warriors of the Enemy, he would know if Fear failed in his part.

* * *

Dave said, "I'm going in. There is something really wrong here."

"Wait, Dave. I think we should pray first. We're not dealing with mere flesh and blood here." Al's voice was sure and clear, though all of them could tell that he was troubled, too.

Mrs. Caffer spoke up in prayer, as though any more discussion would delay this all-important part of their battle. "Lord, we need You more than ever right now. You know what is going on here, and we don't, so we ask for Your power and Your strength to fix whatever is happening here. Give us wisdom and discernment as we face the enemy. In Jesus' name, Amen."

Dave looked at each of the faces in the car, his own face appearing pale even in the dim street light. Dave and Al both opened their doors simultaneously, and Dave heard Mrs. Caffer stifle a small gasp when she realized that her husband was going, too. But what option was there? Dave couldn't insist that the older man stay behind, and Al felt that he was needed in this possibly dangerous situation, too.

They edged between the cars in the garage and approached the door, which gaped open. The garage grew ever darker with each step they took into the shadows. Dave's foot kicked something across the cement floor, making a scraping racket that startled both of them and stopped them in their tracks, hearts racing. His pulse hammered in his ears, making it hard to hear or even to think. Fear coursed through his veins, pounding with each beat of his heart. Again they inched toward the door, stopping at the two steps up into the house. Dave nearly jumped out of his skin, stifling a shout, when Al touched his shoulder to ask in a hoarse whisper, "Should we really be doing this?"

Irritated with his own jumpiness, Dave looked at him, and then back at the empty doorway leading into the hallway. Doubt and Confusion bashed around and around in his head so that all he could think about was helping the Fracks as best he could. They were in danger. He had caused damage to the church body, and he was terrified, but this was something he could do to try to help. The fact that it was dangerous slipped to the back of his mind, overwhelmed by the two demons.

* * *

Pete heard the sudden noise in the garage and froze halfway to the kitchen. He shifted the gun to point farther down the hall and moved closer to the left hand wall to get a better angle through the door into the garage. His finger rested on the trigger, and he checked the safety again to make sure it was off.

* * *

Molech overheard the smaller demons enjoying their work. "Is this great or what?" demanded Confusion as he worked in concert with Doubt and Fear. Molech focused his attention on his own assignment in this project. Bringing the gun closer to the two in the garage was like creating a masterpiece of art. Molech directed Confusion as he stroked Dave's mind again, keeping him from thinking about backing away and calling the police.

Molech's presence kept the guardians of light at bay, giving free run of the area to whatever henchmen he wished to turn loose. Right now, Fear was taking great pleasure in helping his fiends play havoc with the humans involved with this situation. He flitted from one mind to the next, whispering dark things into each ear. Doubt added to the deteriorating situation, questioning beliefs and casting condemnation and false guilt at one heart and then the next.

The arrival of the four in the car had surprised Molech, and he looked for Bagda to berate the humiliated demon for not warning his lord, for that had undoubtedly been what the former city lord had been trying to tell him earlier, but the sniveling coward was hiding somewhere now. The guardians of the four had not been any more of a threat to his tactical situation than the first two had been until the humans began to pray. The angels held their ground with the influx of fresh power from the Enemy, yet they were seemingly content to stand and do only what they must to protect the souls of their charges.

But that was not good enough for Molech. He sent several dozen demons, with swords brandished, to chase the four angels to a distance, giving Fear, Confusion and Doubt more room to work. Soon he would step in, himself, to put the crowning touch on this situation, prompting Pete at just the right moment to pull the trigger and blow away the youth pastor or the old man, or maybe even both of them. The fact that it would happen right before the eyes of their wives was too perfect for words. Molech's mouth watered, thinking of the despair he would cause with this one stroke.

Chapter 17
The soul-rending ache of the pit.

Molly sat, frozen on her bed, the hissing phone receiver still held to her chest. Her mind was locked up like fine gears with sand thrown in. Fear had his claws deep inside her brain, and all she could think about was Pete getting killed in the other room. She couldn't think clearly, could barely breathe, but somehow forced herself to get out of bed and creep to the bedroom door to see where Pete was. She didn't have a clue that Skallum, the demon personally assigned to her, along with Doubt and Fear, were directing her to the place where she too could witness her husband killing a youth pastor and a kind old man in cold blood.

    She reached the door and eased one eye around the corner of the door jam. She could barely see the silhouette of her husband near the kitchen, a stray beam of light from the front of the house glinted off the barrel of the gun in his hands. She, too, heard the sound from the garage and saw him stop in his tracks, shifting the gun to the front. A moan of agony and terror escaped her tightly clamped jaws, and she stepped out into the hallway herself, walking fearfully down the hall, hugging the wall for a false sense of protection.

* * *

Sam and Mrs. Caffer sat in the car straining eyes through the dark to see their husbands approaching the door to the house. They both murmured prayers, but never had God seemed more distant. There was no power in these prayers, no protection or peace to be had from saying the words that had filled them with hope just hours earlier. Fear had sapped their faith, and Doubt had taken the lead in their prayers.

It was so silent that each woman could hear their own heart pounding, could hear each other breathing, could almost hear the clouds as they passed overhead. They saw the men pause in the garage when one of them stumbled on something lying on the floor, saw them speak briefly at the door, and saw them take the step into the dark house.

Suddenly Mrs. Caffer gave a shake of her head. She said, "This is not right!" Then she grabbed Sam's hand and shouted, "In the name of Jesus Christ, I command all evil spirits here to leave Al Caffer alone!"

What they saw next made no sense at all. In the silence which was so intense it was nearly deafening, they heard a voice cry out, whose, they couldn't tell. In the next instant there was a flash of light, the report of a gun shot, and then the unheard, yet somehow audible screaming of many voices in great pain. The cries were at first deafening, yet covering their ears didn't help the women at all, and then the cries faded quickly as though they were blown away on a hurricane force wind. They looked at one another, and acting as one, opened their doors and stumbled toward the house to see what had happened.

* * *

Pete saw the shadows hovering at the doorway leading in from the garage. He heard the strained whispers. With grim determination, a pure terror that froze rational thought processes, he raised the gun to his shoulder, and aimed at the opening. His breath came in ragged gasps, his shoulders and arms quivering with tension and fear. Sweat dripped down his forehead, and he could smell the sour smell of fear on himself. He gripped the gun so hard his knuckles ached, and the sweat dripped into his eyes, stinging and clouding his vision. His breath came in harsh puffs that he tried to silence. All he could see was a blur of motion at the door, perhaps an arm and shoulder reaching into the doorway.

In spite of the terror that gripped his heart, he really had no intention of pulling the trigger. But just as he was about to issue a warning to the person coming in the door, something came over him, and he found that he could scarcely breathe. He lost all volitional control over his muscles. He felt like a puppet in the grip of an evil puppeteer. And for the first time in his life, he truly knew evil for what it was. Every fiber of his being was filled with loathing for whatever it was that had him in its grasp.

He tried to call out, but his voice was frozen. He tried to throw the gun away from himself, but his arms refused to obey his mind, and his hands remained locked around the stock of the weapon. He knew true terror now, intense fear that made the previous fear pale in comparison, and his heart stopped dead still in his chest for what seemed like an eternity.

In horror Pete watched through sweat blurred eyes as his own arms aimed the gun at the figure in the doorway. He saw the look of shock on the face of Dave Merryl as the youth pastor saw the gun aimed at his head. Pete helplessly looked on as he felt his own finger tighten on the trigger of its own volition.

* * *

Al Caffer struggled to put the pieces together. There was something terribly wrong here; that much was obvious. But his head was foggy; he couldn't clear his mind enough to think through what was going on. He followed Dave into the garage, and fought back a shout of surprise when Dave accidentally kicked an empty milk jug across the floor. He felt a ridiculous and uncharacteristic urge to smack Dave for it, but followed him up to the door of the house.

There they paused, and Al asked Dave if he was sure this was the right way to deal with this situation, but Dave just looked at him and then back at the house. He moved woodenly toward the door again. Inside his heart Al fought to understand just exactly what was wrong here, but the fear in his mind spoke louder. None of this made any sense. He watched Dave reach into the house to feel for a light switch, but apparently there wasn't one within reach. With a last look of confused exasperation, Dave stepped into the house.

Just as that happened, Al felt a cold wind as though it was blowing through his soul and heart and mind. It came with sudden force, and seemed to blow the cobwebs out of the nooks and crannies of his mind, suddenly allowing a freedom of thinking and reasoning. Instantly he heard a voice, though he couldn't tell if it was inside his own head or audible, saying, "I am with you always. You have authority here. Use it."

Understanding rushed through him at once. He wondered why he had been so blind, but knew there was no time to think about it. He cried out, "In the name of Jesus Christ, the Son of the Living God, I command all of you evil spirits to be gone!"

Instantly, the noise of dozens of screeching, crying, tormented voices rang out of the silence. Again, he wasn't sure if they were actually audible or something heard only in his heart, but the voices nearly deafened him, and then faded quickly into the distance, disappearing in a matter of milliseconds.

Then there was a bright flash of light outlining Dave's body in the house, and the 'bang' of a gunshot that deafened him again. His ears ringing, he jumped up the step into the house to see Dave crouching against one wall of the entryway and Pete sitting against the opposite wall, a gun lying on the floor beside him.

Al could see little other than shadows in the darkness, and he feared that one or the other was mortally wounded. He looked for and immediately found the light switch. He flipped it on, filling the hallway with warm welcome light, and revealing gun smoke in the air and a gaping hole in the wall - and probably in the side of the refrigerator as well, judging by the angle of the hole. There was, however, no blood, and both Dave and Pete slowly shook themselves and got carefully to their feet.

* * *

Pete heard a powerful shout, and instantly everything changed. The compulsion over his will and body disappeared and with the sudden release he staggered forward and dropped the gun which went off with a huge boom. He fell to his knees in the hall, and then, seeing Dave drop to the floor, covered his eyes and rolled over to sit against the wall, not willing to look at what he had done.

As he sat there, his ears ringing from the blast, he heard the sound of another person coming into the house and he looked up to see Al Caffer walk in. From the corner of his eye he saw Dave sitting against the opposite wall, a shocked look on his face but apparently uninjured. Only then did he realize that the all pervading fear that had gripped his heart since he got home was gone.

* * *

Molech watched the scene from above, waiting for the delicious moment when he would nudge Pete's mind ever so lightly and the man would pull the trigger, scattering parts of the youth pastor all over the wall in the sight of his own wife, the pastor's wife and the older couple. He checked again to be sure that the angelic guardians were still occupied elsewhere; indeed they were still cowering under the threatening eyes and swords of his own demon soldiers. He shifted his eyes back to the man with the loaded shotgun, waiting for Pastor Dave to walk through the door. *Now,* he thought and gently extended his will into Pete's mind.

Suddenly, and with no warning, came a noise and an incredible pain, and an irresistible yank on Molech's being that sucked him immediately from Pete's mind and threw him, armor and all, up through the ceiling of the house and high into the sky. He screamed, dimly noticing the accompanying screams of his demonic army.

His mind remotely placed this terrifying and horrible occurrence as one he had experienced eons ago when the Enemy had thrown him out of heaven along with his lord, Lucifer. Knowing now what was happening and where he and the other demons were going, he screamed again, this time in helpless rage. Across the empty void above the atmosphere, and farther yet he was cast, spinning helplessly through space, still held in the vortex of a pain so acute he could think of little else. He and his fellows passed stars and galaxies so quickly that there was no time to name them. They passed the farthest of the galaxies and went on speeding through deepening cold and darkness. They broke though the farthest limits of the universe into absolutely nothing. The gulf, the abyss, the place where there was nothing, no space, no direction, no time even. Whether they still moved or not, they couldn't tell for there was no reference for motion. The pain eased, only to be replaced by the deeper, soul-rending ache of the pit.

* * *

Al was the first to recover his wits after the fear that had gripped each of them. The strain of walking into the unknown danger, and the shock of having a gun go off practically in their faces left both Al and Dave trembling and weak. The passing of terror and stress was like a physical release, like the sudden removal of tight restraining bands that should have been let loose long before. He pushed himself away from the wall on which he'd been leaning, waiting for his hearing to return. There was still a ringing and a pain in his ears, and he could barely hear the rustling of his sleeve when he reached to pick up the gun. He emptied the magazine with an ease that exposed a familiarity with weapons that a few years hadn't dulled much. He made sure it was unloaded, put the safety on and set it on the kitchen counter.

He saw Molly come down the hall, and then saw a door open from the other end of the house, letting light spill into the darkened hallway.

He could tell there was no bloodshed from the shot, and silently thanked God for His protection. A curious Steve and a frightened, and still shaking, Molly had gathered around Pete and were helping him to his feet, while Dave stuck his fingers into his ears and wiggled them around trying to restore his own hearing. He had been the closest to the muzzle, and he would be hearing-challenged for hours. Now Al could smile at his politically correct euphemism for ringing ears, but three minutes ago, he knew, they were all in mortal danger and under the direct attack of demonic forces the likes of which he had never encountered in all his eighty-three years.

"Just exactly what was that?" muttered Dave, a bit more loudly than was necessary. They all recognized that he was asking about the atmosphere of fear that had held each of them in its grip.

"That," Al stated with conviction, "was an attack of the enemy. It was an attempt by evil rulers and spiritual forces to destroy our lives. That's a paraphrase, but you get the idea, don't you? And it was the most extreme event of the sort that I've ever seen." The others just looked at him, but knew that there was no other explanation. The things that had occurred that evening were beyond any other explanation.

Sam and Mrs. Caffer rushed into the room, asking if anyone was hurt. Steve, also, joined them, and walked to his mom to put an arm around her shoulder.

Molly shook her head, as though to clear the remaining cob-webs. Lifting the phone from the counter and pushing the connect button, she placed the receiver against her ear and heard a normal dial tone. "It works fine now," she said to Pete, but everyone could figure out what she meant from the tone of her voice. "Do you think I should still call the police?"

Pete looked at Dave and Al, and waited for an answer from them. Dave thought a moment and then shook his head. "I don't think we could explain it to them anyway. Let's just leave well enough alone."

The evening seemed so normal now. Nothing threatened. The street lights provided light that was more than adequate. The night was once again a warm and safe time for any who wanted to be out and about. The yard and neighborhood were just another middle American place to live and raise kids.

Mrs. Caffer gave her husband a big hug. They all felt the release of an evil presence, the absence of the stifling fear they had both felt while waiting in the car.

They moved to the living room and settled on the available seating. Pete was amazed and pleased to see Molly aware enough to help him into a chair, shaking as he was. Steve sat on an ottoman that he pulled over near the door to the front entryway, Molly in the matching chair. Mr. and Mrs. Caffer sat on the couch with Samantha. Dave, nerves still making him jumpy, brought in two chairs from the kitchen table for Pete and himself.

After everyone was seated, an easier silence held them for a few additional moments, each contemplating what had just occurred, and trying to make sense of something that defied any natural explanation. Steve found himself looking at his dad with a dumbstruck look on his face, but then looked over at Mr. Caffer, who seemed to have a better grasp on the situation than anyone else. His mom had withdrawn emotionally a bit from the group, but was still much more aware and awake than she had been since Marianne's abduction. She sat at his dad's side, one hand resting lightly on his arm and the other curled lightly in her lap. Mrs. Caffer whispered something in Sam's ear and the younger woman nodded, still with a tight-lipped, serious look on her face.

Each of those present turned to face Mr. Caffer when he cleared his throat. He paused, but then spoke when no one else seemed to have anything to offer to open the conversation. "I guess you all understand that something pretty unusual has happened here tonight." Every head nodded, though Molly's agreement was a bit more vague than the rest. "Even beyond the obvious events, this was a night that will affect us for a long time to come." He paused and looked around at the faces in the room. "I think that we should all agree on a few points here before we do much else. First, I think that we should agree that there was a very real battle fought and won by the forces of God here tonight."

He paused and took the time to look for acknowledgement from each person in the room. Seeing at least the beginnings of understanding, if not complete agreement, he went on. "Second, we need to…"

"Wait!" blurted out Pete. "Wait just a second. Just exactly what happened here? I mean, I can see how it was an emotional or spiritual thing, but how could I have been so stupid, so out of control, as to shoot at an unarmed man - a pastor no less - in my own house?" His words were nearly shouted at the end; passion filled his heart, and tears filled his eyes as he thought about how close he had come to murdering an innocent man. "It wasn't even me. All I could do is watch. I couldn't stop it!"

His words seemed to echo in the room, and each was driven to rethink his or her own part in the activities of the evening. Sam considered her feelings of complete helplessness in witnessing what had occurred. Mrs. Caffer realized that she, too, had done little in the way of being a warrior in this evening's events until it was almost too late. Fear had nearly undone each of them.

Pete was almost completely humiliated and broken by his part in the debacle of this evening's happenings. But somehow, as he gazed at Al Caffer's face, he knew that there was no judgment there, only understanding.

Al looked around again at the expectant faces surrounding him. He saw the need, the confusion, the open frankness of each expression, and he felt compelled to try to explain. "This whole crazy week is a result of three things: God's desire to bring each of us into closer relationship with Him, Satan's desire to keep us from being a healthy effective part of God's kingdom, and our own free will to follow God or to go our own way." He ticked the three off on his upraised fingers. "Those forces are behind every human activity that has occurred since Jesus died on the cross, since Adam and Eve for that matter. Yet, in spite of Satan's plans God has been using every single action that has taken place this weekend for His purposes. Remember He said that all things will work together for good to those who love Him?"

Pete recognized the quote from scripture, and said, "But how does that make any sense out of what happened tonight? I was out of control. I was being controlled by something that wanted me to kill Dave!"

Al continued, "Well, that's the other half of the equation. Satan is a skillful liar and strategist, and apparently he thought that your action would accomplish a victory for him and his cause. So Satan sent demons to try to tease and torment each of us into doing his will rather than God's will."

"Torment is exactly the right word," Pete muttered, thinking of Marianne and the other stresses of the weekend. "But I just recently gave my life to God! How could God desert me into the control of a demon. He's got to care more about us than that!"

"Oh, He does, He does," Al assured them all. "But sometimes we step out of His protection, or perhaps we just haven't learned yet, how to take advantage of His protection. In either case, when Satan sees a chink in our armor, he will attempt to use it to further his purposes." He paused for a moment to let the thoughts sink in, and then went on, "So, tonight - no, this whole weekend - has been Satan's latest attempt at sabotaging God's plans."

"Okay, but how does that explain Pete almost blowing my head off?" asked Dave. "I know that wasn't him doing that," he hastened to clarify and soften his remark, and nodded apologetically toward Pete with a crooked grin. Everyone nodded their support of Pete's character, trying to let him see their affirmation. He still hung his head a bit lower, his cheeks red with shame.

"There are times when Satan and his demons will seize an opportunity, a time when we open a door to them by sinning," said Al. "They will use that opportunity to influence a person, even a Christian, to do something to change history and turn a person or a church or even an entire city away from righteousness and toward Satan's subtle lies. That's what has been happening here this weekend. Satan had decided that this was a pivotal time and place, so he sent greater than usual forces to turn us away from God.

"So everything - Pete's uncharacteristic use of a gun, Dave's unwise directions to the youth group, Steve's disobedience, and Marianne's kidnapping - has stemmed from his evil influence."

At the mention of Marianne's name, silence fell on the room once again as Pete and Molly were reminded of the news they hadn't shared yet. "Just one more thing," Steve broke in, not realizing what his folks were about to share their bad news with the group. "What broke the hold of the demons tonight, Mr. Caffer?"

"God must have gotten through to my mind at the last minute, somehow," he replied with a sigh.

Sam broke in to tell them what Mrs. Caffer had shouted in the car just before the gun shot.

"Ah," went on Mr. Caffer, "That explains why I suddenly knew, even through the fear and panic that had a grip on my heart, that there was something very wrong here. I felt God reminding me of the power that He has given each one of us, the power over Satan, the power to bind and cast Satan away from us. And that is what He reminded me to do. So all I said was, 'In the name of Jesus Christ, the Son of the Living God, I command you evil spirits to be gone.' And I think each of you noticed the result. At that command, Satan and all his demons were forced out of the picture, and the truth was left to make itself known to each of us."

"I have occasionally used that command over the years, and always felt assured that I did have the right to wield such a weapon." He heaved a sigh before going on. "But I've never seen such a dramatic conflict, or been so blinded, or witnessed such a dramatic result from binding evil spirits in the name of Jesus.

"It was close, though. Pete was very close to being forced to pull that trigger. And Dave was very close to stepping foolishly into the path of hot lead. Two actions that neither one of them would ever have done left to their own, much less God's, wisdom. But God won through in time. He kept Satan from destroying these two lives - these two families. And I am certain He kept him from destroying much more than that, judging from the overt nature of his action. It's not common at all for Satan to take such an obvious tactical approach. If he loses, as he did tonight, it just makes it more difficult for him to insinuate his lies into the lives of anyone who witnessed the loss. It's a big gamble for him, and praise the Lord, he lost out tonight."

Pete looked at Molly, and cleared his throat to get everyone's attention. Something in their expressions stopped every motion and sound in the room. Within seconds, every face was riveted to his. He reached out and gently took Molly's hand. Then, after taking a deep breath and letting it out in a long sigh, he said, "They found Marianne's body today."

If they had been still before he spoke, they were quiet as stones now, each holding his breath, wondering what had happened.

"Lieutenant Mochek called this afternoon," Pete went on. "She asked us to come and identify a body downtown. It was Marianne..." His voice broke, and his face crumpled in the agony of remembering what he had seen of his daughter. Molly, too, began to cry again, but softly, as large tears rolled quietly down her cheeks. Pete knelt at her side and held her awkwardly to his shoulder.

Steve's breath caught in his chest, and he bit fiercely on his finger, trying to stop himself from crying or crying out in his despair. He swallowed repeatedly to keep the hard lump in his throat from rising and choking him. *Marianne!* he wailed into the aching chasm of his heart. *My sister! What did they do to you?* Big tears welled up and fell from his eyelashes into his lap.

Dave closed his eyes and felt Sam take his hand and lean her forehead into his shoulder. *What else could happen to this poor family?* he wondered. Every eye in the room was locked on Pete and Molly now, and each heart ached, knowing what was coming.

He started again, "It was her. She was found inside a car at the bottom of the river, and..." again Pete's voice caught, as he struggled to maintain control long enough to get the words out. "At least she's not suffering anymore. At least she's safe with Jesus now." At this, he ran out of words, and ran out of will to keep the tears back. The final walls in his heart crumbled and fell, and sobs shuddered through him, and Molly, too, began weeping openly. Steve half walked, half stumbled over to them, wrapping them in a hug. Then every person in the room made their way to the side of the Frack family and either laid an arm around them or a hand on them in an effort to share what comfort there was to be given at such a time.

* * *

"What can we do?" asked Brilliantly.

Aggrevious, with the wisdom gained from many such pivotal moments, answered, "Watch. Watch and be ready, for this is a critical moment for Molly. You can see, can you not, that she weeps not out of bitterness, but out of loss and grief for the suffering that she is sure Marianne experienced. She is ready, and one of these others will be used to say just the right thing to bring her into the family. This is a rare moment of magic, a jewel of time. It is one of the all-too-rare times when the Lord God is asked to rescue one of these from the clutches of the enemy." He stood silently for a moment, and then whispered, "Watch." He nodded to Patiently, who bent nearer to Mrs. Caffer's bowed head and whispered into her ear. Mrs. Caffer looked up and a small smile crossed her face.

* * *

"Molly, dearest," the older woman whispered into Molly's ear. "You've been so brave these past days. Now it's time to let God in to do His work. He loves you and will heal the hurts that are so painful inside you."

An hour ago Molly would have taken in these words like a sword cutting through her heart. But now things were different. For one thing, she had now surely arrived at the absolute bottom of her reserves of self. For another, at this moment there was no influence from Satan's minions. Right now there were none of the insidious lies that had been whispered in her ear for the last thirty years, no camouflaged and misleading feelings - feelings that had led her on a path that was close to the truth, yet far enough away from it that she had never stepped into a relationship with God.

At this moment the truth shone on her heart, enlightening her eyes and allowing her to hear the truth without interference. Suddenly, so many things made sense to her. There was still the pain of Marianne's loss, but with just those few words, whispered in love from a gentle old woman, the God of love and healing entered Molly's heart.

The words that she had heard all her life in church, that she had taught countless children in Sunday school classes over the years, the words of forgiveness and new beginnings suddenly became much more than mere words. Those words became living words for her, and the Living Word Himself touched her and brought her to life. Fresh tears poured from her eyes, and she reached out her arms toward Mrs. Caffer to wrap her in an embrace that conveyed the words that she was too full of emotion to speak.

Those gathered around experienced the moment as though it were magic come to life. And they knew that, in a way, it was. For the King of all creation had touched yet another life, bringing joy and peace and life, where before there was only dark despair and death.

Through her tears, Molly smiled and enjoyed the first ray of hope that she had felt in days. The support of those in the room was as palpable as their hugs. And though there was grief, it was now felt by each of them to be undergirded by the knowledge that Marianne was indeed safe in the arms of a loving Lord.

Molly closed her eyes and was surprised by a stunningly clear memory - a memory of watching Pete holding Marianne in his arms after she had experienced a particularly frightening nightmare several years earlier. She watched in her memory as Marianne's sobs subsided and peace replaced the fear. She recalled the look on her daughter's face when she looked up at her father's face and sighed in contentment and comfort in his strong arms.

Sitting there, she was given a sweet gift, she envisioned the features of a kindly-faced Jewish carpenter with a twisted circle of thorns on his head. Seated on his head, the cruel thorns looked like a rich crown of some heavenly, precious material. She understood that this was a vision of Jesus, and that He was holding Marianne right at this moment. She too sighed, thankful for the gift of knowing that her daughter was safe in His loving arms.

Chapter 18
Please listen to her now.

At four thirty, on Wednesday afternoon, the auditorium of the First Evangelical Church of Alagonic was filled to overflowing. The memorial service for Marianne Frack had drawn media attention from the Alagonic Herald, and people who wouldn't ordinarily have come, came for a variety of reasons. Some came simply as a heartfelt need to support this family who were experiencing such grief and loss. Others saw it as an opportunity for political gain. The Mayor, several city council members, and the police chief all came to make sure that their faces were seen caring for the people of their community.

Lieutenant Mochek also came, though she came out of real feelings for this family. She had persuaded several of the officers who had worked on the case with her to come along, though it had not taken a whole lot of persuading. They, too, felt something special about this family, and wanted to show support for them in whatever way they could.

The regular membership of the church was out in full number as well, and the overflow crowd was seated in the chapel and the all purpose room with a hastily set up closed circuit television system giving a piped-in view of the service.

The prayer efforts that had started up following the Sunday evening service continued for several days, though with a different focus now that Marianne's body had been found. The prayers of the church members had now shifted to asking God to comfort the Fracks. They prayed for His will and for His kingdom to be furthered somehow by the taking of Marianne's life. Their hope and prayer was that those present at the memorial service would hear the gospel and respond.

Pastor Miller officiated, speaking briefly and movingly about the little girl who had so deeply loved Jesus. The room was entirely silent save one sniffle from Tammy Tesch, who had been in the mall with Marianne that day, and whose brother had just been released from critical care following his accident.

"Marianne has been instrumental in changing our lives," said the pastor. "Her life was a spark of inspiration for those of us who watched her walk with her Lord. But her death has been a blazing torch, written across the entire sky in huge letters, crying out to all who will listen, 'Walk with the Lord now! Don't wait until later, because there may not be a later.'

"Her death has already shocked us. I am certain, though, that she would want her death to be considered a price paid, not a life lost. So let's not allow her death to be a wasted price. Listen to her now. Please listen to her now."

"There are those among this gathering who loved Marianne. There are also those present who didn't know her at all, apart from what you heard in the news reports. But to all of you I say, and I think Marianne would join her voice with mine; take the time now to examine your own heart, and see if you have a relationship with God, the loving Father. Ask yourself if you've ever seen that deepest need of your heart in light of His truth. And ask yourself if you have accepted His offer to meet that need."

"If there are any of you here today who would like to take the first step in a life-long walk with God, please stay after this service and meet with us here at the front of the sanctuary. We'll be happy to stay with you and help you find the peace and strength that Marianne spent her life in demonstrating."

"And for those of you who already know Jesus as your Lord and Savior, I believe she would say, "Hold fast! Press on! It is worth it – whatever you are going through."

Toby walked quietly to the front of the platform and sang Amazing Grace, an aged song with an ageless message. The silence following his song continued throughout the packed room, but then after a few moments, moments in which those present considered the state of their heart and the words of the song, they stirred and then came. First an individual from the far right, almost in the back row. Then a couple came together, a young man and woman, both crying silent tears. Then more and more, people from all walks of life and all ages came in response to what God had done in the life of a twelve-year-old girl. Hearts young and tender, hearts cold and calloused, whatever their state, God reached down that day and gave brand new life to each one who answered the call.

Chapter 19
Those demons who dared.

    Lives were changed that day. In fact the city was changed. Aggrevious still watched over the city. Though some of the enemy had snuck back into the city, welcomed back by human hosts of long standing, the tenor of the city had changed. This was now a territory occupied by righteousness, and those demons who dared to return, knew that they were trespassing on land held by their Enemy.

    Aggrevious cherished the memory of that Wednesday afternoon, when the Son had brought light and life to dozens of cold, dry hearts. And the work went on. Those who had responded to the invitation to new life that day had done so with a deep commitment, and indeed their lives were visibly and permanently affected.

    They still worked the same jobs and went to the same schools that they had previously. But there was something markedly different about them, and the difference was contagious. The ranks of the saved swelled practically every day, and as the day of the Son's return to rule over the earth drew closer, the bride grew and became more complete, more full, more and more beautiful and perfected for her King.

Made in the USA
Charleston, SC
16 October 2013